W9-BYQ-651

FATALITY WITH FORSTER

Also by Katherine Bolger Hyde

Novels

THE DOME-SINGER OF FALENDA

Crime with the Classics

ARSENIC WITH AUSTEN
BLOODSTAINS WITH BRONTË
CYANIDE WITH CHRISTIE *
DEATH WITH DOSTOEVSKY *

Other titles

LUCIA, SAINT OF LIGHT
EVERYTHING TELLS US ABOUT GOD

* *available from Severn House*

FATALITY WITH FORSTER

Katherine Bolger Hyde

**SEVERN
HOUSE**

First world edition published in Great Britain and the USA in 2021
by Severn House, an imprint of Canongate Books Ltd,
14 High Street, Edinburgh EH1 1TE.

Trade paperback edition first published in Great Britain and the USA in 2022
by Severn House, an imprint of Canongate Books Ltd.

severnhouse.com

British Library Cataloguing-in-Publication Data
A CIP catalogue record for this title is available from the British Library.

ISBN-13: 978-0-7278-9035-1 (cased)
ISBN-13: 978-1-78029-791-0 (trade paper)
ISBN-13: 978-1-4483-0530-8 (e-book)

All Severn House titles are printed on acid-free paper.

MIX
Paper from
responsible sources
FSC® C013056

Typeset by Palimpsest Book Production Ltd.,
Falkirk, Stirlingshire, Scotland.
Printed and bound in Great Britain by
TJ Books Limited, Padstow, Cornwall.

ONE

If Emily had been a fraction more English in her character and upbringing as well as in her tastes, she might have been able to keep a stiff upper lip when she and Luke landed at Heathrow the second day after their wedding, only to discover that the rental car they had reserved to carry them to Oxfordshire was not, in fact, available. But Emily was American, and therefore accustomed to things working properly. Also, she was rich, but she had not been rich long enough to know instinctively that all inconveniences give way to money, provided there is enough of it and it is wielded with sufficient arrogance and complacency.

As it was, however, nouveau-riche American Emily, little experienced in the ways of transatlantic travel, had barely slept a wink on the two-stage, twelve-hour overnight flight from Portland, and her reserves of sangfroid were exhausted. She sagged against her new husband, berating herself for poor planning and fighting a losing battle against tears.

Fortunately, Luke's reserves of quiet strength and un-flappable amiability ran deep. He was able both to support his wife – at this point quite literally – and to conduct a calm and rational negotiation with the rental car company's apologetic representative.

'I'm terribly sorry, sir,' the young man said. 'I can't imagine how this happened. We'll find you some alternative. Are you staying here in London?'

'No, Oxford. Well, near there.'

The man's face brightened. 'In that case, I suggest you take the Oxford Tube and pick up a car at the station there. I can reserve one for you now.'

Emily controlled her voice enough to say, 'The Tube goes all the way to Oxford?'

The attendant chuckled. 'Oh, I see what you mean. No, not the Underground. The Oxford Tube is a bus, oddly enough.

Or rather a coach – quite comfortable. It's about a ninety-minute ride, so you'll be able to rest for a bit before you have to start driving. We'll credit the fare against your rental fee.'

Luke glanced at Emily, who allowed her head to bob affirmatively, then said, 'Right. Where do we get the bus?'

The attendant directed them, and Luke gave a heave to get the luggage trolley going again. Emily hardly knew how they got to the bus.

In the Tube, which was indeed comfortable and partook of the soothing motion of wheels on road, Emily finally dozed as still-vivid scenes from her wedding drifted through her mind. Her home church, St Sergius Orthodox Church in Portland, ablaze with light and overflowing with white and yellow flowers. She in her ivory silk ankle-length dress of Edwardian cut, embellished with dozens of minuscule tucks and enough subtle lace to make Mrs Bennet drool. Luke standing upright and solemn beside her, slightly adjusting his shoulders in his uncomfortable rented tux. Father Paul facing them with a smile that beamed through his voluminous beard as he pronounced the opening prayers.

The timeless Orthodox service – standing at the back of the church for the betrothal and exchange of rings, then moving up to the front of the nave for the crowning. Luke looking truly regal in his symbolic crown, where a lesser man might have looked ridiculous – then cutting his eyes toward her and giving her a subtle wink that reminded her of his teenaged self.

They'd been through so much over the years, together and apart – a summer of tumultuous young love, followed by thirty-five years of separation and another year of finding their way back to each other. Now, at last, she and Luke were really and truly man and wife. She reached for his hand and he squeezed it, half asleep himself. Their years on earth were more than halfway over, yet their life's true adventure was just beginning.

Emily came to full consciousness only when the coach arrived at Oxford railway station. There they finally got their car – a tiny thing of an unfamiliar make with standard shift and barely enough room for Luke's long legs, but at least it had a GPS. Luke set it for Fitzhugh Manor, near Binsey. As he navigated the left-sided streets of Oxford with only the occasional curse, sudden swerve, or slam on the brakes, Emily thought she'd fallen through the looking glass into a mirror-image nightmare of unintelligible road markings, nerve-wracking roundabouts, and one-way streets that each took on a series of different names and directions. She barely had leisure to glimpse the dreaming spires of the university before they finally found themselves on the A24 highway, heading north.

From there it was only a few miles to their destination, the village of Binsey. Tiny and picturesque, with venerable thatched-roof cottages and an ancient stone church, Binsey exemplified Emily's anachronistic but cherished vision of England – a country of fields, hedgerows, and quaint, time-weathered villages, of cows, horses, and sheep, of farmers and landlords leading a slow and contemplative life governed by centuries-old traditions. She'd never voiced it to Luke, but she harbored a secret hope of inserting herself into this vanishing way of life by finding a cottage somewhere that she might buy. They could use it as a vacation home for now, and maybe – if she could ever bring Luke around to the idea – as a retirement home at some point in the future. She had already retired from her job as a professor of literature, but it was difficult to envision Luke stepping down from his post as lieutenant sheriff of Stony Beach. He and the town had grown up together; his whole life was embedded there, and he loved his work.

They passed through the village in a tantalizing instant. A few more turns on narrow country lanes bound by hedgerows brought them to the gates of Fitzhugh Manor – their home from home for the next four weeks.

Emily had fallen in love with the place from the pictures on Airbnb, and the reality did not disappoint. A drive of about a quarter mile through a stand of ancient trees in full leaf brought them in sight of the house – a Tudor-era construction of Cotswold yellow limestone, like the university buildings in Oxford. Of middling stature as English manor houses went, the structure was still many times the size of Windy Corner, with enough gables and turrets, pointed arches and diamond-paned windows to satisfy even Emily's Gothic-loving heart.

'I feel like Catherine in *Northanger Abbey*,' she said to Luke, gripping his arm. 'Don't let me get carried away and start looking for secret passageways and skeletons in old chests, will you?'

Luke shuddered. 'No way. I'm counting on this being a corpse-free honeymoon. If we happen on a skeleton in a chest, we're going to drop the lid and never mention it to a living soul. It'll just be part of the furniture.'

A corpse-free honeymoon was certainly what Emily wished for as well. In fact, she'd be quite happy never to encounter another dead body as long as she lived. She and Luke had seen quite enough of them since she moved back to Windy Corner. They'd chosen England for this trip partly because it was five thousand miles out of Luke's jurisdiction as a lawman. If anything untoward did happen, at least no one would expect either of them to take a hand in solving it.

A fine mist was descending as Luke pulled the car into the wide drive in front of the house and got out, stretching his legs with a groan. Emily had half expected a whole queue of servants standing ready to greet them, as in *Downton Abbey* when an important guest arrives. But there was no one to be seen.

They mounted the few steps to the front door and pulled the bell. Emily couldn't resist lifting the lion-shaped knocker as well and was slightly disappointed that it did not transform into Marley's head.

A couple of minutes passed before the door was opened – not by the standard-issue ancient retainer, but by an attractive young woman dressed in jeans and a T-shirt with her dark hair in a ponytail. She looked like a casual version of Kate, Duchess of Cambridge, which doubled Emily's shock when she spoke with an American accent.

'Hi, I'm Allison Fitzhugh. You must be the Richardses.' She put out her hand. Luke took it first, then Emily, when she'd recovered a bit from her bewilderment.

'You're American?' she blurted, then repented her rudeness.

But Allison only laughed. 'Yeah, I'm the import. Don't worry, though, the rest of the family is as British as you could ever want to meet. I married in.' She glanced at their rented car, then called back into the bowels of the house, 'James! Come get our guests' bags, would you?'

Turning back to Luke and Emily, she said, 'Come on in. I'll show you to your room. James will bring your bags and put the car in the garage. Did you leave the key in it?'

'Uh, yeah.' Luke seemed as bewildered by this level of service as Emily had been by the lack of ceremony on their arrival.

They entered a hall that answered all Emily's ideas of what a manor house hall should be – dim, spacious, chilly, with a slate floor and paneled walls darkened by the smoke of centuries. Over the enormous fireplace hung a coat of arms surrounded by swords, daggers, and antique guns, which gave Emily a chill as it recalled too many country house mysteries in which a decorative weapon became a real one. A wide staircase with elaborately carved banisters ascended to a landing, then split to continue to either side.

They followed Allison up the staircase to the right and down a long gallery that took a right-angle turn into another wing. Allison opened a heavy paneled door and said, 'This is you. You're our only guests at the moment, so you'll have the wing all to yourselves.' She led the way into the room.

Emily nearly gasped at the size of it. Even the Forster room, the largest and most luxurious bedroom at Windy Corner, was nothing to this. The immense four-poster bed barely made a dent in the space. At one end was a fireplace, not quite as huge as the one in the hall but still impressive, with two wing chairs and a round table arranged in front of it. The outside wall held several ceiling-high diamond-paned casement windows flanked by pale-green velveteen drapes. A tall inlaid desk stood between them, replete with small drawers and cubbyholes. Although the walls were paneled in dark wood, the high molded-plaster ceiling and light-colored upholstery and bedding, combined with a pastel Aubusson rug, kept the room from feeling dark or oppressive. Emily was completely enchanted.

Allison pointed out the amenities. 'Cupboards there' – she

indicated a whole wall full of them, then opened a door at the end of it – 'and this is your bathroom.'

Emily glanced in and sighed with pleasurable anticipation at the sight of a clawfoot tub with center tap, plenty big enough for two. In one corner was a modern shower.

A young man appeared in the doorway, lugging their bags. 'Oh, thank you, James,' Allison said. 'Mr and Mrs Richards, this is my husband, James Fitzhugh. Technically, *Sir* James, but he doesn't much care for the "Sir."'

Luke shook their host's hand. 'And I don't much care for "Mister." Call me Luke.'

Emily blinked in shock – she'd expected a footman or butler. If such people still existed. But she recovered herself before James turned to her with a smile and outstretched hand.

'I'm Emily. Pleased to meet you.' She took in his tall, lanky form, fair hair, and aristocratic features. If she'd met him when he didn't have his arms full of luggage, she'd have known him for the lord of the manor right off. But his smile forestalled any awkwardness.

'Welcome to Fitzhugh Manor.' James's Oxbridge accent confirmed his full membership in the privileged class. 'You're our very first PGs – did Allison tell you?'

'Paying guests,' his wife explained. 'No, I didn't want to frighten them. But I promise, we have plenty of experience with guests of the non-paying variety – we'll take excellent care of you while you're here.'

'I don't doubt it,' Emily said. 'This room is amazing.'

'Allison's worked hard to make it comfortable. I hope you'll be happy here.'

'We'll give you some time to get settled,' Allison said. 'It's past formal teatime, but I can bring you up a little something if you'd like.'

'Please.' Tea had become a beloved ritual at Windy Corner, and Emily was parched.

'Later on, you can join us for dinner. The dining room is just off the main hall at the bottom of the stairs. We eat at seven thirty.' She gave a small grimace. 'And if you don't mind, Lady Margaret – James's grandmother – likes everyone to be prompt.'

*   *   *

Emily set her purse and jacket on the bed and sank down beside them. 'Mmm, this bed is perfect,' she mumbled.

Luke sat beside her, leaned over, and kissed her. 'For sleeping, or . . .'

'Both, I think.' She returned his kiss with interest. 'But sleeping will have to come first.'

Luke consulted his watch. 'Five o'clock. We should have time for a little nap before dinner.'

'I was thinking of napping in the tub, actually. If I can stay awake through tea. I am famished.' The food on the plane had not been to Emily's taste, nor had there been nearly enough of it.

Luke rose and went to the window. 'This place is pretty amazing. Who'd'a thunk we'd get a lord for a bellboy?'

'I know. Or that we'd be the only guests in a family home. From the Airbnb listing, I thought this whole place was run like a hotel.'

He turned to her. 'Not disappointed, are you?'

'As Marguerite would say, *pas du tout*. Quite the reverse, in fact. It should be much easier to live out my fantasy of being a nineteenth-century noble lady under these circumstances. We can pretend we're friends of the family invited for a long visit. Only without the valet and lady's maid.'

'There must be some actual servants, don't you think? Place as big as this?'

'I think there must. A cook and a maid or two, at least. Behind-the-scenes people. James and Allison can't do everything by themselves.'

A knock came at the door, followed by Allison bearing a tray laden with tea service and a plate of cakes and finger sandwiches. Emily didn't know much about such things, but based on the preferences of Bertie Wooster's Uncle Tom, she guessed the silver teapot and tray might be Georgian and the china probably of the same period. The cups were made of such fine porcelain she could see the light through them. The family might be comparatively impoverished – she assumed they wouldn't be renting out rooms otherwise – but apparently they had not yet been reduced to selling off all their treasures.

'That looks heavenly,' Emily said. 'Luke and I were just speculating about how you keep this place running. You must have some servants, surely?'

Allison smiled. 'We don't call them servants anymore. We call them staff. But yes, we do have some. A cook and two cleaners who come in by the day. A couple of groundskeepers and several people to run the stables – that's our main income producer: we give riding lessons and board horses. But the only live-in now is Lady Margaret's personal maid, Cadwallader. We call her Caddie. She's about a hundred and fifty years old, but neither she nor Lady Margaret can imagine her retiring.'

Ah, so there was an ancient retainer, after all. Now if Emily could only ascertain the existence of a family ghost, the picture would be complete.

'Wow. That must leave a lot of work for you and James. Is there anyone else in the family?'

'Only Uncle Roger. He's a dear, but fairly useless as far as actual work is concerned. But James and I are young and healthy, and we like to keep busy. We'd far rather put the work into keeping this place going than give it up and get ordinary jobs.'

'I admire your dedication, especially considering Fitzhugh Manor is not your own ancestral home.'

'No, but I fell in love with it the first time James brought me here. I feel like I was born for this life.' She smiled. 'Now, if you'll excuse me, I need to set the table for dinner. And we don't want your tea to get cold.'

TWO

After tea and a doze in the capacious bathtub, Emily felt ready to face the world – or at least those representatives of it who resided at Fitzhugh Manor. She did wish she'd consulted Allison about what to wear, though. Allison's jeans suggested a casual dinner, but Lady Margaret sounded like a traditionalist who would expect formal attire. Too tired to iron anything, Emily compromised with an olive-green travel-knit dress she'd bought for the trip. She dressed it up with Aunt Beatrice's long string of pearls. At her suggestion, Luke donned a sport coat and chinos with his dress shirt instead of his usual jeans.

Allison was waiting for them in the hall, wearing a simple black dress that fitted as if it had been custom-made. Her smile was a bit too bright, causing Emily to suspect some nervousness underneath, but she seemed to relax when she saw Emily's outfit.

'Oh, good,' she said. 'I realized too late I'd forgotten to ask you to dress for dinner. The days of formal gowns and dinner jackets are over, thank God, but Lady Margaret does insist we change into something presentable.'

Emily returned her hostess's smile. 'I suspected that might be the case. I'm glad I guessed correctly.'

'There's just one thing before we go in.' Allison darted a glance through the dining-room door and lowered her voice. 'Lady Margaret is under the impression that you are old family acquaintances of mine. I don't like deceiving her, but she would never have agreed to our having paying guests. She's an earl's daughter, and her aristocratic pride wouldn't allow it.' When Emily registered alarm, Allison hastened to add, 'Don't worry about fielding questions or anything – I'll take care of all that. Just, please, if it's not asking too much, don't mention anything about money changing hands.'

Luke and Emily exchanged a glance, then nodded. 'Of course. We'll play along as best we can.'

Allison's whole body relaxed. 'Thank you so much. I knew as soon as I saw you that you were the right sort. Shall we go in?' Allison gestured for them to precede her, then led them to the small group clustered around the empty hearth.

James stood at one side, carelessly handsome in a navy blazer and khaki slacks, with a red ascot tucked into the neck of his crisp white shirt. Opposite him, a short, skinny, middle-aged man in a baggy tweed suit and bowtie fidgeted with a pipe, filling and tamping it, then jamming it into his mouth without lighting it. He glanced up as they entered and blinked with a vague smile, passing a hand over his sparse, flyaway gray hair.

In the depths of a high wing chair, Emily could just make out the tiny but upright form of a woman who looked to be anywhere between eighty and a hundred. Her black lace dress fell to the floor; rows of small diamonds encased her withered neck, and a blinding assortment of jewels encrusted her gnarled fingers. One translucent hand gripped the carved bronze head of an ebony cane while the other lay curled in her lap. Her pale eyes appeared as sharp as her body was frail, and they held no trace of welcome as she stared at Emily and Luke. Emily adjusted Aunt Beatrice's pearls, summoning all her ancestor's self-possession to keep herself from quailing physically under that piercing glare.

Allison made the introductions. 'Lady Margaret Fitzhugh, allow me to introduce our guests, Mr and Mrs Luke Richards.' Emily bit her tongue to stop herself inserting her own first name. There would be no first names with Lady Margaret.

The dowager gave the barest inclination of her prominent chin. 'Welcome to Fitzhugh Manor,' she said, her voice rasping as if she were forcing out the words against her own formidable will. 'I hope you will enjoy your stay.'

'Thank you so much for having us,' Emily said. 'It's a wonderful house, and Allison is taking good care of us. I'm sure we'll be very comfortable.'

Lady Margaret ran her eyes up and down Emily, then turned away. Clearly, the audience was over. Emily had the feeling she had narrowly avoided being figuratively cast into outer darkness. It must have been the pearls that saved her.

Allison turned to the middle-aged man, who shoved his unlit pipe into his pocket and held out his hand. 'Luke and Emily, this is Uncle Roger. He's a Fitzhugh, too, but he missed the title.'

Roger took Emily's hand in both of his and pressed it warmly. 'I assure you, I don't miss it a bit,' he said. 'The title sits much more handsomely on young James, even though he prefers not to wear it.' He gave his nephew a smile of pure affectionate pride.

Emily beamed at Roger, liking him already. Though he was

of her own generation – perhaps a few years older – she was ready to adopt him as her uncle on the spot.

Luke pumped Roger's hand. His usual question on meeting another man was 'What do you do for a living?' but in this case he must have realized that was inappropriate; Roger wasn't the sort of person who would need to earn a living, or even be capable of doing so. Instead, he asked, 'How do you spend your time around here? I'm guessing you're not the horsey type.'

Roger looked as startled as if a stallion had reared in front of him. 'Heavens, no. Can't stand the brutes.' He gave himself a little shake. 'I'm a butterfly man. Happy to show you my collection later on.'

'I look forward to it,' said Emily, though she much preferred her butterflies alive.

'Dinner is served,' announced a sepulchral male voice from the opposite end of the room.

Emily turned, startled at the presence of a servant – or rather staff member – she hadn't been informed about.

Allison whispered in her ear, 'That's Witherspoon. He used to be our full-time butler, but he's retired now. He only comes in when we have dinner guests. Lady Margaret can't stand us serving ourselves in front of other people.'

James offered a formal arm to Lady Margaret. He saw her to the chair Witherspoon pulled out for her, at the foot of the long table, and helped her into it, kissing the hand she held out to him as she patted his cheek with the other. The smile she bestowed on him held more true affection than Emily would have thought her capable of.

James went to sit at the head of the table himself. Allison gestured to Luke and Emily that they should be the next to follow Witherspoon. He led Emily to the chair on James's left and Luke to the next one down on James's right, pulling out each chair with slightly trembling, white-gloved hands. Finally, Allison walked to the table on Roger's arm and took her place on James's immediate right, while Roger sat next to Emily. Acres of table stretched between their group and Lady Margaret – Emily counted six empty chairs – but the matriarch showed no sign of disliking the arrangement.

After the soup was served – while Emily was trying to instruct Luke silently and invisibly in the art of sipping from the side of the spoon – Lady Margaret spoke. Her voice, undimmed by age, carried the length of the table with no apparent effort. 'Mrs Richards, I believe you are an acquaintance of Allison's mother. How did you meet?'

Emily shot a panicked glance at Allison, who piped up brightly, 'Oh, they met at Smith. Inseparable they were, Mother says – LucEmily, people called them, one name. But after college Emily moved out West and they lost touch for a long time. Isn't that right, Emily?'

She cleared her throat. 'Yes, we'd lost touch completely. We reconnected online quite recently, and Lucy told me Allison was living here. Luke and I wanted to honeymoon near Oxford, so it was quite fortuitous when she invited us to stay.'

Lady Margaret raised one finely arched brow. 'I see. So is this the thin end of the wedge, Allison? Are we now to play host to every slight acquaintance of yours who wishes to visit England?'

Allison grimaced an apology to Emily. 'I promise you the house won't be overrun, Lady Margaret. I don't know *that* many people.'

James put down his spoon and smiled down the table at his grandmother. 'Granny, I hope I don't need to remind you that Allison is the mistress of this house. She does have the right to invite whatever guests she pleases.'

Lady Margaret shifted her shoulders as if something pained her. 'Why don't you invite some of your friends, James? Surely you know people from Balliol who have moved away and would like to visit the area again.'

'My friends all lead busy lives, Granny. Everybody has to earn a living nowadays – it isn't like when you were young. Country-house parties are a thing of the past.'

Lady Margaret held a lace handkerchief to the end of her nose. 'Next you'll be telling me families are a thing of the past. In my day, gentlemen married within the extended family in order to preserve their property, but now it's all about "love." As if romance ever survived beyond the honeymoon.'

Luke and Emily exchanged a glance. Their love had survived

for thirty-five years before their honeymoon even began. And as far as Emily could tell, James and Allison looked pretty solid as well. There must be more behind that barb than met the eye.

'All this change . . . I am thankful I shall not be here to see much more of it.' Lady Margaret addressed herself to her soup. Her pronouncement had an air of finality, and Emily hoped that wouldn't be the end of all conversation for the meal.

But Allison was equal to the occasion. 'Do you have plans for your time here? Places you want to visit? Or are you just going to play it by ear?' she asked Emily.

'We want to tour Oxford, of course. The Bodleian in particular. And Blenheim Palace is a must. I'd like to tootle around the Cotswolds a bit, see *Father Brown* country. But honestly, I've been so busy the last few months planning the wedding and whatnot that I didn't have as much time to research as I would have liked.'

Allison grimaced. 'I can tell you, Oxford is swarming with tourists this time of year. If you want to tour the Bodleian or any of the larger colleges, you'll need to reserve ahead. Since you're here for a whole month, you shouldn't have a problem getting a space, but I'd suggest you do that as soon as possible.'

Emily swallowed. 'Thanks for the warning. It would be awful to have come all this way and not get to see the university properly. What about Blenheim? Does one need a reservation there?'

'Oh, no. They do self-guided tours. It will be packed too, of course. But it's an enormous place, so you shouldn't feel too crowded.'

Witherspoon noiselessly cleared the soup and served the main course – some bird Emily didn't recognize, but it was delicious. After a few bites, she asked Allison, 'Is there any other place you'd recommend?'

'I don't know exactly what you're interested in, but if you like William Morris, his country house, Kelmscott, is nearby. It's definitely worth a visit.'

Luke looked blank, but Emily said, 'Oh, I love William Morris! We'll have to put that on our list. Will we need a reservation there?'

'No, but they do have rather limited hours, I think, so by all means plan that in advance.'

Allison turned to Luke. 'What about you, Luke? Is there anything you're especially interested in?'

Luke shrugged. 'This is mainly Emily's trip. I'm just along for the ride. Usually when I take a vacation, it's to hunt or fish, but I don't suppose that's an option around here.'

James brightened. 'Hunting season isn't till autumn, but we can get you all the fishing you want. We have a small lake here on the estate. I keep it stocked with roach, carp, and bream. And I've got plenty of gear you can use. I'll even keep you company if you like.'

Allison gave her husband an affectionate smile. 'James will take any excuse to go fishing. I keep him too busy most of the time.'

'I'd love that,' Luke said. 'And there is one English thing I really want to do – go to a pub.'

James laughed. 'That's a must. We've got a famous one right here in Binsey – the Perch. People come from Oxford and all over to eat and drink there. It's a seventeenth-century inn – thatched and everything.'

Luke grinned at Emily. 'Thatch for you, English beer for me. Win-win.'

The main-course plates magically disappeared, and fruit and cheese appeared in the center of the table. Emily helped herself to a slice of a wedge labeled *Wensleydale*. It was delicious.

'About meals,' Allison put in. 'We're assuming you'll want to breakfast here each day. We do that buffet-style so everyone can eat when they're ready. And you're welcome to lunch and dine with us as often as you like. Other than the Perch, we don't have much in the way of restaurants close by, but if you're out and about, you'll probably be lunching elsewhere most days. I'd just ask that you let me know each morning what your plans are for the day so we can prepare accordingly.'

'Of course,' Emily said. 'Tomorrow I think we'll stick around here, rest a bit and get our bearings, make some more definite plans for the rest of our stay.'

'Excellent,' Allison replied. 'I expect you'll want to sleep in tomorrow, so we'll have breakfast laid out till . . . shall we say ten?'

'I doubt we'll sleep that late. But thank you, it will be nice not to have to rush.'

A lull in the conversation ensued. Lady Margaret, who had eaten only a few tiny bites of dinner, rose and said, 'You must excuse me. I am an old woman and need my sleep.' She left the table without waiting for a reply.

Emily barely had time to wonder whether this was their cue to rise as well before Witherspoon materialized again, this time bearing small crystal dishes full of some gorgeous confection that appeared to contain chocolate. Emily was quite full by this time, but she always had room for chocolate.

The first bite went down like a small taste of paradise. She closed her eyes and savored it. 'Your cook is amazing,' she said after the bite had melted in her mouth. 'Everything was delicious, but this dessert is to die for.'

Allison smiled. 'Mrs Terwilliger is a treasure. We're very lucky to have her. Not many top-notch cooks want to work in private houses these days – they want the glory of running their own restaurants. But like everything else around here, Mrs Terwilliger is getting old. We may not have the privilege of eating her food much longer.'

'Nonsense,' James said. 'Mrs Terwilliger will last forever. Just like Caddie, and Granny, and Witherspoon. They're fixtures. The world may be changing, but they're all as immutable as time.'

THREE

The next morning, Luke and Emily slept in as expected. Emily didn't want to drag herself out of the cushy feather bed, but eventually her growling stomach won out.

No one was in the dining room when they entered, but soon Allison came in with a fresh pot of coffee. She was dressed in riding breeches and her cheeks glowed. 'Good morning,' she greeted them. 'I had a feeling you'd sleep in. James and Roger ate hours ago, and Lady Margaret always has toast and tea in her room.'

'Have you been out for a ride already?' Emily asked.

'If I don't get my ride in early, the day gets away from me and I never have time. Besides—' She stopped herself, biting her lip, then made a 'what the hell' gesture. 'My riding days are numbered. We're not telling the family yet, but I'm bursting to tell someone – we're going to have a baby!'

Emily was momentarily speechless. News of anyone's pregnancy was always bittersweet to her. She felt genuine joy for the parents-to-be, but at the same time the event brought back painful memories – she had miscarried Luke's baby when they were young and had never been able to conceive again. It was the great sorrow of her life.

She found her tongue to say, 'That's wonderful, Allison. I'm so happy for you – and honored that you would entrust us with your confidence. But why the secrecy? Surely Lady Margaret would be glad for James to have an heir?'

'That's just it. The moment she hears the word "baby," she'll be counting on it being a boy. A girl couldn't inherit because the estate is entailed on the next baronet. So we're going to try to keep it from her until we can determine the baby's sex. If it is a boy, she'll be able to rejoice freely, and if it's a girl, she'll know right away and won't be entertaining false hopes.'

'I see. But won't you be showing before then?'

'Possibly, but the women in my family never get really big pregnant bellies – we're tall and long-waisted, so it doesn't show till late. And anyway, Lady Margaret avoids looking at me more than she can help.' Allison's face tightened slightly on those words, and Emily knew she wasn't as indifferent to her grandmother-in-law's resentment of her as she tried to let on.

'I'll be praying for a healthy pregnancy – and a healthy son. But isn't riding dangerous, even early on?'

Allison shrugged. 'I'm an experienced rider, and my horse is the gentlest thing in the world. My doctor gave me permission to ride, only at a walk, till the end of the first trimester. But that's coming up soon.' She took on a wistful look. 'The baby will be worth the sacrifice, of course, but I will dearly miss my morning ride.'

Emily speculated that might be the only time of the day Allison felt free from the looming disapproval of Lady Margaret.

Allison looked them over. 'Luke, I'm guessing you know one end of a horse from the other, am I right?'

'You bet. Haven't had time for a while now, but I used to ride a lot.'

'James will set you up with a mount if you'd like to brush up your skills at some point.'

'I'd love it. Today, if possible. But I ride Western style – not sure I could handle an English saddle.'

'Don't worry. We have both kinds of tack. We get plenty of American tourists as customers at the stable.' She held up one hand. 'Your rides, of course, will be complimentary as guests of the house.' She turned to Emily. 'How about you? Are you interested in riding?'

Emily swallowed. 'I've never been on a horse in my life. I think I may be a little old and out of shape to start now.' The truth was that she loved horses – from a distance, as aesthetic objects. Up close and personal, they terrified her.

'Would you like to explore the estate on foot, then? I'd be happy to take you on a tour once you've eaten.'

'That would be perfect. Thank you.'

'We'll stop first at the stables, and James can show Luke around there and find him a mount. That is, if you two love-birds can stand to be apart for one morning.'

They exchanged a smile. 'I think we can manage that much,' Emily said.

Luke and Emily both did justice to a full English breakfast – though Emily skipped the baked beans, which she didn't think she could stomach at that hour – and lingered over a second cup of coffee and a newspaper. Then they went upstairs to change their footwear – Luke into the custom-made cowboy boots Emily had given him the previous Christmas, and Emily into some stout walking shoes.

Allison, wearing jeans again, met them in the hall and led them out the back on to a flagged terrace. From there a gravel path led past a stand of trees to a large courtyard bounded on two sides by stables. The path intersected a lane that led to the main road, and the fourth side of the courtyard opened on to a paddock.

In the courtyard, a young, ginger-haired man was leading a gleaming black horse in a wide circle as James looked on. 'Good,' James said. 'He's not favoring that foreleg at all now. Let's put him out in the paddock today, and I'll ride him a bit tomorrow.'

'Darling,' Allison called. 'I've brought Luke for a stable tour and a ride, if you can fit him in. Emily and I are just passing through – she prefers a walking tour of the estate.'

'Certainly. Glad to accommodate you, Luke. We've got a light day today, so I can ride with you and show you around. Conan can hold the fort.' He turned to the ginger fellow. 'Conan O'Donnell, these are our house guests, Luke and Emily Richards. Conan's our stable manager. You won't find anyone within a hundred miles who knows more about horses.' Emily noticed Conan's eyes flick toward James with an expression she couldn't quite read, but it didn't seem to fit with appreciation of his praise.

'Pleased to meet you,' Emily said. She wasn't about to approach close enough to shake hands as long as Conan still held the black horse's reins.

'Likewise,' said Conan in a faint Irish accent, shooting Emily a special fellow-ginger smile. 'Lucky's happy to see you, too.' The horse nodded its head and huffed by way of greeting.

James rubbed the horse's nose fondly. 'His full name is Luck of the Fitzhughs. Prize racehorse in his day – his winnings founded our whole stable. He's getting a bit long in the tooth now, but he's earned his retirement many times over.'

Luke joined in the equine lovefest for a minute, then James said, 'We'd best get him out to the paddock. Winky!' he called at the top of his voice.

A minute elapsed, and he called again before a faint Cockney voice answered, 'Comin', guv'nor!'

Following the voice, a wizened old man emerged from the stable, walking with a severe limp – his left leg was noticeably shorter and more bowlegged than his right. Emily saw the reason for the nickname – he wore a patch over his left eye. Winky grinned toothlessly up at them from his height of about four foot nine.

'Take Lucky to the paddock, would you?' James said, handing him the horse's reins.

'Right you are, guv'nor,' Winky said, nodding at the newcomers. Emily nodded back.

Allison said, 'Have a good ride, Luke. We'll see you chaps at lunch.' She steered Emily back the way they'd come.

'I see you're picking up the lingo,' Emily said when they were out of earshot.

Allison laughed. 'Yeah. I used to say "you guys," but around here a "guy" is a straw man like the ones they set on fire for Guy Fawkes Night. I got some really strange looks until I figured that out.'

They passed the stand of trees again, and before them were the house on the right and a mass of shrubbery on the left. The terrace came almost up to its edge. 'That's the labyrinth,' said Allison. 'Do you want to go in? No danger of getting lost – I know the key. You turn left whenever you can going in, and the reverse coming out.'

Emily had all sorts of fictional associations with labyrinths – none of them pleasant. For all she knew, the center could contain a minotaur, a trophy cup that was really an enchanted portkey, or even a man-eating tiger. But she had promised herself that on this trip, which she had been looking forward to for a lifetime, she would not miss out on any new experience due to groundless fear. 'Sure, sounds like fun.'

Allison led the way. Emily wished she had a red thread with her, in case Allison had misremembered the key, but it wasn't worth unraveling her handmade sweater just for insurance. They passed uneventfully through the narrow lanes between the head-high rows of yew and were rewarded at the center with a lovely pocket rose garden, where a white-painted iron bench invited the visitor to stop a while and admire the riot of pink and red and peach and yellow blooms.

But as they approached the bench, a figure appeared from

behind a rosebush – Lady Margaret, in a broad-brimmed straw hat and gardening gloves, brandishing a pair of pruning shears. Emily took an involuntary step back and shivered as a cloud crossed the sun.

Allison started visibly as well. 'Lady Margaret. I thought you'd be finished by now.'

'The Birthday Boy has a bad case of blackspot. I've been consulting with Perkins about it. He's going to do another fungicide spray.'

Emily's imagination did a series of backflips in the course of this speech, but she landed on the idea that the Birthday Boy must be a type of rose.

'I see,' Allison said. 'We didn't mean to disturb you. I can show Emily the roses another time.'

'Nonsense. I have finished, and I will show her the roses myself. You don't even know their names.' Lady Margaret's tone and accompanying glare suggested this was a breach of etiquette comparable to failing to learn the names of one's nieces and nephews.

She turned to Emily. 'Are you a gardener, Mrs Richards?'

Emily gave an apologetic grimace. 'I'm afraid not. I love to look at flowers, but I'm absolutely incapable of growing them.'

'It is merely a matter of early training. I take it your parents did not educate you in the art?'

'No. We moved around a lot, and my mother died when I was quite young. My father had no time for gardening, and he died relatively young as well.'

From her expression, Emily half expected Lady Margaret to quote Lady Bracknell's line from *The Importance of Being Earnest* – 'To lose one parent, Mr Worthing, may be regarded as a misfortune; to lose both looks like carelessness.' However, she merely turned to the bush nearest her and began to expound on its unique qualities.

Beauty of form and scent Emily could appreciate, but the finer points of rose breeding were lost on her. The names, though, were as colorful as the blooms, and she filed some of them in her memory – Oranges and Lemons (a lovely mottled orange and yellow), Eye of the Tiger (yellow with a red center),

Rhapsody in Blue (which was purple), and Life Begins at Forty – pure white, and her favorite name of all.

At last, when Emily felt she would be seeing roses in her sleep, should sleep ever be permitted her, Lady Margaret came to the final bush. Its lush deep-red blooms were streaked with a delicate pink, and Emily thought she had never seen anything so lovely. 'And this' – Lady Margaret drew herself up to her full height – 'this is the Fitzhugh Pride.'

Emily glanced at Allison, who seemed to be signaling that she should react in some way. Emily took a stab in the dark. 'Did you breed this one yourself?'

Lady Margaret condescended to allow the corners of her mouth to rise a millimeter. 'Indeed I did. It won the county show in 1986.'

'I think it's the most beautiful rose I've ever seen.' Emily's sincerity rang in her voice. She leaned in to catch the fragrance. 'And the scent is lovely, too. I'd say your win was very well deserved.'

Lady Margaret inclined her head graciously. 'And now I must rest,' she said. 'Allison, you may continue with your tour.' She walked slowly off into the labyrinth, leaning as little as possible on her bronze-headed cane.

Allison sank on to the bench, exuding relief. Emily sat next to her.

'Thank you,' Allison said. 'You were a good audience for her. She may even forgive me for invading her sanctuary. In general, she resents any outsider enjoying her roses – that's why they're hidden away inside the labyrinth.'

Emily wondered if she might venture a personal observation. If Allison had been British-born, she never would have dared, but she'd been fairly open about family matters so far.

'I get the feeling Lady Margaret rather resents *you*, period,' she said. 'Is it just because you're American, or is there more to it?'

'It's all sorts of things. Being American is an unforgivable sin, of course, given that I didn't bring a fortune into the marriage. Money would have covered a multitude of sins. My parents are reasonably affluent, but they're hardly in the Vanderbilt category. But on top of that, Lady Margaret doesn't approve of monetizing the estate. That was as much James's idea as mine, but since he's her golden boy, she prefers to blame me.' Allison leaned back on the bench, lifting the hair off her neck. 'The third strike against me was determined before James and I even met – I'm not remotely connected to the Fitzhughs. She wanted James to marry some umpteenth cousin or something so the estate would be kept in the family.'

'I see. And do such umpteenth cousins abound?'

'Not to say abound, but we've got one highly eligible one living right here on the estate. Penelope Fitzhugh – they call her Bunty. She's our main riding instructor and co-owner of the stable. I'm sure you'll meet her soon.'

'James doesn't care for her, I take it?'

'Oh, he's quite fond of her, but in a purely brotherly way. They're third cousins several times removed, I think, but they pretty much grew up together. She's a few years younger, and he's always thought of her as the little sister he never had.'

'But Lady Margaret doesn't see it that way?'

'Not at all. To her, Bunty was the obvious match for James. They clearly didn't hate each other, and to her mind that was all that was necessary for a successful marriage. "Successful" being defined as one that produces an heir, keeps up appearances, and doesn't end in scandal or divorce.'

'But James wanted more.'

'Always. He wanted genuine love. He's quite the romantic under that placid upper-class exterior.' Allison gave a little private smile as her hand rested on the barely visible swelling of her belly.

Emily was happy for Allison, but she had her own romance and preferred not to dwell too much on the subject of her hostess's pregnancy. 'So do you and James have further plans to monetize, beyond the stables and the Airbnb?'

'We do indeed. If you're rested, let's move on and I'll show you some more of our plans.'

They exited the maze without difficulty and turned left to go around to the front of the house. Here they strolled through extensive gardens laid out in the formal eighteenth-century style of Capability Brown, with statuary, fountains, and geometrically arranged flower beds – beautiful in their way, but Emily preferred the wild profusion of the typical English cottage garden, which worked with nature rather than attempting to beat it into submission.

'We give garden tours every weekend in the summer,' Allison said. 'Eventually, I hope to do house tours as well, but that will have to wait until Lady Margaret passes on to her mansion in the sky. We're asking a lot of her as it is – admitting the hoi polloi of all Europe, America, and Asia to wander through her home would be a bridge too far.'

'Do you really get so many tourists here?'

Allison hooted. 'You haven't spent time in Oxford yet, have you? The city is positively overrun in the summertime. And Binsey is easily accessible, with a famous pub in the village, so a lot of them spill over into the countryside around here. Blenheim Palace is the big draw, of course, up in Woodstock – their gardens are incredible. But we're less expensive and less intimidating, so we get our fair share.'

Emily made a mental note that she and Luke should time their excursions to hot tourist spots for weekdays, when the crowds might be a little more manageable. She knew that being lost in a crowd would ruin her enjoyment of all the sights she'd come so far to see.

Around the back of the house again, they passed a walled kitchen garden, which Emily declined to explore – she had little interest in the private life of produce before it appeared on her plate. From there Allison led the way across a broad downward-sloping lawn toward a stand of trees in the distance. Although the morning was cool, exertion was making Emily warm enough that she thought she would welcome their shade.

Allison stopped at a point where the lawn began to slope more steeply. 'I don't know how far you want to go,' she said. 'If you're up for the walk, I could show you our building site. It's just beyond that little copse.'

'Building?' Emily had an interest in architecture, so her ears pricked up at the word.

'This is hush-hush, you understand – the dragon doesn't know about it yet.' Allison put a hand to her mouth. 'Oops

– didn't mean to let that out. "Dragon" is my private name for Lady Margaret. You won't tell, will you?'

Emily assured her of her secrecy, only hoping she could keep herself from letting the nickname slip. It was too appropriate.

Allison went on. 'Anyway, she never ventures that far from the house, and the trees buffer the noise, so we've gotten away with it so far. We're building a small housing development. Now, before you jump to any conclusions, let me assure you we're doing it in the most respectful way possible. We're building cottages in the traditional style of the Cotswolds – with all mod-cons inside, of course – priced to be affordable for the locals as well as for people from Oxford or London looking for a home in the country. The cottages will be spaced out with proper gardens, not crowded together like a lot of developments, and they're being built to the highest possible standard.'

She smiled in satisfaction. 'James hinted around that he'd be open to building on the estate, and I took it from there. The stables are his baby, and this development is mine.'

Emily was getting a little tired, but she couldn't resist the offer to see the project up close. 'I'm up for the walk, I think, if we can rest a bit once we get there.'

'Sure. There's a canteen for the workers, so we could even sit down with a bite of something and a cup of tea.'

'Perfect. *Allons-y!*'

They tripped down the steepish slope the rest of the way to the wood. As they passed under the refreshing shade of the ancient deciduous trees, Emily glimpsed a figure with its back to them in a baggy brown corduroy coat and disreputable soft hat, carrying a butterfly net in one hand and a large leather case in the other. She pointed him out to Allison. 'Roger?'

'Yes,' Allison whispered. 'Don't speak to him, though; he doesn't like to be disturbed when he's hunting. Scares away the butterflies.'

Emily nodded sagely and tried to tread more softly, though the debris underfoot made that difficult.

The wood ended all too soon, and they came out on to a dusty road lined with construction vehicles. Emily could see foundations being dug at intervals along the road, and a couple of stone shells of houses were being erected at the near end.

'Come, I'll show you the plans,' Allison said. She led the way into a portable shed that served as an office. A young man in jeans and a hard hat, sporting a trendy trimmed beard, looked up from a set of blueprints as they came in. 'Morning, Adam,' she said. 'This is our new guest at the house, Emily Richards. I'm just showing her around.'

Adam shook Emily's hand and said a rather absentminded 'Pleased to meet you' in an American accent. Then his eyes fastened on Allison and stayed there as she turned away. His dark, shadowed eyes burned with an intensity that seemed uncalled for by the situation.

'Adam's our architect,' Allison explained. 'And here's what the whole development will look like when it's done.'

On a large table was spread out an elaborate scale model showing a curving road lined with about a dozen cottages, ending in a small green and what looked like a pub. The cottages were mostly two-story, squarish structures of Cotswold yellow sandstone with tiled roofs, covered doorways, and rows of multipaned windows. The modeler had included tiny trees and gardens surrounding each home. Emily was completely charmed.

'Do you have any floor plans I could see?' she asked.

'Sure.' Allison turned to another, smaller table and opened a large album. 'All the plans are in here. Each cottage is a little different – no cookie-cutters in our development.'

Emily leafed through the album, nodding approvingly. The floor plans and interior elevations were modern in layout but included traditional details, such as arched passageways between the main rooms, built-in sideboards and bookcases, and big farmhouse kitchens. She could easily see herself and Luke living in one of these houses. However, she reminded herself, half the point of living in an English cottage was to breathe in the history embedded within its walls. These cottages would have considerable appeal, but history would not be part of it.

'I'm going to show Emily our progress,' Allison said to Adam. He nodded without speaking, that same intense light burning in his eyes. Emily glanced at his desk in passing and saw a photograph of him and a fresh-faced Allison together, smiling. Allison's hair was shorter and Adam's longer than they were now, and Adam's younger-looking face lacked a beard. Allison might see Adam as only a colleague in this project, but Emily would have been willing to bet that at some point in their past he had been something much more.

They left the office shed and strolled down the road, noting the progress on each property. Allison stopped at the one that was furthest along. The walls were complete, with gaping holes where the windows and doors would go, like the empty eye sockets of a skull. Emily shivered. A building in progress ought to hold a sense of hope and possibility, but she always found them slightly creepy.

'This is going to be our model home,' Allison said. 'It isn't far enough along yet to look like much, but by the time you're ready to leave Fitzhugh, it should be nearly finished – you'll be able to see one of those little models come to life.'

Emily made appropriate admiring noises, then they headed back to the canteen, which consisted of a food van with several portable tables in front of it. Emily's stomach told her it was time for elevenses, so she opted for a double-crusted berry pastry along with her tea. Allison chose a more nutritious breakfast wrap. 'I can't eat an early breakfast these days – morning sickness – so by this point in the day I'm always ravenous.'

'Morning sickness shouldn't last too much longer, I would hope,' said Emily. 'You're almost through the first trimester, right?'

'Right. And I've had a fairly easy time, all things considered. I have friends who could hardly leave the house for months.'

Emily's long-ago pregnancy had been so brief that she had barely had time to experience any of the typical unpleasantness; all she remembered was the agony, both mental and physical, of the miscarriage itself. She hastened to change the subject.

'I'm really impressed with what you're doing here. It all seems quite tasteful and appropriate. Have you encountered any opposition from the locals?'

'Nothing serious. A bit of grumbling from a few old curmudgeons who hate change of any kind, but most of the locals are supportive. Over half the cottages are informally spoken for already.'

Emily almost choked on a bit of pastry. 'Really? Any chance you might have one left for me and Luke?' The words came out involuntarily. Although she'd just been telling herself she wanted an old cottage, the prospect of missing out on these made them suddenly more attractive.

Allison looked at her, wide-eyed. 'Are you serious? You're actually thinking of moving here?'

'Well, not moving completely. We'd probably just be vacationers, at least to begin with – until Luke is ready to retire. And to be completely honest, I'm the only one who's thought of it at all – I haven't gotten around to mentioning the idea to Luke yet. He's probably never remotely considered the possibility of leaving Stony Beach. I expect I'd have an uphill battle to convince him.'

'Forgive me, but is it something you could afford? A second home overseas?'

'Oh, yes. I inherited a good income from my great-aunt. And if we did decide to relocate here completely, we could sell my house – Windy Corner. It's large and old by American standards, with a nice bit of land, right on the beach. It'd bring a pretty penny.'

Emily stopped herself with another bite of pastry and a long sip of tea. 'But I'm just dreaming. There's so much to consider, even if Luke would ever warm up to the idea. It's kind of crazy, really. I'm just so charmed by all this.' She swept an arm around to include not only the development but the woods and estate beyond, even the whole countryside up to and including Oxford. 'I've dreamed of England all my life. I can hardly believe I'm finally, actually here.' She giggled. 'I'm tempted to kiss the ground.'

Allison laughed. 'Well, maybe do that closer to the house. In the grass, where not so many people have walked on it.'

Her look grew thoughtful. 'But you know, I feel much the same way. As soon as I arrived in Oxford – I came to the university on a Rhodes scholarship – I knew I'd found my real home. Meeting James there, falling in love first with him, then with this place – it was all like a story that had been written before I was born. I was just acting my part in it. My parents weren't thrilled, but I've never looked back.'

Emily's heart swelled. She'd felt that way when she inherited Windy Corner. But was it possible the past year was only one chapter in her story? Could there be a major plot twist in her future?

FOUR

Luke watched Winky lead Lucky out toward the paddock. 'Finest piece of horseflesh I've seen in years,' he said. 'Too bad he's not up for riding.'

'Don't worry,' James replied. 'We've got plenty of excellent mounts to choose from. How experienced a rider are you?'

'Used to ride all the time as a kid, but I haven't been in the saddle for a while. Too busy.'

'What line are you in?'

'I'm a lawman. Lieutenant sheriff. Quiet little town, or used to be. But we've got a small staff so I don't get a lot of time off.'

James grinned. 'I have to admit, my picture of an American sheriff comes from old Western movies, and it always includes a horse. But I suppose that's a bit outdated.'

Luke laughed. 'Yeah, by about a hundred years. Only Bronco a sheriff rides nowadays is an SUV.'

James joined in the laugh, though it occurred to Luke he might never have heard of a Ford Bronco. 'Let's see . . . What do you think, Conan? Shall we put Luke on Ginger?'

'You've got a horse called Ginger?'

'I named him,' Conan said. 'He's a chestnut, and he's got a bit of ginger in him – no real mischief, you understand, but spirit. He'll give you a workout, but he won't challenge you too much until you get your riding mojo back.'

'Sounds perfect.'

Conan led the way into the stable block. Before reaching Ginger's stall, they passed a dapple-gray pony being saddled by a pretty young blonde.

'Morning, dar— Bunty,' Conan said, his fair cheeks reddening. 'This is the new PG up at the house, Luke Richards.' As Conan passed to the young woman's other side, Luke caught a movement he wasn't supposed to see – Conan's hand lightly brushed her buttock. That plus the aborted word that might have been 'darling' told Luke all he needed to know about their relationship.

The blonde smiled at Luke as she finished tightening the girth, then turned to him with outstretched hand. 'Penelope Fitzhugh. Everyone calls me Bunty. Welcome to Fitzhugh Stables.'

'Pleased to meet you,' Luke said, shaking her hand. 'What do you do around here?'

'I'm the riding instructor. I have a pupil coming in any minute, so excuse me if I get on.' She slipped the bit into the pony's mouth and buckled the bridle.

'Of course. Child, I take it? Your pupil?'

'Yes, a little girl from Oxford. Lily Braithwaite. She's my star pupil in her age group. A real joy.'

'So you're another Fitzhugh, but you don't live at the manor?'

'No, I live in the gatehouse. I'm just a poor relation, not one of *the* Fitzhughs.' She grinned to show she did not resent her position.

James had followed them in and now draped his arm casually over Bunty's shoulder. 'Nonsense, you're my little sister. Only Granny and *Debrett's Peerage* insist on calling you my third cousin twice removed.' He dropped his arm so she could finish her task. 'Bunty and I grew up together. I got her into all sorts of trouble, but for some reason she still seems to like me.'

Bunty gave James a playful punch on the arm. 'That's what you think. I'm secretly plotting to bump you off and take over the estate. Then I'll pull down the house as a symbol of feudalist oppression and build the biggest stable in the country.'

James wagged a finger at her. 'Ah, but you'll have to get rid of Roger, too. He's the heir after me. Not to mention—'

He stopped himself, and Luke surmised he might have been about to spill the beans about the expected baby. 'Not to mention the entail. Anyway, you could never bring yourself to harm old Roger.'

Bunty released an exaggerated sigh. 'No, I suppose I couldn't. Oh, well. So much for that plan. Your head and your title are safe.'

They all laughed. 'Lily's due any minute,' Bunty said. 'You'll have to excuse me.' She took the pony's reins and led her out into the courtyard.

Conan said, 'This way, Luke,' and led him around into the other wing of the stable block. In the first stall, a beautiful chestnut nickered in greeting.

'Here you are, old boy,' Conan said, stroking the horse's nose. 'Got a new rider for you. Luke, meet Ginger.'

Luke took Conan's place with the horse. Conan called, 'Winky! Got a customer for you!' When no one appeared, he muttered to himself, 'Where is the old devil?'

'Probably still in the paddock with Lucky. He didn't seem to move too fast.'

'True. Ruined his leg in the same racing accident that cost him his eye. Another rider cut too close and Winky's horse went down. The other horse's hoof caught his eye on the way, and his own horse fell on his leg and crushed it.'

Luke winced. 'I'm surprised he's still working. He must be, what, getting on for eighty?'

'About that. He's not good for much these days – I find him most mornings in an empty stall, sleeping off the previous night. But Lady Margaret won't hear of him being let go.'

They both glanced into the courtyard and saw Winky limping his way back. They waited for him to reach them.

'Mornin', guv'nor,' Winky said. 'What can we do ya for?'

'This is Luke Richards, Winky. Guest at the manor. He's going to ride Ginger. Get her ready, will you?'

'Course, guv'nor, right away.' He sized Luke up with his one eye, taking in the jeans and cowboy boots. 'Western saddle, am I right, sir?'

'Please.'

Winky hefted a saddle off a hook on the wall and edged

around Luke and Conan into the stall. Luke could see he'd only be in the way if he stuck around to watch. He heard the sound of a car on gravel – a powerful sports car, if he was any judge – and followed Conan back into the courtyard, where James and Bunty were waiting with the pony.

The car – a royal-blue Porsche convertible – crunched to a stop opposite the stable office. Out of it climbed a rather frail-looking blond girl of about eight or ten and a tall, dark man who looked as if he considered driving his daughter to her riding lesson to be an unforgivable intrusion in the busy day of an important man.

'James,' the newcomer said with a curt nod.

'Simon,' James returned, not coldly but with less friendliness than he'd shown toward everyone else.

'Let's get this over with, shall we?' Simon said to Bunty. 'I have to be in Oxford in an hour.'

Bunty opened her mouth to protest, but Lily forestalled her. 'Daddy, my lesson always takes a whole hour. How am I going to win the junior dressage if I don't get my whole hour?'

Simon's frown faded slightly. 'All right, then, one hour, but I want you in this car at exactly' – he consulted his expensive-looking wristwatch – 'eleven twenty-eight. Now go!' He gave his daughter a gentle push.

She ran toward the pony. 'Come on, Blossom! We've got work to do!'

Conan gave the girl a leg up to mount, and Bunty walked alongside as Lily rode Blossom toward the paddock.

James followed them with his eyes. 'I see she has your drive, Simon.'

Simon humphed. 'She does that. Along with her mother's wheedling ways.'

'Care for a ride yourself while you wait? You could go out with Luke here. He's our new PG.'

Luke stuck out his hand, but Simon only turned slightly toward him and nodded. 'Lord, no. Do I look as if I'm dressed for riding?' He indicated his immaculate gray suit. 'Besides, I've got work to do. I'll sit in the office, if you don't mind.' Without waiting for an answer, he grabbed a briefcase from the back of his car and strode off toward a door at the far end of the stable block.

'Nice guy,' Luke said in a tone that allowed James to take the words as he would.

James sighed. 'Believe it or not, Simon and I were once close friends. Back at Balliol. But I gave him some financial advice that turned out not to be as good as I thought it was, and he's never forgiven me.'

'Seems to be doing all right for himself now.'

'Oh, yes. He went into finance, mostly to prove me wrong, I think, and now everything he touches turns to gold.'

'You'd think he'd be able to let the past go, in that case.'

James gave a wry smile. 'Perhaps he could – if I didn't live in the Big House. Simon wasn't born into wealth and station as I was, and that's another thing I fear he'll never be able to forgive.'

Emily and Allison returned to the house just in time for lunch. Emily went upstairs to change her shoes and leave her sweater. She met Luke coming out of their room; he had changed as well.

She gave him a kiss. 'How was your ride?'

'It was great. Couldn't take it for very long, though. I haven't used those muscles in longer than I care to remember. I may have to join you in that bathtub tonight.'

'Fine with me.'

More kisses ensued. Then Luke asked about her walking tour with Allison.

'It was . . . interesting.' She gave him a rundown of the salient points, ending with their visit to the new development but omitting her thoughts about the possibility of buying in. She wanted to see if Luke would come to share any part of her love for England before she broached the subject of a vacation cottage. Luke was Stony Beach born and bred; he'd never lived elsewhere except during his brief stint in the army after high school. It wouldn't be a simple thing to wean him away.

At lunch, Lady Margaret was silent as the two couples chatted about their respective morning activities. As they were finishing their meal, Roger asked if Luke and Emily would be interested in seeing his butterfly collection.

'For goodness' sake, Roger,' his mother said, speaking for the first time during the meal. 'Leave the poor people alone. When will you learn that no one but you has any interest in your juvenile hobby?'

Roger opened his mouth and shut it again, tempting Emily to quote, 'Close your mouth, please, Michael. We are not a codfish.' But of course she didn't say it aloud. She felt far too sorry for Roger to do that.

'James and I have a date with a couple of fishing poles,' Luke said. 'Some other time, I hope.'

Roger turned a crestfallen face to Emily. 'And you?'

Emily felt obligated to accept, under the circumstances. She liked Roger and felt he needed encouraging. How bad could it be?

He led her to a small outbuilding on the other side of the kitchen gardens. Surely in a house the size of Fitzhugh Manor there must be a spare room he could have used for a workshop. Emily suspected that either Lady Margaret refused houseroom to her son's dead butterflies or he himself preferred to work far from his mother's critical eye. Or both.

The room was sparsely furnished, with bookcases on one windowless wall. Against another wall stood racks of shallow cubbies occupied by wooden trays. A large, high table took up most of the remaining space. Only one stool stood at the table. Roger offered it to Emily and began lifting trays out of the rack one at a time.

As he named and described the moths and butterflies one by one – a dozen or so to a tray, tray after tray and rack after rack – Emily felt she was repeating her experience with Lady Margaret in the rose garden, except that Roger's butterflies, being small and individual, were far more numerous in their variety than his mother's roses. Each was a small miracle of color and pattern, so she tried to focus on that rather than on the fact that they were dead. Besides, she reminded herself, most butterflies had such brief natural lifespans that Roger could only have shortened their lives by a matter of hours. On the other hand, those hours could have constituted half of each creature's mature winged life.

In the space of ten minutes, her eyes had glazed over, and

her brain refused to accept a single additional appellation, classification, or description of habitat. But when she detected a change in Roger's tone as he named one particular butterfly that inhabited a tray all its own, she seized on it.

'Roger, did you by any chance *discover* this butterfly?'

He blushed with a charming, bashful smile. 'I can't say I was the first to discover it. But to my knowledge, this is the only specimen whose capture has ever been recorded in England.'

'But that's marvelous! Congratulations! Where did you find it?'

'Incredibly enough, right here in our own little wood. Most of my specimens were found somewhere on this estate. The Fitzhugh property comprises a remarkable variety of habitats, from wetlands to meadow to forest. No desert or tundra, but you don't find a lot of butterflies in those places anyway.' He smiled at his little joke.

'Amazing,' she said, looking more closely at the delicate patterning on the wings. Roger was no doubt regarded as a mere eccentric by his family and acquaintances, but given more scope – more encouragement from his dismissive mother, more ambition – he might have been a reputable scientist in his chosen field. At the very least, Roger's butterflies deserved as much respect as his mother's roses.

She watched him puttering happily about, rearranging his trays of wings frozen in flight. No, he was probably happier this way. Human accolades would mean nothing to him in comparison with the freedom to roam daily through his vast ancestral estate, which held everything he would ever need.

FIVE

When Roger at last released her to return to the house, Emily headed to her room, feeling the need for some time alone and possibly a nap. She knew Luke and James would be fishing right up until it was time to dress for dinner. She had not yet had time or energy to finish unpacking, so she addressed that first, reveling in the beautiful craftsmanship of the wardrobes with their drawers especially sized for every conceivable type of garment. She would have to get something like this built at Windy Corner. Maybe she could clear out one of the attics and turn it into a closet-cum-dressing room.

Her musings were interrupted by a knock at the door. She called 'Come in!' and heard the door creak open, but no one spoke. She looked around to see a woman who made Lady Margaret look young. The woman had more wrinkles than skin, and her shrunken frame looked as if it could have no internal support. And yet she stood upright and unaided; her severe black dress fell in unbroken folds to her lower calves.

'Her Ladyship requests that you join her for tea in her sitting room, madam.'

'Her Ladyship? Oh, you mean Lady Margaret. You must be Cadwallader.'

'The family call me Caddie, madam. I am her Ladyship's personal maid.' She stood a little taller as she said it. Emily sorted through her memories of shows like *Downton Abbey* and *Upstairs, Downstairs* to retrieve the servants' pecking order: a lady's maid held a position of trust with a status just below that of butler and housekeeper. In this house, where the roles of butler and housekeeper had been relegated to history, Caddie must hold a power greater in some respects even than Allison's.

'I see.' Emily glanced at her watch – ten minutes to four. 'Does Lady Margaret wish me to come now?'

'Her Ladyship takes tea at precisely four o'clock, madam. You will have time to dress.' Caddie cast a reproving eye over Emily's chinos and sweater. Emily felt a rush of profound gratitude that she had packed a variety of dresses and skirts, even though she hadn't been sure she would need them. 'I will return to escort you to her sitting room.'

'Thank you, Caddie. I'll be ready.'

Only after the door had shut behind her did Emily realize what an extraordinary honor was being paid her by this invitation. Although it might be less an invitation than a prelude to an inquisition.

She dressed in a brown tweed skirt and a quickly steamed ivory silk blouse, fastening the last button as Caddie's knock came again at the door. The house was chilly, so she threw a hand-knitted fawn-colored shawl around her shoulders before following the old woman out.

They traversed the whole width of the house in silence and passed through double doors that echoed those leading to the wing where Luke and Emily were staying. The door at which Caddie stopped was positioned in mirror image to their door.

Caddie entered without knocking. Emily passed between burgundy velvet curtains – meant, she supposed, to keep out drafts – and saw a round piecrust table replete with tea things, presided over by Lady Margaret in a black silk dress only a little less ornate than the one she had worn the previous evening. A vacant chair that might have been genuine Louis XV stood at the table across from her.

'Mrs Luke Richards,' Caddie announced, and then departed. Emily was left alone, facing the incarnation of something between a stern schoolmistress and Medusa. In fact, a dragon.

'Thank you for joining me, Mrs Richards.' Lady Margaret indicated the empty chair.

Emily sat, feeling for perhaps the first time since adolescence that her feet and hands were too big for her body. 'Thank you for inviting me.'

Lady Margaret poured milk into both cups without asking, then added the tea. Emily preferred her tea without milk but now felt like a barbarian for doing so. 'One lump or two?'

Again, Emily preferred her tea without sugar, but she said, 'One, please.'

The tea service was, if possible, more elegant than the one Allison had brought to their room the previous afternoon, and the tiered stand was piled even higher with every imaginable delicacy. Emily wondered who would eat all this – she wanted no more than perhaps one cake and one sandwich, and she felt sure Lady Margaret would eat only crumbs. Perhaps an army of well-dressed, well-mannered Beatrix Potter mice would emerge after her departure to finish up what was left.

'Did you enjoy your tour of the estate?' Lady Margaret asked when the formalities had been completed.

'Very much,' Emily said, selecting a cucumber sandwich from the stand. 'It's all quite lovely.'

'The gardens especially, perhaps.'

Emily's favorite part had actually been the building project, but she could hardly mention that. 'The gardens are quite impressive. But your little rose garden is the loveliest of all.'

Lady Margaret smiled as if the compliment were nothing more than her due. 'It is a labor of love.'

Emily bit into her sandwich, wondering whether the rose garden was the only thing Lady Margaret had ever loved. Her husband? Maybe for the length of the honeymoon, not longer. James's father? She seemed to have no affection left for her younger son, so perhaps she had spent it all on the elder. But she had betrayed some feeling for James – perhaps deep feeling – even though she constantly criticized his choice of a wife.

'You seem to be a sensible, right-thinking woman, for an American. You see, do you not, why I love this estate? And why I wish to have it preserved for posterity?'

Ah. Here was the minefield. She was expected to take sides between Lady Margaret and Allison. Hardly fair, since she was supposed to be Allison's family friend.

She chose her words with care. 'I can certainly understand that the estate should be preserved. It's a unique legacy. And I'm sure James and Allison want that, too. But I suppose it depends on what you mean by preservation – keeping it exactly as it has always been but risking its ultimate loss, or preserving it in a form that is viable in today's economy.'

Lady Margaret frowned, and Emily felt a thundercloud building. 'I know what that woman considers "preservation." I can live with the public stables – at least keeping horses is a gentleman's occupation. But letting the house go to rack and ruin with no servants to care for it? Opening the grounds to all and sundry to trample over and abuse? And the house too, no doubt, eventually, though I hope she'll have the decency to wait until I'm gone for that.' She paused to fan herself with her lace-trimmed handkerchief, overcome by the very thought.

Emily held her breath and concentrated on choosing one cake from the tempting variety offered, hoping this was the extent of the old woman's prescience. Surely she had not divined the existence of the building project? Or, for that matter, Luke and Emily's status as paying guests.

But the next thing Lady Margaret said took Emily completely by surprise, so that she fumbled the cake with her fingers and had to retrieve it from her plate.

'I believe Allison is having an affair.'

Emily was shocked to her bones not only that Lady Margaret could think such a thing but that she would share the thought with a stranger – and one whom she might expect to take Allison's side. She must be desperate to enlist some ally in her battle.

When she had recovered her composure with the aid of a bite of cake, Emily said, 'Oh, no, Lady Margaret. Surely you're mistaken. It's obvious how much she loves James.'

The dowager went on as if Emily had not spoken. 'She receives secret phone calls that she won't answer in my presence. She disappears for hours every day with no hint of where she is going. She glows continually with some hidden satisfaction. She is furtive, I tell you. A sure sign of an affair.'

So Lady Margaret had, in fact, observed the effect of the building project on Allison's behavior, as well as the effect of the pregnancy on her emotional state, and given them both a completely wrong interpretation.

'I'm sure if you were to ask her about it, she could set your mind at rest.'

Lady Margaret applied the corner of her handkerchief to the tip of her nose as if blocking out an unpleasant smell. 'I would never stoop to such a conversation. I thought perhaps that you, as an old family friend, might see your way to giving her a hint.'

'A hint?'

Lady Margaret huffed as if annoyed at Emily's obtuseness. 'That her activities have not gone unremarked. That she should conduct herself as a respectable married woman and the mistress of a great estate.'

Emily wondered whether Allison's true alleged offense was having an affair or merely being discovered in it. She knew the British upper classes had a long tradition of discreet adultery.

'If I thought your suspicions were justified, Lady Margaret, I might do that. But I'm certain they're not.'

Lady Margaret banged her stick on the floor. 'I tell you she is having an affair, and I believe I know with whom.'

Now Emily was completely baffled. 'Whom . . . I mean, who is it, do you think?'

'A man she used to be engaged to. Before she hoodwinked my grandson into marrying her. I believe his name is Adam Marshall. She is clearly still attached to this man. She even invited him to the wedding. She married James only for his wealth and position.'

A lightbulb went on as Emily remembered Adam, the architect, following Allison with his eyes. She could believe there was still an attachment there – but it went only in the opposite direction.

'Lady Margaret, I'm sorry to contradict you, but I'm quite sure you're wrong. Allison married James for love. She loves the estate, too, but only because it's a part of James. She would never do anything to hurt him.'

Lady Margaret made a dismissive gesture. 'You have known the woman less than twenty-four hours. I have known her for five years. *Five years* in which she has yet to produce an heir. What loving wife could fail to conceive a child within five years? Penelope would have had three or four strapping sons by this time.' Lady Margaret sank back into her chair, coughing with her handkerchief to her lips.

Emily was stung by the injustice of this. Even if it had been true that Allison had not yet conceived, she could hardly have been blamed for it; Emily was sure it wasn't for lack of trying. She had to bite her tongue to avoid revealing James and Allison's secret. Lady Margaret would find out in time, and God willing she would live to see her great-grandson.

Cadwallader materialized out of nowhere, smelling salts in hand. 'I think you'd best go, madam,' she said, and set her mouth in a thin, reproachful line. Emily could not but agree.

Lady Margaret did not appear for dinner but sent Caddie with the message that she was indisposed. Emily found an opportunity while James and Luke were reliving their day's fishing for Roger's benefit to give Allison a précis of the first part of her tea with the dowager – her complaints about Allison's handling of the estate. The rest would have to wait for greater privacy.

'Oh dear.' Allison sighed. 'I keep hoping one day she'll come around – warm up to me and see the value of what we're doing – but things only seem to get worse. One day she'll fret herself into the grave, and I'll be left feeling guilty all my life for having driven her there.'

Emily patted her arm. 'You're not driving her there. She's doing it herself. If she would only face reality, she would be much happier, and live longer.'

'I suppose you're right.' Allison glanced at James, who was spreading his arms to show Roger the size of the one that got away. 'It's James I'm concerned about. His parents died when he was quite young, and his grandmother has really been a mother to him. Underneath that crusty exterior, she loves him to distraction, and he dotes on her. It will be such a blow when she goes.'

'At least you'll both have a new little life to care for,' Emily said with a smile. 'When all is said and done, Lady Margaret represents the past. Your baby is the future.'

Allison returned a teary smile. 'You're right, of course. Don't mind me. It's the hormones – they make me all weepy. It won't be long before we can tell her about the baby, and then, knock on wood, everything will be all right.'

Emily glanced at the men. They were engrossed, but even so, Emily didn't want to risk making the rest of her communication in their presence. They had finished eating, so she said to Allison, 'Could we be really old fashioned and retire to the drawing room ahead of the men? There's something more I need to tell you in private.'

Allison looked startled but nodded and rose. 'We've had enough of your fish stories, gentlemen. We're going to have a civilized coffee in the drawing room. Please don't hurry on our account.'

James shot her a sheepish grin, while Luke raised an interrogative eyebrow toward Emily. She tried to signal with her eyes that something significant was up, then followed Allison out of the room.

When they were settled on a Georgian sofa and Witherspoon had come and gone with coffee, Emily said, 'Allison, I don't know how to tell you this, but Lady Margaret told me she thinks you're having an affair. With Adam.'

Allison clattered her cup into its saucer. 'With *Adam*? But that's insane. I mean, yes, we were once engaged, but I couldn't be more over him. We grew up together, and our families always assumed we'd marry. I'll always regard him as a friend, but as soon as I met James – well, that was it. I knew I'd been kidding myself that I could ever love Adam that way.'

'I tried to tell her that, but she wouldn't listen. And . . . I'm not sure if you're aware of this, but I don't think Adam is over *you*. I saw the way he looked at you when we went to the building site – hungry, as if he wanted to devour you. You might want to be careful around him.'

Allison waved a hand. 'Adam may still have a bit of a thing for me, but we have a perfectly good understanding. It's been almost six years since I broke it off with him. I hardly saw him after my wedding until about a year ago, when I hired him for this project. And anyway, Lady Margaret has never seen us together and never will. She just fastened on him because she knew there was another man in my past.'

'That's reasonable, I suppose. I tried to dissuade her, of course. It's obvious to me that you and James are very much in love.'

Allison beamed. 'Yes, we are. Thank you. And thank you for telling me. I don't know what she intends to do with this fantasy of hers, but forewarned is forearmed.'

'She also implied – no, actually, she said outright – that if you truly loved James, you would have given him an heir by now. Ridiculous, of course, but I did wonder if telling her about the baby sooner rather than later might help.'

'Hmm . . . you may be right. I'll talk to James about it.'

'You'll tell him all of it? The supposed affair and everything?'

'Of course. We always tell each other everything. James has perfect confidence in me. He'll know there's nothing in it.'

Emily hoped she was right. She knew first-hand how harmful to a relationship an unfounded suspicion could be.

Later that evening, as they both luxuriated in their capacious bathtub, Emily filled Luke in on her tea with Lady Margaret. 'In a weird way, she reminds me of a Forster character.' Early in their renewed courtship, Emily had forced Luke to watch several films based on her beloved novels by E.M. Forster – *Howards End*, *A Room with a View*, *Where Angels Fear to Tread*. 'She's not exactly a Wilcox – certainly not Ruth, the mother. Lady Margaret has Ruth's attachment to place, but I don't think it's a genuine love like Ruth's was – it's more about position and appearances. In that way she's more like the rest of the family. They were determined to keep control over Howards End even though they didn't particularly want to live there. It even led to murder in the end. Well, manslaughter, anyway.'

'You're not thinking things could get that bad here, are you?'

She shuddered. 'Good Lord, I hope not. But that old woman is a seething mass of repressed emotion. If she were younger and fitter, and I were in Allison's shoes, I wouldn't feel any too safe in this house.' She ran a meditative sponge over Luke's leg. 'Actually, the best Forster parallel is probably the grandmother in *Where Angels Fear to Tread*. That woman had such an intense investment in her family honor that she ordered the virtual kidnapping of another man's child – one who had no blood relationship to her at all and only a tenuous connection through her widowed daughter-in-law. That led to death, too. I tell you, this whole class-and-land-and-family thing can make people crazy.'

'Yeah. I guess that's part of the reason it's on the way out. Turn around and I'll get your back.' She turned, and he scrubbed gently as he went on. 'But the idea of family being important and being tied to the land – that in itself is something I think we Americans could use more of. I don't like the way people move all over the place and lose touch with each other.'

Luke's extended family had mostly stayed in Tillamook County, or at least in Oregon, and they all got together for holidays. Emily knew he was thinking of his son, Aaron, who had moved to California as soon as he finished high school and had rarely been in touch since. He had come to their wedding, though, and Emily felt the relationship was in a fair way to being restored.

'Yes, I agree with you there. We could use a little more tradition and stability in our culture. Your turn.' They switched positions and she scrubbed his back. 'I think where the evil comes in is in being so obsessed with position and reputation, with how other people see you. If that starts to come before actual relationships with loved ones, then you have a serious problem.'

'Can't argue with that. And speaking of relations with loved ones . . .' He turned around and took the sponge from her hand. 'Think you're rested enough to make good use of that perfect bed?'

SIX

The following morning, Luke and Emily prepared for their first excursion – to William Morris's home at Kelmscott. Emily had looked it up online the night before – since becoming computer-literate the previous winter, she had discovered the vast usefulness of Google – and found that the manor was open only on select Wednesdays and Saturdays. This was one of the Wednesdays, so it seemed like a good time to go.

If Oxford had been a grueling initiation into English town driving, the route to Kelmscott was an equally baffling, though greener and quieter, introduction to driving in the countryside. Binsey lay just to the northwest of Oxford while Kelmscott was significantly farther to the southwest, in a land that the modern highway system forgot. Narrow lane opened out of narrow lane until Emily was sure they must be lost in a labyrinth of hedgerows that had no convenient key. But at last the name *Kelmscott* appeared on a sign. They drove through a tiny village that seemed deserted, found the designated parking area after more confusion, and walked about a quarter of a mile to the actual Morris estate.

Emily had subconsciously been expecting another manor on the scale of Fitzhugh, but Kelmscott proved to be much more modest in size. In sheer beauty, though, she thought it unequaled by any house she had seen. Its yellow Cotswold stone had been weathered gray by the passing of centuries, while ivy meandered about its walls as if, dreaming, it had lost its way to the sky. The L-shaped mass of the house with its graceful gables spoke of solidity without stolidness, of tradition without petrification, of a firm but adaptable welcome that was the quintessence of 'home.'

Once inside, she could see that the scale of the house – its medium-to-small-sized rooms and lower ceilings – was more human, more 'homely' (in Tolkien's sense) than that of Fitzhugh Manor and its ilk. While Fitzhugh was a lovely place to visit, Kelmscott was the kind of house Emily could imagine actually living in.

They learned from the docents that the manor, which had begun life as a humble farmhouse, was not exactly as it had been in Morris's day. By the time of his death, the structure was crumbling from the foundations up and had to be largely rebuilt. The current furnishings had been gathered from various sources, but everything in the house, from furniture to pictures to tableware, had been designed and made by Morris, his family, and his colleagues in the Arts and Crafts movement of the late nineteenth century.

Emily was in textile heaven, gazing at all the intricate tapestries, upholstery, wall coverings, bed coverings, and especially the phenomenally skilled and detailed needlework created by Morris's wife, Jane (whom Emily had previously known only as a favorite model of the pre-Raphaelite painters Edward Burne-Jones and Dante Gabriel Rossetti), and their daughter May. The collection of the two women's needlework included several nearly life-size embroidered panels depicting great women of history.

Luke made polite noises as Emily effused over the textiles, but he was genuinely interested in the furniture and other woodwork. 'This workmanship is incredible,' he said, examining an inlaid desk. 'They don't make stuff like this anymore.'

'I know,' Emily said. 'Morris's motto was "Have nothing in your home that you do not know to be useful or believe to be beautiful." Here, even the useful stuff is elevated to an art form.'

'Kinda makes you think about the way we live, doesn't it? I mean, Windy Corner has some pretty good craftsmanship, and we call it old by American standards. But heck, the Pilgrims hadn't even landed when this place was built. This is *history*.'

'And that's exactly why I've always wanted to visit England. Wanted to live here, really. To have that sense of roots that go back centuries.' She was tempted to take this opportunity to bring up the idea of buying a home in England, but she stopped herself. Better to wait and let Luke's current thinking take deeper root in his mind.

From the house they moved on to the tearoom for lunch and then to the gift shop, where Emily went a little wild. It was simply too difficult to choose between all the lovely designs and the various useful objects on which they had been employed.

'You know we have to cart all this stuff home, right?' Luke said as she piled his arms high with cushion covers, tea towels, serving bowls, and books.

'We can mail it. Hang the cost. You just can't get this stuff at home.'

Luke rolled his eyes and shifted his load. But Emily had pity on him after that.

They took their purchases to the car and then strolled through the village, stopping to look at its ancient church, before they headed back to Fitzhugh. Emily had spent the perfect day. If she had died that night, she would have felt she had accomplished a good part of her dreams. And they still had almost a month to spend in England.

The following day, Thursday, dawned on a heavy, settled rain. All the plans they'd made involved being as much outdoors as in, so Luke and Emily opted to spend the day at Fitzhugh.

Allison offered to show them the house in greater depth and
extent than they'd yet seen. 'I need the practice at being a tour
guide,' she said. 'For later.'

Emily was enthralled as they walked through room after
room, each one containing heirlooms that went back centuries
within the Fitzhugh family. If Kelmscott had wafted the scent
of history, Fitzhugh Manor positively reeked of it. If Allison's
plans for monetization had required destroying any of this,
Emily would have found it difficult to sympathize with her.
But since her changes simply involved sharing all this beauty
and timelessness with a wider audience, Emily could find no
fault with that. If none of the old families opened their homes
to the public, she would never have been able to see anything
like them.

As they were touring the vast, partially underground kitchens
with their innumerable offshoot rooms once dedicated to
purposes such as plucking poultry, spinning wool, and storing
a bewildering array of rifles and shotguns, Emily asked how
many people had been on the staff when it was at its height.

'About a hundred, I think,' Allison replied. 'Including the
outdoor staff, the stables, and so forth.'

'All those people to serve one family?' Luke said. 'No
wonder people rebelled against the class system.'

'That is one way to look at it,' Allison said. 'But you can
also consider that the estate was like a village in itself. The
landlord gave work to all those people when they might not
have had it otherwise. And think of all the people who
were employed to build this place, all the craftsmen who made
the furniture, the artists who painted the portraits. None
of them would have had the opportunity to exercise their
skills to their fullest extent without rich patrons to hire
them. I know it seems offensive to our American populist
sensibilities, but, at its best, it was a system that brought
about a lot of good.'

Luke shook his head, clearly unconvinced but too polite
to say so. As a confirmed Anglophile, Emily had learned to
overlook a good deal in England's history – not merely the
class system but the imperialism, the xenophobia, the attitude
that no one else in the world was quite as human as the English

themselves. In her view, British culture – centuries of great literature, art, architecture, and more recently film – redeemed those crimes to a large degree. But Luke was American to his back collar button, and he had no time for any of it.

By this time they had finished with the kitchens and ascended to the second-floor portrait gallery. 'Of course, like any other system, the British landowning system was subject to abuse. Take this fellow, for example.' Allison stopped before a large full-length portrait of a man in seventeenth-century dress. That he had been a Royalist rather than a Roundhead in the English Civil War was clear from the embroidered satin of his coat, the deep lace adorning his collar and cuffs, and the long, elaborate curls of his wig. He had the reddened, puffy features that spoke of a life of decadence, and his piggish little eyes held only disdain.

'Percival Fitzhugh, the fifth baronet. A complete and utter hedonist. He nearly bankrupted the estate with his orgies and gambling. It was said after his death there wasn't a family in the county, high or low, that did not have his blood in their veins – and you have to think most of those liaisons were nonconsensual. He worked his servants to the bone and neglected to pay them, and the farmers on the estate starved because he took all their produce for his own table. He kept his woods stocked with enough game to feed the whole village, but poachers were hanged or shot on sight. A real charmer, that one.'

Luke's hands balled into fists. 'I'd like to have gotten my hands on a fellow like that. Legally speaking, I mean.'

'Good luck with that. He did hardly anything that was actually illegal; the law of the time favored the rich. And of course he was the magistrate, so there was no one to call him to account when he did cross the line.' She paused with a slight smile. 'He did finally get his comeuppance, though. At the hands of his own mother.'

Emily gasped, unable to conceive of a mother deliberately harming her child.

Allison led them on to the next portrait. 'Lady Letitia, daughter of the Earl of Somerset and wife of the fourth baronet. She was a formidable lady.'

Emily could well believe that. Lady Letitia had been painted as a young mother before she had fully lost the bloom of youth and beauty. She had excellent bones, the kind of face that ages well, and a lovely figure, shown off by a costume less elaborate than her son's. There was something in her eye and the set of her jaw that reminded Emily of Lady Margaret, though both being Fitzhughs by marriage, they were unlikely to be blood relations.

Allison continued her narrative. 'Percival was ruining the family, as I said, but he had a son – the only legitimate one – whose mother had died giving birth to him, so he had always been under his grandmother's care. She had protected him from his father's influence, and he had grown up into a fine, decent, responsible lordling. Lady Letitia was determined that he should come into the title before his father had wasted his inheritance completely and brought irrevocable dishonor to the family name. So she arranged a little accident.'

Emily's mind flew immediately to the accident that had once been arranged for her but fortunately had not succeeded in killing her. The brakes on her car had been disabled. That was the easiest sort of accident to arrange in modern times, but, of course, in the seventeenth century people would have had to be more creative. 'What sort of accident?'

'One night when she knew he would be traveling a particularly treacherous road, she loosened a wheel on his carriage.'

Not so different after all.

'She confessed it on her deathbed, with her grandson present. The wheel came off as expected, and Percival was sent flying into a ravine, where rocks made mincemeat of his evil little head.' A tiny smile played about Allison's mouth as she added, 'Rumor had it he was castrated in the fall as well. Most likely apocryphal, but it would have been poetic justice.'

Luke shuddered. 'I guess so, but – wow. That woman was ruthless.'

'She did what she thought had to be done to preserve her family. She sacrificed the one to save the many – the Fitzhughs of the future. I'm not saying I approve – or could ever imagine acting that way myself – but I can see her point of view.'

Allison paused with a slight smile. 'In fact, Percival's son, Augustus, turned out to be the founder of a line of much-reformed Fitzhughs. I doubt my James would have been possible without him. So, in a peculiar way, I owe Lady Letitia a lot.'

SEVEN

The tour of the manor ended in the library – none too soon for Luke. 'I can't tear myself away from these gorgeous books,' Emily said with an apologetic smile. 'Aunt Beatrice's library is nothing to this. You don't mind, do you?'

Luke didn't mind at all. He'd had enough of being indoors, let alone looking at stuff acquired over centuries by people he'd never met and hearing stories of people he'd like to lock up, or maybe punch in the face. He left her to her raptures and borrowed an umbrella from the hall to walk to the stables. It might not be a good day to ride, but at least he could admire the horses. He'd only seen a couple of them on his previous visit.

He didn't see anyone in the courtyard – not surprising, given the weather – so he stuck his head into the office, hoping to announce himself and maybe get James or Conan to show him the rest of the stock. But the office was empty, too.

Luke figured he couldn't hurt anything by poking around on his own; he had enough horse sense not to mess with anything he shouldn't. He headed first down the row of stalls where the riding-school horses were housed, stopping to get acquainted with each one. They were all good-tempered and friendly, as they had to be to serve the public, and they all appeared exceedingly well kept.

As he neared the end of the row, he heard rustling in the next stall, and heavy breathing that didn't sound like a horse's. His lawman's sense was alerted to the possibility of trouble, but when he heard a woman's sigh of pleasure, he realized he was not about to interrupt a crime but to trespass on an intimate moment – at a guess, between Conan and Bunty. He smiled to himself and turned away – only to see Lady Margaret walking with her deliberate step down the length of the stable toward him.

'Lady Margaret!' he exclaimed a little more loudly than was strictly necessary for her to hear. 'I didn't expect to see you here. Do you still ride?' The sounds from the next stall indicated that his ploy to alert the lovers had been successful. He didn't know for certain how the dowager would feel about their relationship, but given her frustrated designs for Bunty and James and her generally strict adherence to class distinctions, it wasn't hard to guess she would not take to it kindly. Especially not to the two of them cavorting in her stables.

'Mr Richards. No, I haven't ridden for some years, thanks to this cursed arthritis.' She flourished her cane. 'But I still like to visit the horses as often as I can. I was quite an accomplished horsewoman in my prime.'

'I can imagine,' Luke said. 'I've been saying hello to the horses, too. Maybe you wouldn't mind giving me a proper introduction.'

Lady Margaret's forced smile suggested she'd had a different purpose in coming, but her duty as a hostess was paramount. 'Certainly, if you wish.' She turned back with him and gave him the name – Fonteyn – and pedigree of the first horse they came to.

Out of the corner of his eye, Luke saw Conan slip out of the last stall and nip over to the other wing, where the board horses were housed and where he properly belonged. A minute later, Bunty emerged, looking flawlessly turned out except for one stray wisp of straw in her hair. Lady Margaret was focused on the horse, so Luke made a motion as if removing something from his hair, and Bunty got the message. She blushed and mouthed the words 'Thank you.' Luke grinned back.

Bunty gave her jacket a final tug and came toward them. 'Granny! I didn't expect to see you here today, given the weather. What brings you out in the rain?'

Luke was confused by the 'Granny,' since James had said he was the only one who regarded Bunty as his sister. But he supposed it was a courtesy title, since Bunty had grown up under Lady Margaret's eye.

The dowager allowed herself to be kissed and eyed Bunty with a mixture of affection and suspicion. 'I might ask you the same, young lady, since clearly you have no lessons to give today.'

Bunty's voice was a shade too carefree. 'Oh, I just love these horses so much I can't stay away.' She stroked Fonteyn's nose, and the mare nickered as if to confirm her story. 'Besides, we're a groom short today, and a rainy day is a good opportunity to give them an extra brushing and a special feed.'

'A groom short?' Lady Margaret looked unexpectedly concerned. 'Is Bill Pollard sick again? I wanted a word with him.'

'No, Winky— Bill's around here somewhere. Jenny has a bad cold, that's all.'

Lady Margaret looked momentarily relieved, then her expression resumed its accustomed sternness. 'Isn't it Mr O'Donnell's job to cover any shorthandedness?'

'He takes care of the board horses when needed. Jenny works on my side, so I'm filling in for her. I imagine Conan's probably over in the other wing now.'

'You imagine.' Lady Margaret narrowed her eyes. 'Be careful, Penelope. You know the dangers of fraternizing too much with the staff.'

Bunty's jaw tightened, but she controlled her voice. 'If you want to get technical, Granny, Conan's status in these stables is exactly equivalent to mine.'

'Do not split hairs with me, young lady. Your status is neither here nor there. You are family. He is not.'

Bunty dimpled and kissed Lady Margaret's withered cheek a second time. 'All right, Granny. Whatever you say.'

Lady Margaret softened visibly but did not relent. 'Since you're here, then, Penelope, perhaps you could introduce Mr Richards to the rest of the horses as he asked. I find I am getting tired.' Without waiting for a response, she passed them and rounded the corner into the other wing of the stable block.

Bunty turned to Luke. 'Do you really want to meet all the horses? I'm happy to do the honors if you do, but . . .'

Luke grinned. 'Nah. That was just a ruse to distract Lady Margaret. I already said hello – I don't need to know all their pedigrees.'

She laid a hand on his arm. 'Thank you again. I can't tell you how much Conan and I are in your debt. If she ever found out about us . . .'

Luke didn't need her to finish that sentence. 'I can imagine. But you can't go on this way forever. What are you going to do?'

Bunty shrugged helplessly. 'Just wait for her to die, I suppose. It sounds callous, but that's about the size of it. We could look for jobs elsewhere – we're both well qualified, so it wouldn't be difficult – but Fitzhugh is my home. Conan's, too – his father worked here before him. He grew up with James and me, never went away except to university. Neither of us can imagine leaving. But Granny will never see him as my equal. And horrible as it sounds, I think she still cherishes some irrational hope that James and I will marry someday.' She shook her blond ponytail. 'For an intelligent, fundamentally sensible woman, Granny can do denial like nobody else I know.'

Bunty returned to her work. Luke hadn't yet met all the horses in the other wing, so he rounded the corner and stopped at the first stall, Ginger's, to say hello. He'd taken a liking to the horse, partly because its color and name reminded him of Emily.

From farther down the row he could hear voices – Lady Margaret's aristocratic contralto and Winky's Cockney whine – but couldn't catch the words. Not that he was trying. After he'd shown Ginger a reasonable amount of attention, he moved on down the row to Lucky, and the voices grew more distinct. They seemed to be coming from the next stall but one.

'So you have nothing to report today, Bill?'

'Nothin', milady. Ain't seen much of 'erself around 'ere last few days. Just in and out, like, fer a ride.'

'Mmm. I suppose the stable is primarily James's preserve. But I'm still concerned she may influence him in some way. You will keep your eyes open?'

Winky suddenly cleared his throat and upped his volume. 'Afternoon, *yer Ladyship*.' He put a strange emphasis on that title. 'Not goin' ter ride in this weather, are you?'

Allison's distinctive American accents responded. 'No, not today. Just checking on Jackie. She looked a bit off color yesterday.'

'Now, don't you worry none about Jackie, *yer Ladyship*. Winky takes good care of 'er, 'e does.' The words were submissive but the man's tone sounded defensive, even hostile.

'I'm sure you do, Winky. I simply want to see her for myself.' Allison's tone shifted slightly. 'Lady Margaret – is there anything I can help you with?'

'No, thank you, Allison. I am *just checking on* our horses.' She repeated Allison's words in a parody of her accent and inflection. 'I wish to speak with you outside,' she said in a lower voice, presumably to Winky, and Luke heard her cane tapping its way out of the stables. Winky's uneven step followed her.

Luke decided it was time to stop hiding, even though he hadn't done so deliberately. He came out of Lucky's stall as Allison was about to enter Jackie's.

'Hello again,' he said. 'Couldn't help overhearing just now. Am I imagining things, or is Winky not your biggest fan?'

Allison started at seeing him, then relaxed. 'You're not imagining anything. Winky and Lady Margaret are thick as thieves, always have been. He used to ride her prize racehorse back in the day. So, of course, he hates me, because she does. Did you notice he calls me "your Ladyship" instead of "my Lady," as he calls her? That's improper protocol. Not that I care, but it's his way of underlining that he doesn't consider me legitimate nobility.' Allison ran a hand over Jackie's withers and down her back.

Luke took a good look at the horse. Her coat did look a little dull. 'You suspect him of not taking good care of Jackie?'

She shrugged. 'Nothing I can put my finger on. I think he maybe shorts her on her oats a bit, doesn't give her all the supplements the vet prescribes. Nothing serious, you understand – just a bit of petty malice. He doesn't dare do anything to me directly, so he takes it out on Jackie.' She scooped some oats from a barrel in the hallway into the horse's manger. 'That's why I come to check up on her every day, even if I'm not riding her.'

Luke suspected Allison might like to be alone – visiting the stables was probably her only respite on days she couldn't ride. 'I was just saying hello to all the horses myself. I'll let you get on.'

She flashed him a smile. 'Thanks for listening. I don't think anyone else quite believes me about Winky – not even James.'

When Emily finally managed to tear herself away from the library – which she did only because it was nearly time for tea – she heard voices as she approached the main hall. Allison's, raised in anger, and a man's, muffled as if coming from farther away. Not wanting to interrupt anything, she stopped in the corridor – not on purpose to listen, but soon both voices were clearly audible.

'Adam, I've told you never to come to the house! I can't risk the dragon finding out about it. She has eyes and ears all over this place.'

'I had to talk to you. You didn't answer your phone.'

'That's because I was with Lady Margaret. I told you there would be times I wouldn't be able to answer.'

'I tried three times.'

'And I was with her for an hour. She insisted on going over the menus for the week, since we have guests, even though they're my guests and it's really nothing to do with her. She insists on making sure "the honor of the house is not compromised" by an inferior menu.' Emily could almost hear the eye-roll that followed that statement.

'Well, since I'm here, can I at least ask you my question?'

'Not here. Go back to the site and I'll get down there as fast as I can.'

Allison shut the door and went into the dining room. Emily emerged from the corridor and headed toward the main stairs. Just disappearing up the flight that led to Lady Margaret's wing, she saw the unmistakable swish of Caddie's black dress.

* * *

At dinner that night, Lady Margaret was again absent, and James and Allison were more subdued than Emily had yet seen them. Although Allison had been so open with her, she did not quite feel she could pry into what might be wrong – especially in the presence of the more reserved James and the likely uninvolved Roger.

But Allison could not contain her emotion indefinitely. After Witherspoon had deposited the cheese and departed, she burst out, 'Well, we told her.'

Emily started. 'You mean you told Lady Margaret about the baby?'

'Baby?' Roger said with more animation than he'd yet shown about anything other than his butterflies. 'You're having a baby? But that's marvelous! My dear, congratulations!' He jumped up and planted a kiss on Allison's cheek.

She managed a pale smile. 'Thank you, Uncle Roger. I'm glad someone's happy about it.'

Emily's stomach contracted. 'You mean Lady Margaret wasn't?'

Allison shook her head, eyes on the cheese she was crumbling but not eating.

James spoke for them both. 'My grandmother did not take the news quite as we expected,' he said in a strangled voice. 'In fact, she accused Allison of – no, I can't repeat it. In short, she is not fully persuaded the baby is mine.'

'Oh, how awful for you!' Emily was flooded with guilt as well as dismay, since telling Lady Margaret had been her suggestion. 'I'm so sorry, I never dreamed . . .'

'It's not your fault,' Allison said flatly. 'It was our decision. It seemed like the best thing to do, after you told me what she'd said to you. I thought it would convince her. But instead it's made everything a thousand times worse.'

'Granny had one of her spells after we told her,' James said. 'The doctor came and ordered her to stay in bed for at least forty-eight hours, or until he tells her otherwise.'

'You mean she actually takes orders from a doctor?'

'When it suits her. And this time it suits her because she wants to punish me.' Allison pushed her plate away. 'But she really did look ill last night. I don't think she was faking this time. She'll follow orders because she wants to live long enough to see James chuck me out and marry Bunty.'

Emily pressed Allison's hand. She knew that would never happen, and therefore it was entirely on the cards that Lady Margaret might live, and go on plaguing the life out of Allison, for years to come.

Allison pushed her chair back. 'I'm sorry, I'm lousy company tonight. Please excuse me.' She left the table and dragged herself out of the room.

'I'd better go with her, if you don't mind,' said James, and he followed his wife out.

Luke and Emily were left with each other and Roger. None of them had any clue what to say. Eventually, Roger mumbled something about being sorry they had gotten caught up in the family drama.

'Please don't apologize,' Emily said. 'Luke and I have a way of getting caught up in other people's drama wherever we go. I just hope in this case—' She stopped herself. She'd been about to say, 'I hope in this case it doesn't lead to murder.' Instead, she finished lamely, 'I hope it will all be satisfactorily resolved. James and Allison deserve to be happy.'

'I agree with you,' Roger replied. 'Unfortunately, other people's happiness has never been my mother's top priority.'

EIGHT

Friday dawned fine, so in an attempt to escape the drama for a while, Emily and Luke set off for Blenheim Palace. Emily was more interested in the architecture, Luke in the history. Blenheim had been the childhood home of Winston Churchill and featured exhibits about his life and work.

Not even Emily was prepared for the size of either the palace itself – the 'palace' moniker was no exaggeration – or of the grounds. The drive from the outer gates to the entrance felt like a mile, though it was probably only a quarter of that. The inner gates constituted a fortress in themselves, and when she and Luke finally emerged from the gauntlet of the admissions line to pass into the main courtyard, Emily felt as if she were in an unusually compact and cohesive city. The palace extended across three sides of the gigantic courtyard, with the fourth side looking out across the extensive lawns to a fair-sized lake.

The tour comprised only relatively few of the public rooms on the first floor of the central wing of the palace, but within half an hour Emily was so dazzled by all the splendor that she couldn't take in any more. It was splendor, for the most part, rather than the highest form of beauty – splendor in the form of ornate carving and gilding, inlaid floors and luxurious carpets, painted ceilings so high one could barely make out what the paintings depicted. She was glad to have had the chance to see it but felt it was unlikely she'd ever want to return.

Until they came to the library. The library took her breath away. The room took the shape of a long, narrow gallery with tall windows filling one long side and flooding the room with light. The walls, where they were not covered in bookshelves, were plastered in a pale peachy beige that reflected the light all around, and the room was topped at one end with a dome supported by more windows. Under the dome, a life-size statue of Queen Victoria reigned over all she surveyed, while the opposite end of the room was filled by a baroque organ with an impressive array of pipes. Emily felt she could have lived in that room.

The library was currently being set up for a wedding reception, and Emily whispered to Luke, 'Imagine having your wedding here. I wonder who you have to be to rate that?'

'Just rich, I reckon. Money talks, even in a class-based society.'

'Maybe. But I'd bet it talks louder if you're the Duke of Omnium and Gatherum marrying the daughter of Lord High Everything Else.'

'You may be right.' Luke huffed and ran a hand over his buzzed hair. 'I wouldn't want to get married here. This place is way over the top in my book. Windy Corner's plenty grand enough for me.'

Emily thought back with fondness to their so-recent reception in her Victorian home on the Oregon coast. Katie, her young housekeeper, had made it festive with yards and yards of white tulle and gold ribbon festooned from the ceilings and over the tables and chairs. They'd kept the party as small as possible, with only family and close friends, but between them they had enough of both to fill the house nicely. It had been a lovely reception, both in terms of trappings and in terms of the spirit of the gathering, and Emily wouldn't have traded it for all the Blenheim libraries the world could hold.

The other highlight of the visit came from the historical quarter. From the library they passed into a space – not a room, exactly, more of a wide, open-ended passage furnished with couches on either wall – with a sign proclaiming it *The Birth Room of Sir Winston Churchill.* Apparently, the infant Winston – displaying an impatience, love of theatricality, and disregard for the convenience of others that would characterize his whole life – had decided to make his precipitous entrance into the world in the middle of a party, not giving his poor mother time even to reach a bedroom where she might have given birth in decent privacy.

By the time they finished touring the palace itself, Emily was too tired to explore the gardens at any length. Instead, they had lunch in the tearoom overlooking one of the smaller gardens, then boarded a conveyance that was billed as a 'carriage' but turned out, to Emily's immense disappointment, to be a sort of glorified golf cart rather than an elegant horse-drawn equipage. This took them around the formal gardens that lay beyond the house and back past the lake. There the guide informed them that the supporting structure of the bridge over the lake contained rooms where certain less reputable activities of the young scions of the house had been known to take place.

'Shades of Sir Percival,' Emily whispered to Luke in response to this story.

'You know it,' he responded. 'I don't think much of the British aristocracy, all things considered. James may be the only decent one of the lot.'

'I wouldn't go that far. But certainly excess and self-indulgence do seem to be the rule rather than the exception. No wonder the system fell into decline.'

Luke nodded. 'Give me America every time. We have our problems, but at least the average Joe has a chance to make good, and you don't get away with murder just because your blood goes back a thousand years.'

Emily's confidence in her ability to sell Luke on a vacation cottage in England took a severe blow at that speech. But she hadn't used up her arsenal yet. The humbler delights of the Cotswolds hills and villages might yet succeed where Blenheim's splendor had failed.

When they turned into the drive at Fitzhugh Manor late that afternoon, Luke had to swerve suddenly on to the grass to avoid colliding with a blue Porsche that was speeding toward them, driving exactly in the middle of the narrow lane.

'That was a close one,' he said when the cars had cleared each other. 'My instincts were screaming at me to swerve to the right. If I'd done that, we would have collided for sure.'

Emily was looking back at the other driver. 'Who was that?'

'I wasn't looking at the driver, but it looked like Simon Braithwaite's car. Was there a little girl with him?'

'I didn't see a child, only the driver.'

'Thank God for that, anyway. Poor kid mighta been traumatized for life.'

'Who is this Simon? How do you know him?'

'Met him at the stable the other day. His daughter Lily takes lessons with Bunty. He and James have some kind of history.'

They put the car away, and when they came out of the garage, they met James coming back from the stables. His gait was slow and labored.

'Hard day?' Luke asked. 'We just saw Simon flying out of here like a bat out of hell. Practically ran us off the road.'

James pushed his blond hair back off his forehead. 'I'm sorry about that. He always drives fast, but he's furious with me today.'

'What for? If you don't mind me asking. None of our business, really.'

James waved that quibble away. 'He thinks I cheated him in a deal on a horse.'

'I thought Lily just used the school horses.'

'She did, but she and Blossom have developed a wonderful working relationship. They have every chance of sweeping all the prizes in the next county show. Simon feels they ought to own Blossom – he says it's so there will be less chance of the partnership being broken up, but I know it's because he couldn't bear to have my name mentioned in the prizegiving as the owner of the pony.'

'So what's the problem?'

'I quoted him a fair price, and he paid it. Then he found out a similar pony had been sold at a nearby stable for a much lower price. Now he wants me to refund the difference.'

'But you had good reasons for the price you set, I'm sure.'

'I certainly did. The other pony is considerably older than Blossom and doesn't come from nearly as good stock. And besides that, having sold Blossom to Simon, I now have to find a replacement for the other young students to ride. It won't be easy in the current market. So I had to factor in the loss we'll have to absorb until we can find one.'

Luke humphed. 'As a finance guy, you'd think Simon would understand all that.'

James sighed. 'You'd think. But to him it's all part and parcel of the same old grudge. I'm the big landowner taking advantage of the little guy.' He gave a sharp bark of laughter. 'Even though he's worth two of me now. One of these days he's going to try to get his hands on the whole stable.'

'You'd never sell that, though, would you?'

James's face hardened. 'He'd have to take it over my dead body.'

That evening Luke and Emily were invited to dine at Bunty's cottage along with James and Allison. The four of them had a lovely stroll down the drive, past the formal gardens and through a grove of trees, to the gatehouse. Emily caught her breath at the sight of it. From the outside it looked like just the sort of venerable cottage she was looking for, with diamond-paned windows trimmed in a cheery green set amidst the weathered stone of the ivy-covered walls – like a smaller version of Kelmscott. But of course, the gatehouse was already taken.

Once they were inside, the Olde England impression faded considerably. Bunty had modernized the interior, creating an open floor plan with plenty of light-colored polished wood, white leather upholstery accented with red throw pillows, and black-framed photographs – mostly including horses – dotting the white walls. At least she had stuck with organic materials instead of going all metal and glass; still, Emily's cottage-envy was effectively nipped in the bud.

Conan welcomed them to the living room while Bunty finished up in the kitchen. Allison went to help her set the table. No staff in this house to cook or wait on them – just a casual gathering of friends with simple, fresh food and inexpensive wine. Emily felt honored to be included, as not only a PG of the manor but a member of an older generation. She was a little afraid she and Luke might cramp the young people's style.

But the conversation flowed freely as they all talked about the work at the stables and further plans for the estate. Once they were seated at the table and the food had been passed around, Luke said, 'You all talk like you're in this together. Do you two' – he nodded toward Conan and Bunty – 'have a share in all this as well? I thought it all belonged to James. Being lord of the manor and all.'

'The estate does belong to James alone,' Bunty replied. 'But Conan and I are buying in as partners in the stables. I had some family money, and Conan' – she glanced at her beloved, whose face had darkened as he bent over his plate, shoveling in pasta for all he was worth – 'is making payments as best he can.'

'Which means he's just as much a partner as you and I,' James said breezily. 'He'll get his part paid off eventually.'

'You mean when my mam pops her clogs,' Conan grumbled. 'Not likely to happen before that.'

Bunty laid her hand on his, but he reached for his napkin, letting her hand fall. 'You see,' she said, 'shortly after we drew up the papers, Conan's mother had a severe stroke and had to go into a nursing home. So his funds are rather tied up in her care for the time being.'

Emily was startled. 'I thought all that sort of thing was covered by your National Health Service.'

Conan sighed. 'Unfortunately, no. They contribute a bit since she has medical needs, but it's mostly on me. And a decent home costs.' He rubbed his thumb and first two fingers together. 'Big time.'

'We completely understand,' Allison said reassuringly. 'We know you'll pay when you can. And in the meantime, you're an equal partner with the rest of us.'

Emily, who was sitting next to Conan, barely caught his next words. 'Right. All partners are equal, but some are more equal than others.' She recognized the altered quote from *Animal Farm* and wondered at the bitterness behind it. Did Conan just have a chip on his shoulder because he wasn't a Fitzhugh? Allison had mentioned Conan's father had worked on the estate before him – perhaps as a lowly groom. Was this class envy aggravated by the humiliation occasioned by his false financial position? Or was there something more complex between Conan and James? Did he suspect the affection between Bunty and James went beyond the honorary-sibling variety?

Emily watched the dynamics between them all for the rest of the evening. She was fairly certain that if Conan did harbor such suspicions, they were unfounded. Allison and Bunty acted like BFFs, which surely could not be the case if they both loved the same man. And James teased Bunty merci-lessly, which certainly seemed more like a brother than a lover – as did the equanimity with which she gave as good as she got. Conan, however, continued to brood, but the cause of his brooding remained uncertain.

After a couple of glasses of wine, though, his humor improved, and once they left the table, Conan entertained them all with comic Irish songs. Bunty acted out the part of the girl where there was one, showing considerable dramatic flair. They were all convulsed with laughter by the time the grandfather clock – the only antique piece of furniture in the house – tolled ten o'clock, and Luke and Emily decided it was time for them to retire.

James and Allison, accustomed to later hours, stayed on. Luke and Emily strolled back to the manor hand in hand.

'That was fun,' she said.

He made a nonverbal, noncommittal noise in his throat.

'Didn't you enjoy it? You were laughing hard enough.'

'Oh, yeah, the songs were a riot. But I'd rather have been alone with you.'

She lifted her face and kissed him. 'We'll be on our own all day tomorrow.'

'And I'm looking forward to that.'

NINE

Saturday dawned drizzly and cold. Bed was warm and cozy, and at first Emily was tempted to postpone their Cotswolds outing to a more auspicious day. But Luke had seen enough of the manor house and was eager to be out and about. So Emily dragged herself into the shower and down to breakfast.

James and Allison were just finishing their coffee, both dressed in riding clothes. They seemed to have regained their good spirits. 'Today is the absolutely last day my doctor will let me ride,' said Allison, 'and I'm not going to waste it because of a little rain.'

Emily was apprehensive on Allison's account, given the weather and the consequent slickness of whatever ground they planned to ride on, but it was hardly her place to offer any caution. If James was agreeable to her riding, Emily could only keep silent and pray. At least he was going with her.

'I'm not letting you out of my sight today, darling,' he told her. 'This is pushing the boundaries, and you know it.'

'I know. But it's going to be such a long six months with

no riding. Longer than that, I suppose, since I don't plan to ride with a baby strapped to my chest.'

'I'll tell you what. Why don't you ride Buttercup? She's as gentle as they come, and I never saw a more sure-footed beast.'

Allison rolled her eyes. 'Gentle? I think you mean plodding. She couldn't do more than amble if her life depended on it.'

'And that's exactly what you need right now.'

Allison sighed theatrically. 'All right, darling. I'll do it for you.' She leaned across the table for a kiss.

'We'll see you two lovebirds tonight,' Luke said. 'Emily's taking me on a tour of the Cotswolds. Which she has never seen. With no particular destination. And where most of the roads are apparently not on the map.'

Emily gave a nervous laugh. She would have preferred to use public transport for this trip, but it wasn't available. She felt as if she should strap on her explorer's boots for a journey into the back of beyond. But she had to put on a brave face. 'We made it to Kelmscott and back, and that was fairly convoluted. I'm sure we'll be fine.'

'Of course you will,' James reassured them. 'You have satnav, right? Just set it to come back to Fitzhugh, and you can wander all you please along the way. And if worse comes to worst, call us and we'll send out a rescue party.'

Equipped with umbrellas and walking shoes, and provided with snacks against the possibility of failing to encounter civilization, Luke and Emily climbed into their rental car, and Emily turned on the GPS. 'Hmm. Where shall I tell it we want to go?' She asked the system to show her a map of the Cotswolds. She couldn't exactly ask it for *Father Brown* country, though that was in fact what she was hoping to find.

'If only Kembleford were a real place. But I have no idea where they film *Father Brown*. It may not even be a single village.' She scanned the map for any familiar name of a real settlement. 'There's Gloucester,' she mused. 'But that's a biggish place, I think. As I recall, the cathedral's there. We want villages . . . Oh, here's Cirencester – Father Brown mentions that, so it must be in the general area. Let's try that. It's probably a market town, but we're bound to pass through some villages on the way.' She entered the name into the GPS.

'Here goes nothing,' Luke said as they set off down the drive.

The GPS offered them the option of a route that was mostly highway, but Emily rejected that in favor of the more pictur- esque minor roads and lanes. The journey was much more important than the destination. So they meandered among the hedgerows and byways for an hour or so.

Along the way, Emily decided it was time to let Luke in on her idea, now amounting almost to a plan, of buying a vacation cottage somewhere in the area.

He reacted much as she expected. 'A cottage? In England? Why would you want to do that?'

'Because I love England. I love the land and the people and the accents and the architecture. I love the whole feeling of history that permeates this place. I feel like I could really put down roots here.'

'I thought we had roots in Stony Beach.'

'*You* do. And our relationship does, in a way. But it was never my home until a year ago. That's not long enough to grow real roots.'

'If you can't grow roots in a solid year, you sure as heck couldn't grow them in a couple weeks every summer. That dog won't hunt, Em.'

'Well, maybe not in that sense. But I've always felt as if I belonged in the British Isles, all my life. I've felt like a stranger in a strange land in America.'

Luke was silent, but Emily could see the muscles clench in his jaw. This was an abyss between them they'd never be able to bridge, because Luke was as American as apple pie, corn- bread, and the Fourth of July all rolled into one.

'It would only be for a few weeks a year. You know the money's not an issue. We have your Stony Beach for eleven months out of the twelve. Couldn't you give me that one month to be in England?'

They were just coming to a lay-by, and Luke pulled the car over, put it in park, and turned to face her. 'Is this what you need to make you happy?'

She swallowed. 'Marrying you has made me almost as happy

as I'm capable of being. But there is just this one little corner
of longing left, and I do believe buying a cottage here would
satisfy that.'

He leaned over and kissed her. 'Then we'll see what we
can do.'

Emily hugged him as well as she could around the gear
shift and steering wheel. Her heart was full. 'You're a keeper,
Luke Richards,' she whispered in his ear.

Once their moment was over, they drove on for a few miles
until they came to a village that suited Emily's idea of the
quintessential Cotswolds village: no modern structures,
everything built of stone or brick, a high street only a few
blocks long lined with quaint little pubs, shops, and cottages.
The sign at the top of the high street said *Welcome to Lower
Gloaming*. The sun at last defeated the drizzling clouds and
glinted off the bells in the tower of the church at the end of
the street. And, of course, the shops included the obligatory
tearoom advertising cream teas.

It was mid-morning – time for elevenses rather than high
tea – but cream teas were served from ten till five, so Emily
was able to partake of this delicacy she'd heard so much
about. It turned out to consist of a melt-in-your-mouth scone
filled with sugared strawberries and a generous dollop of
Cornish clotted cream – a cream so heavy it was almost butter.

'We're eating Mrs McCarthy's award-winning strawberry
scones!' she said after the first bite. 'Or some descendant of
hers that she passed the recipe down to. I wonder if it's
possible to get this kind of cream at home, or make it somehow.
Katie could manage the rest.'

Luke was too busy eating to answer, except with an ecstatic,
'Mmm.'

They finished their tea and lingered a bit to digest it, then
strolled down the high street. Emily was overjoyed to find a
yarn shop, where she dawdled until Luke started to fidget. She
forced herself to decide on something and chose a skein of
gorgeous autumn-gold Shetland wool. Next they came to a
sporting goods shop, where Luke contemplated investing in
a fishing pole of his own to use while they were in England.
But although Emily encouraged him to indulge, his frugal

common sense won out – it would be difficult to get the pole home, and he could always use one of James's. She could easily have bought the pole for him and paid to ship it, but in the course of their engagement she'd already learned that Luke did not appreciate her throwing her money around too much on his behalf.

After that, Emily caught sight of an estate agent's office and paused to examine the listings displayed in the window. One of them was for a cottage right here on the high street of this perfect village.

'Oh, look, Luke,' she said, 'this cottage is right across the street. Let's go take a look.'

He followed her, his easy strides keeping pace with her excited scurry. They found the cottage with a *For Sale* sign coyly peeking from a front window.

It truly was a lovely cottage – picture-perfect in fact, with twin casement windows above the tiny entrance porch turning the façade into a face that invited them in. Delicate pink roses climbed up the trellises that supported the porch roof, while ivy half covered the yellow stone walls. Kelmscott notwithstanding, Emily felt she had never seen a homier-looking house in her life.

'Not bad,' Luke said. Emily knew that from him that was a high compliment.

'Luke, let's ask to see inside it. Can we?' She locked her arms in the crook of his elbow.

He cocked an eyebrow at her. 'Will that make you happy?'

'Absolutely. Ecstatically happy.'

He turned and marched back to the estate agent's. 'Hi there,' he said to the bored young receptionist. 'We'd like to see the house across the street.'

The girl took the earbuds out of her ears, and he repeated his request. 'Oh. OK.' She called back to an inner office. 'Dad! People here to see Rose Cottage.'

A middle-aged man in a dark suit bustled out, stopping to hiss to the receptionist, 'How many times do I have to tell you? Come into my office or use the intercom – don't yell. And call me Mr Forsyth!'

She gave a 'whatever' eye-roll and put her earbuds back in.

Mr Forsyth gave them a nervous smile. 'Charles Forsyth. How may I be of service?'

Luke repeated his request. 'We'd like to see the house across the street. Rose Cottage, I guess it's called?'

'Of course.' Forsyth made to consult an appointment book that lay open on his daughter's desk, reading upside down. 'Would tomorrow at three o'clock suit you?'

'We were thinking more like right now. If you're not too busy, that is. We're staying near Oxford, see, and quite frankly I don't have a lot of faith we'll be able to find this place again if we have to come another day.'

'The village sort of rose out of the mist. Like Brigadoon,' Emily put in with her most winning smile.

Mr Forsyth looked at her in a way that showed he had no idea what she was talking about, but professional avidity won out. 'Certainly,' he said. 'I can show you the cottage now. Just give me a minute to – ah . . .' He gestured vaguely toward the inner office, then darted in there and fussed around a bit, probably to suggest he was not as completely unoccupied as in fact he was.

In a moment he emerged, smoothing his hair and clutching an old-fashioned skeleton key. 'Shall we?' He smiled them out the door and across the street.

'Here we are!' he sang out when they reached the cottage door, as if they had come a great distance. After a couple of fruitless attempts he managed to unlock the door, then stood back to usher them inside.

The sitting room was fully furnished in all the cabbage-rose chintz, pouffy pillows, and lace curtains one might expect, with a fireplace that stretched across half the room. Luke had to duck slightly to get through the doorway, and once he was inside, the sagging beams in the ceiling nearly brushed the top of his head. All the pictures appeared to hang crookedly because they had to choose whether to line up with the ceiling, wall, or floor; some of the pictures had patches of damp peeking out from behind them. But Emily was completely charmed at first sight.

Forsyth babbled on about the features of the house, but Emily was way ahead of him, dashing through all the rooms at first and then taking them more slowly, one by one. She opened all the drawers and cupboards (most of which stuck a bit), tried the taps (which choked out brown water before running clear) and the light switches (one of which sparked), and flushed the single toilet (which whined like a sleepy banshee). Mentally, she was apportioning the rooms to their various purposes. The farmhouse kitchen – obvious. They could eat in there and use the dining room for a library. A small room at the back of the ground floor would do for Luke's den. Upstairs were a master bedroom and two smaller rooms – one could be a guest room, the other a study for her. The single bathroom would be a minor inconvenience if they had guests, but they could cope. At least there was a clawfoot tub.

All thought of Allison's new but old-looking houses with their solid, perpendicular walls, state-of-the-art systems, and all mod-cons faded in the face of this embodiment of old-world history and charm. 'I love it,' she said to Luke.

'It's a money pit,' he replied, then proceeded to point out to her all the drawbacks she had overlooked.

Her spirits drooped momentarily, then perked up again. 'Who cares? I have plenty of money. This is the one. I want to buy it.'

Luke took her by the shoulders and turned her to face him. 'If you want to waste your money, I can't stop you. But I can tell you, I have no intention of staying in this place until every last solitary thing is fixed to my satisfaction.'

'But Luke—'

'Listen, Em. You know I would do just about anything on earth to make you happy. But I honestly don't think this will do it in the long term. You're like a kid in a candy shop right now. But if you jump into this thing without thinking it through, you're gonna end up with the worst bellyache of your life. And I don't want any part of that.'

She closed her eyes and took a deep breath. Some part of her knew he was right, but that didn't stop her from feeling she simply had to have this cottage.

'All right. I won't jump in right away. I'll think it over. But promise me if I still want to in a few days, we can come back.'

'I promise.'

'All right. Let's go then and not waste any more of Mr Forsyth's time.'

Emily's spirits plummeted after they left the cottage, and the return of the morning's drizzle, now graduated to actual rain, did not help to raise them. They got back to Fitzhugh Manor around five o'clock – past teatime – and she was ready to go straight to their room for a hot bath and a nap before dinner. But Roger met them in the hall, fluttering about like one of his winged treasures before it was pinned to his board.

'Have you seen James and Allison?' he asked breathlessly. 'No one has seen them for hours.'

'We saw them at breakfast,' Luke said. 'They were just going out for a ride.'

Emily's heart flooded with trepidation. 'Do you mean to say they never came back from their ride?'

'No, indeed they did not. Conan says the horses are still out, too. What shall we do? I don't know what to do.' His hair flew about his jiggling head, and his arms waved like those of the robot in the sixties TV show *Lost in Space*, who was always saying, 'Danger, Will Robinson! Danger!'

Luke took Roger by the upper arms and gently held him still. 'We're going to go out and look for them. Let's go get Conan and the gardeners and anybody else you can round up. Conan will probably have some idea which way they went.' He turned to Emily. 'You better wait here. Make sure there are hot drinks and blankets ready. They'll be wet through for sure, maybe in shock if they're injured. As soon as we find them, I'll call you, and if necessary, you can call an ambulance.'

Emily nodded. Though part of her wanted to be among the searchers, she would never dream of questioning Luke's judgment in an emergency. Emergencies were his job, and nobody could keep a cooler head when things went wrong. She would stay behind, provide for everyone's warmth and comfort, and pray.

'What about Lady Margaret?' she asked Roger. 'Does she know?'

'Mother? No, Mother doesn't know. Don't tell her anything

until we know for sure. Yes?' He looked from Emily to Luke as if to confirm this was the right decision.

Luke nodded, and Emily was relieved. She wasn't sure she could deal with Lady Margaret when she was in fear for her grandson's life.

Luke grabbed a waterproof jacket off the rack for himself and another for Roger. He strode out of the back of the hall toward the stables, Roger scurrying to keep up. Roger would be worse than useless in the search, but he had to give the poor fellow something to do or he'd go mad.

They found Conan in the stable block, giving the horses their evening feed. 'We're going out to look for James and Allison. You coming?'

Conan dropped what he was doing immediately. 'Thank God. I would have gone before, but I was afraid on my own I'd never find them, or be able to help if I did. Besides, it was hard to know exactly when to start panicking, you know?'

Luke wasn't entirely convinced by this reasoning – it might have held up until lunchtime, but not for the whole day. But there was no point in going into it now. 'Who else can we rope in? We've got a lot of ground to cover.'

'Bunty's here, and Winky, though I doubt he'll be much good. The other grooms have gone home, but I expect the groundskeepers are somewhere around. I'll see who I can rustle up. Meet you back here in ten.'

Luke turned to Roger. 'Any idea which direction they'd be likely to ride?'

Roger twisted his hands. 'No idea at all. I don't ride, you see, so I don't know where people go. Somewhere on the estate, I expect. I'm sorry I can't be more help.'

Luke patted his shoulder. 'No worries. Conan or Bunty will know.' He called, 'Bunty? You here?'

'Coming!' came her voice from inside the stable. In a few minutes she emerged, leading three saddled horses, one of which he recognized as Ginger. Bunty's upper lip was stiff, but Luke could see a tightness around her eyes that betrayed how worried she really was.

'I heard you and Conan talking. I had these two saddled up

already – it seemed like well past time we were out there searching. Then I threw a saddle on Ginger for you.'

At least someone in this stable had good sense, Luke thought. 'Good work, Bunty.'

Winky followed on Bunty's heels, grinning nervously. Conan raced back into the courtyard, followed by two other men.

Luke looked from Conan to Bunty. 'Either of you have any idea which direction they might have gone?'

Bunty nodded. 'They have two favorite rides. One is down towards the lake, around it, and back along the edge of the woods on that side. The other is the path through the copse on the far side of the lawn. Since it was cloudy this morning, I'm guessing they'd take the more open route, towards the lake.'

'Right. You, me, and Conan will ride that way. You two' – he indicated the gardeners – 'and Roger go on foot to the copse and check out that path.' He considered Winky, who stood shifting his weight from foot to foot and looking as if he dreaded being included in the search. 'Winky, you stay here in case they come back.' They all exchanged cell numbers so they could keep each other informed. 'Let's get moving!'

Luke swung into Ginger's saddle. Bunty mounted Fonteyn, and Conan took a white horse Luke didn't recall seeing before. 'Come on, Fionn, let's go get James and Allison now,' he said to the horse. Luke assumed Fionn was Conan's own.

They set off toward the lake and circled it, seeing nothing untoward. But as they entered the path that skirted the wood, Luke, who was in the lead, spotted an indistinct shape in the grass on the other side of the path. 'Up ahead!' he called back to the others, pointing. He tapped his heels against Ginger's sides and trotted toward the shape.

As he suspected. Feared. An inert body lying on the ground, clothes covered in dirt and leaves, hair matted with blood. Near it was a large, rough stone embedded in the ground. The rain had nearly washed the stone clean, but Luke thought he could see traces of blood in its crevices.

He dismounted, went up to the body, and gently turned it over. It was James.

TEN

When her phone rang, Emily jumped, spilling hot milk out of the pan in which she was making cocoa. Fortunately, the milk missed her feet.

'Luke? Did you find them?'

A heavy pause. 'We found James.'

His tone answered her next question, but she had to ask it anyway. 'Is he . . . dead?'

'I'm afraid so. Looks like he may have been thrown from his horse.'

Emily crossed herself and breathed a prayer. Lord, have mercy on James. Have mercy on Allison. Have mercy on everyone at Fitzhugh, all of them losing so senselessly someone they loved so well.

'And Allison? The baby?'

'No sign yet. Conan and Bunty are going on while I stay with the body. I already called the police.'

'You'll let me know as soon as you know more?'

'Of course.'

Emily quailed at the thought, but asked, 'Should I tell Lady Margaret?'

'Best not. I think it'd be better coming from one of the family.'

'Yes, of course.' She was ashamed of how relieved she felt.

She paced the dining room, end to end, windows to fireplace, around the table and back again. It seemed like hours before her phone rang again.

'What news?'

'We found Allison. She's alive. They're taking her straight to the hospital.'

'Is it bad?'

'Hard to say. Looks like she was thrown, too. She's unconscious – concussed, no doubt – but her pulse is strong. My guess is she'll make it, but who knows about the baby.'

'Lord, have mercy. Are you heading back now?'

'Yeah. Police and ambulance are here. Nothing more for us to do. I called Roger and his bunch with an update, so they'll be back, too.'

'I've got the fire lit, cocoa and blankets waiting. Sounds like you're all going to need them.'

'Yeah. See you soon.'

Roger and the groundskeepers returned first, and Emily ministered to them. Roger seemed deeply shocked. Another eternity passed before the three mounted searchers stumbled into the hall. Luke fell into Emily's arms. This kind of thing might be his job, but that didn't mean discovering the body of a man he knew and liked was easy for him. He would need her comfort tonight.

Conan and Bunty clung to each other, still in their water-proofs – Bunty sobbing, both oblivious to the rest of the world. Minutes passed before they separated and removed their gear. Their eyes were red.

After they'd all sipped their cocoa and wrapped up in their blankets, Bunty and Roger locked haunted eyes across the room.

'Granny.'

'Mother.' They spoke simultaneously. 'Who's going to tell her?'

Roger stared in horror. 'She's still in bed from her turn the other day. This could finish her.'

'Still, she has to be told.' Bunty squared her shoulders. 'I'll do it,' she said, and headed for the main stairs.

'I'll go with you,' Roger said, and Emily thought that was probably the bravest action of his life.

A few minutes later, a keening wail pierced through the foot-thick, solid-built floors and walls and flooded the house with pure anguish. Lady Margaret Fitzhugh, having outlived her husband, favorite son, and all joy in living, had lost the only remaining thing she truly loved.

Since the police had questioned Luke, Conan, and Bunty at the scene where the body was found, and no one else was likely to know much about the incident itself, they postponed further investigation until the following morning.

When the knock came, as Luke, Emily, and Roger were finishing breakfast, no lowly police inspector stood at the door. Emily heard Roger greet the visitor. 'Colonel Allan! Do come in.'

Luke and Emily went to the hall door, wondering whether they ought to emerge. Roger turned to introduce them. 'Luke, Emily, this is Colonel Allan, our chief constable. Colonel, allow me to present Mr and Mrs Richards, our guests. Mr Richards led the search last evening.'

The chief constable was a heavyset, sixtyish man of medium height with military bearing and haircut, dressed in a tweed suit rather than a uniform. He shook their hands with a raised eyebrow. 'That was good of you. As a guest, you had no responsibility to do such a thing.'

Luke shrugged. 'I'm a lawman myself. Kind of second nature to take charge in a situation like that, and it didn't look like anyone else was going to do it.'

'I see. I'm sure the family is very grateful.' He turned to Roger. 'I'm sorry for your loss, Roger. Would it be possible to see Lady Margaret?'

Roger turned pale and flapped his arms. 'Mother? Oh dear. I very much doubt it. She hasn't emerged from her room, you see. She was devastated when Bunty and I gave her the news last night. She actually went into hysterics – a thing I've never seen her do in all my life. We had to leave her with Caddie and call the doctor.'

The chief constable registered concern but said, 'Nevertheless, I do need to talk to her as soon as she's able. Do you think you could ask her maid when that is likely to be?'

'I–I suppose so. I'll just be a minute.' He darted up the stairs and took the flight that led to Lady Margaret's wing.

Emily took the hostess role since there was no one else to do it. 'Won't you sit down, Chief Constable? We were just finishing breakfast. Would you like some coffee?'

'Please. And call me Colonel. Barely had time for a sip before I came over here. Wanted to see Lady Margaret first thing.'

He dropped into a chair with a heavy sigh. 'Terrible thing, this accident. James was a fine man. Leaves the place without an heir – not counting Roger, that is. Somehow one never does count Roger. At any rate, he's not likely to marry at his age, so once he's gone, the line will die out.'

Emily wondered how much she should disclose, but with Allison in the hospital, surely her pregnancy could not remain secret for long. 'That may not be entirely true, Colonel. Allison is three months pregnant – or was, before the accident. You haven't heard anything about her condition, have you?'

He shook his head, sipping the coffee Emily had handed him. 'Not yet. Hospital's my next stop. Got to see if she's awake, remembers anything about what happened.'

Emily and Luke exchanged glances. 'Would it be appropriate for us to visit her once she is awake? We've become friendly in the short time we've been here.'

The colonel shrugged. 'Not my call. She went straight into critical care, so if she's still there, they may not let you in. Not being family. Best for Roger to go.'

'Of course.' But maybe they could tag along. Emily doubted Roger could even drive.

Roger returned looking relieved. 'Mother will see you now, Colonel. She's much calmer, apparently. Quite her old self.' He looked a little baffled by that fact, but Emily was less surprised. Lady Margaret could hardly have become the force of nature she was today without iron self-control.

'Thank you, Roger. I know my way.' The chief constable strode out.

Roger collapsed into a chair. 'Does he know anything about Allison? Did you ask him?'

'We asked, but he doesn't know. He said the hospital was his next stop.'

'I have to see her. I'm all she's got.'

Emily realized for the first time that was true. Poor Allison. Roger was well intentioned, of course, but hardly a rock one could lean on.

She exchanged glances with Luke. 'We've been wondering whether we should find another place to stay,' she said tentatively. 'We don't want to be a burden. But if we can be of any help . . .'

Roger sat up in his chair, eyes wide. 'Oh, you must stay!

Please! The housekeeping may suffer a bit, I'm afraid, but please, please stay as long as you meant to. At least until Allison gets home.' He didn't utter the words 'I'm helpless on my own,' but they were clearly written across his face.

Emily smiled. 'Of course we'll stay if you want us to. And don't give a thought to the housekeeping. We're not here to be catered to. We want to be of use.'

Before Roger could stammer out his gratitude, the chief constable returned. 'I'm off to the hospital now. Have to interview Allison before we can say for sure, but I'm ninety-nine percent certain this is just a tragic accident. That's what I'll say at the inquest.' He cut his eyes upward. 'Remarkable woman, Lady Margaret. Strong as they come. This would have destroyed a lesser woman, but she'll outlive us all.'

He addressed himself to Luke. 'We'll need you to stay for the inquest, since you found the body. I can get you a room at the Perch if it's inconvenient for you to stay here.'

'Oh, no, Colonel, they're staying.' Roger smiled at them. 'We've just arranged it.'

'Good.' The colonel gave a brisk nod, no doubt aware that Roger would need their support.

'Do let us know about Allison's condition, won't you?' Emily said. 'And whether she can have visitors? Roger at least will need to be there if she's regained consciousness.'

'And I'll need you to take me, if you don't mind,' Roger said to Luke. 'I never learned to drive. Never needed to. My whole life is here on the estate.' His eyes widened as if he was just beginning to realize how much his life was about to change in the wake of James's death.

Immediately after the chief constable left, the doorbell rang again. This time Emily went to answer it.

She opened the door to see Adam on the threshold – hair wild, eyes dark with worry. 'Is Allison here?' he said, looking past Emily as if he suspected her of hiding Allison from him.

'No, I'm afraid she isn't. There was an accident yesterday.'

'Oh my God, she's dead, isn't she? The men were talking about an accident, but nobody was sure what really happened.

I knew in my heart she must be dead.' He turned in circles on the doormat, his arms clutching his body.

Emily laid a hand on his arm, hoping to calm him. 'She is not dead. At least she was alive last night, and we haven't heard otherwise today. She was badly injured, though – she's in the hospital. And James – it was James who was killed.'

Adam stilled, blinked, and took a deep breath. Then he looked at Emily as if seeing her for the first time. 'You came to the site the other day. With *her.*'

'That's right. I'm Emily Richards. My husband, Luke, and I are guests in the house.'

He sagged against the doorframe. 'I've got to see her. But they won't let me, will they? I'm not *family.*' A world of bitterness was infused into that word.

'Come in. You look like you could use a bite of something. Have you eaten today?'

He looked confused. 'Eaten? Uh – no, I guess not. I don't think I can.'

'Well, come on in and try.' She led Adam into the dining room and introduced him. 'Luke, this is Adam – I don't know your last name.'

'Marshall. Adam Marshall.' He shook Luke's hand and turned to Roger.

Roger said with a nervous smile, 'I believe we've met. Didn't you come to the wedding?'

'Wedding?' Adam snorted. 'More like funeral. Funeral of all my hopes. But yeah, I was there. Had to convince myself it was all real.'

Emily gently pushed the young man into a chair. She put some toast, eggs, and sausages on to a plate and set it before him. Was coffee a good idea in his state? He was terribly agitated, but perhaps the simple familiarity of a ritual like drinking coffee would help to calm him. She poured him a cup.

Once the food was in front of him, Adam tucked in like a starving man. The others watched him warily, unsure what to do with him, under the circumstances, beyond feeding him. On the one hand, his distress excited Emily's sympathy. But on the other hand, if there had by any unlikely chance been

foul play involved in James's death, Adam could have been
the one with the best motive to perpetrate it.

He was wiping up egg yolk with his fourth piece of toast
when they all felt a presence in the doorway. Incredibly,
Lady Margaret stood there, fully dressed and in possession
of all her faculties. Her eyes skimmed the room, then
fastened on Adam with a furious glare that threatened to
vaporize him on the spot.

'*You?*' she bellowed. Her arm raised and pointed to him
like the finger of death. 'Get that man out of my house! He
killed my grandson!'

Adam was too shocked to speak. He scrambled to his feet
and backed away, but he couldn't get out of range of those
blazing eyes.

Roger rushed to his mother's side. 'Let's not get irrational,
now, Mother. Nobody killed James. It was an accident. Colonel
Allan said so.'

Lady Margaret turned to her son, her expression morphing
into one of contempt. 'Colonel Allan is a fool. I told him
it was an accident, and he agreed. But now I will tell
him James was murdered – by *that man*.' She pointed at
Adam again.

Adam found his tongue. 'Murdered? No way. I haven't even
seen James in – I don't know – months. Why would I kill
him? And for God's sake, why would I do it in some way that
put Allison in danger, too?'

'I have no obligation to answer your foolish questions. I
know you killed him. Now get out of my house!'

Luke exchanged glances with Emily and said, 'We were all
just leaving for the hospital anyway. Adam, you may as well
come along with us.'

Lady Margaret focused on Luke as if she hadn't noticed
his presence before. 'What are these people still doing here?
This is a house of mourning. Surely even Americans can see
when they are not wanted.'

'But they are wanted, Mother,' Roger piped up. 'I want
them. In fact, I can't manage without them.'

'Manage? Who asked you to manage? This is my house,
and I do not want strangers in it at this terrible time.'

Roger cleared his throat and drew himself up to his full modest height. 'I'm sorry, Mother, but I must remind you that in fact this is *my* house. I am the baronet now, and the estate is entailed on me. And I have asked Luke and Emily to stay.' He fixed his eyes on her without wavering. Emily was proud of him – the mouse had become a man.

Lady Margaret blinked several times. 'You. You, the baronet.' She spoke slowly, in a low voice, as if trying to convince herself. At last, she appeared to succeed. 'Very well. If they must stay, they must. I shall retire to my apartment. Messages may be sent through Caddie if required.' She turned and stalked out of the room.

They all let out a collective breath. 'Thank God she's bound by tradition,' Emily whispered to Luke. 'If she were to act on her own will, we'd be out of here on our ears, alternative accommodation or no. And what on earth would become of poor Roger?'

ELEVEN

Under the circumstances, none of them felt like waiting around for the chief constable's call. Luke and Emily, along with Roger and Adam, squeezed into the rental car, and Adam directed them to the John Radcliffe Hospital in Oxford. There, Roger, as the only family member, was told that Allison was still in critical care and had not regained consciousness. Nor was she allowed any visitors.

'Ask about the baby,' Emily prompted him.

'Oh, yes. She was pregnant – is the baby OK?'

The nurse consulted her notes. 'I'm afraid not. She miscarried before she was brought in.'

Emily's heart sank into her shoes. Immediately, she was sixteen again, hunched in the bathroom as her unplanned pregnancy trickled away, trying to stifle her sobs so her father and brother wouldn't hear her and ask what was wrong. She'd never told anyone about the baby she lost until she was married to Philip and had to explain why she could not conceive.

Her tragedy had been amplified because she had lost Luke – but years later she had found him again. Allison had lost James, and he was never coming back.

Roger seemed even more heartbroken than Emily. His newfound assertiveness evaporated, and he was dithery Roger again. With that baby had vanished his hopes of ever avoiding the baronetcy with all its unwelcome responsibilities.

Luke surveyed the group. 'Well, since we're here, we might as well stick around a while. Maybe we can find a doctor to give us more information.'

Emily nodded. Luke asked the nurse for the name of the doctor in charge of Allison's case.

'Doctor Mirama,' she responded. 'You'll find her on the critical care ward. But don't expect much information.'

They all traipsed off in search of the ward. There they found the chief constable waiting outside a room Emily assumed to be Allison's. 'They told us she's still unconscious,' Luke said. 'You heard anything else?'

The chief constable shook his head. 'Well, a bit. She has concussion, obviously, and a couple of cracked ribs, and a broken ankle. Concussion is the only thing to worry about. No internal injuries.'

'Except to the baby,' Emily said softly. 'They told us she lost the baby.'

Colonel Allan cleared his throat. 'Yes. Of course. The baby.' He looked at Roger, who had sat in the chair next to him. 'I suppose that makes you Sir Roger.'

Roger nodded, looking as if he was about to cry. 'Last thing in the world I ever wanted.'

The colonel rested his hand on Roger's shoulder. 'I know, old boy. I know.'

They all sat together in silence – all except Adam, who paced the corridor from one end to the other – until a woman in a white coat with a stethoscope around her neck entered Allison's room, stayed a few minutes, then came out again.

'Any change, Doctor Mirama?' the chief constable asked, standing.

'No change,' she said in a slight African accent. 'But at this point that's a good thing. There's still every reason to hope she will recover.'

'But you can't say when?'

The doctor shook her shoulder-length dreadlocks. 'I can't say when. We must simply let nature take its course.'

Colonel Allan looked at the others. 'If you're all planning to stay a while, perhaps I'll get on about my business. Inquest to arrange and so forth. Here's my number.' He handed the doctor a business card. 'You'll call me if there's any change?'

She nodded.

'Right, then. See you all later,' he said, and walked off.

'And who are all of you?' Dr Mirama asked.

'I'm Roger Fitzhugh,' Roger said. 'I'm Allison's uncle. Uncle by marriage, but I'm her only family on this side of the Atlantic.'

Dr Mirama made a note on her clipboard. 'Does she have family in the US? Or Canada?'

'Parents. In Boston, I think.' He looked helplessly at the others. 'Oh Lord, I can't even remember her maiden name.'

'Booker,' Adam put in from the back of the group, where he had been hovering. 'Randall and Lucy Booker. They live in Cambridge, Massachusetts. I could probably find their phone number at home somewhere.'

'I'm sure Allison would have it in her address book, wouldn't she?' Emily suggested. 'Or in her phone?' She'd forgotten for the moment that she was supposed to be an old friend of Allison's mother.

The doctor nodded. 'Perhaps you could find that for me. We will need to inform them.' She looked back at Adam. 'And you are?'

'Adam Marshall. Her . . . her friend. I knew her back in Boston, knew her parents.'

'Perhaps you would like to inform them, then.'

He shook his head. 'Not a good idea.'

She looked at him quizzically, then turned to Luke and Emily. 'Are you family friends also?'

'Well – not exactly.' Emily didn't see the point in keeping

up the fiction for Roger's benefit. 'We're Luke and Emily Richards. We're guests at Fitzhugh Manor. We're just concerned for Allison, trying to help out as much as we can.' She gestured to Luke. 'My husband led the search for her and James last night.'

'I see. Well, you are all welcome to wait, but as I said, I have no idea how long it might be. And even when she does wake up, I may not be able to allow any of you to see her. At most, it will only be Mr Fitzhugh who can go in.'

They all nodded acquiescence and sat back down, except for Adam, who returned to his pacing. Luke picked up a magazine and leafed through it without stopping to read, while Roger leaned his head back against the wall and appeared to doze. Emily devoutly wished she had brought along her knitting – she hadn't been thinking ahead.

A jingle emitted from Roger's direction. When he didn't react, Emily said, 'Roger, I think your phone's ringing.'

He sat up, blinking and patting his various pockets. 'Oh, is it? Dear me. Allison got me a mobile just recently so she wouldn't have to go searching for me when I'm out hunting. It's hardly ever rung before.'

At last he found the phone in an inside pocket of his coat. 'Hello? Hello? Roger Fitzhugh here . . . No, no word. We're all at the hospital now. Luke and Emily drove me. Allison's condition hasn't changed. She's still unconscious . . . Yes. Yes, of course I will. Thank you, Bunty. Goodbye.'

He stared at the phone as if uncertain what to do next, but Emily saw the screen change, so apparently Bunty had hung up. Roger shrugged and put the phone back in a different pocket.

'That was Bunty,' he said unnecessarily. 'Asking about Allison. Remind me, would you, to call her when we hear something?'

'Yes, of course.' Emily was a little surprised Bunty hadn't come herself, but perhaps she thought that as a distant relative by marriage she wouldn't be allowed in to see Allison.

Silence ensued. When Emily could bear the inactivity no longer, she said, 'I think I'll go in search of coffee. Anybody else want any?'

'Sure,' said Luke. Roger shook his head. She repeated her question to Adam as she passed him, but he did not slow his pacing to answer.

After wandering through much of the hospital, Emily finally found a cafeteria. She got a latte for herself and a plain black coffee for Luke, and went back in.

When she found the critical care ward again, an army of medical personnel was buzzing about Allison's door, while Luke, Roger, and Adam stood clustered a few yards off, out of the way.

'What's happening?' she asked, handing Luke his coffee.

'I think she's waking up,' Roger replied. They were all whispering, though no one could say why.

'Oh God,' Adam groaned. 'I can't take much more of this. I have to know if she's going to be OK!'

Luke placed a hand on his shoulder, both reassuring and restraining him. 'It won't be long now. I'm sure they'll let us know as soon as they can.'

What seemed like an eternity, but was probably about five minutes, passed before the bustle died down. Dr Mirama emerged from the melee and came toward them, smiling.

'Allison is awake,' she said, addressing herself to Roger. 'She is a little foggy still, but she wants to see you.' She turned to Emily. 'I told her you were here, and she asked for you as well. She's asking about her husband and the pregnancy, but we have put her off.' She looked from Roger to Emily as if sizing them up. Roger had gone all fluttery again, spinning in circles and clutching at his hair. The doctor said to Emily, 'I think perhaps it will be better coming from you.'

Emily swallowed. Telling Allison her whole world had collapsed was the last thing she wanted to do, but she had to admit the doctor was right – it probably would be best coming from her. She was the closest thing Allison had to a mother right now – which in itself was sad.

Dr Mirama checked her clipboard and found Colonel Allan's card. 'I must call the chief constable. You two may go on in.'

Emily felt as if she were being invited to face a firing squad.

*   *   *

Emily opened the door slowly, half hoping to see that Allison had dropped into a normal sleep so her dreaded task could be postponed. But she lay staring at the ceiling. Odd bruising patterned her otherwise pale face, perhaps caused by blood seeping from her concussion. Her head was mostly covered in bandages. An IV was hooked up to her left arm, and her right foot and ankle, poking free of the bedclothes, were encased in a cast.

Emily quietly approached the bed. 'Hello, Allison,' she said. 'It's good to see you awake.'

Allison turned her eyes toward Emily but not her head. 'Emily. Thank you for coming.' Then she glimpsed Roger hovering in the doorway. 'Roger. I'm so glad you're here.' She reached her free hand toward him. He scurried up toward the bed and took it.

'But where's James? Why isn't he here? They won't tell me anything.'

Roger shot Emily a panicked glance. 'It's all right, my dear,' he crooned to Allison, evading her question. 'James can't come right now. You're going to be fine.'

'So they tell me.' She attempted a smile. 'Doesn't really feel like it just yet.'

She licked her lips, and Emily offered her a sip of water from the cup by the bed with a bendable straw. Allison bent her head forward to sip, then fell back again, her face screwed up in pain. 'This damned head. What happened to me, anyway?'

Emily and Roger exchanged a glance. 'We were hoping you would be able to tell us,' Emily said. 'Nobody else was with you when it happened. Whatever *it* was. They only found you hours later.'

Allison's eyebrows twitched as if she meant to draw them together but it was too much effort. 'What about James? James was with me. Why doesn't James know? Was he hurt, too? Where is he?' Her agitation increased with each question.

Emily took Allison's left hand, careful to avoid the IV. 'Allison, honey, I'm so sorry. James . . .' She took a deep breath. Best get it over with. 'James didn't make it.'

'Didn't make it? What do you mean? Didn't make it where?'

Roger took over. 'James died, dearest girl. In the accident. He was dead when Luke found him. I'm so very sorry, my dear. James is dead.'

Allison's whole body seemed to deflate. 'No . . . Not James . . . No . . .' Her head turned from side to side, then she clutched it and groaned in pain. Her limbs began to thrash instead. '*No!*' she cried. 'Why are you lying to me? What have you done with him? He can't be dead. He has to be here to look after our baby. We had so many plans . . .' She sat up suddenly and yelled as if sure he was in the building and would hear her if only she could shout loud enough. 'James!'

Alarmed, Emily pushed the call button. A nurse rushed in, shooed them both from the bedside, and injected something into Allison's IV. Gradually, she subsided into a stupor.

The nurse frowned at them. 'She'll sleep now. She needs time to recover. You'll have to leave.'

Emily meekly turned to go. She didn't know whether to be glad or sorry that the revelation of the miscarriage was still to come. It must be for the best. Let the poor girl absorb one loss before she was confronted with another.

In the corridor, Emily reminded Roger to call Bunty while she filled Luke in. She was in the middle of her account when the chief constable returned. Apparently, he hadn't gotten very far.

'The doctor said Allison's awake,' he puffed. 'Have you talked to her? What did she say? What does she remember?'

'She doesn't remember much beyond going out for the ride, apparently. She didn't realize about James. When we told her, she got so upset they had to sedate her again. I'm afraid she won't be able to talk to you for a few hours more. And even then she may not remember what you need to know.'

He huffed in frustration. 'But she does remember something? She knew you, knew who she was?'

'Oh, yes. It's just the details of the accident itself that may take a while to come back.'

'And here I am with an inquest to organize and not a shred of eyewitness testimony. Who'd want my job? Well, if we have to adjourn, we have to adjourn. I promised Lady Margaret we'd get it over with as quickly as possible, and fortunately we both know the coroner. The timing's a little unorthodox, but nonetheless the inquest is set for fourteen hundred hours tomorrow, whether she wakes up and tells us what happened or not. I'll need you three there.' He cast a curious glance at Adam but didn't include him in the request.

The chief constable turned on his heel and strode away before Emily could ask why he needed her specifically. She wasn't a witness to anything except a certain amount of family drama that couldn't be connected with a riding accident. Could it?

TWELVE

Roger, Luke, and Emily returned to Fitzhugh Manor soon afterward, having been assured that Allison would sleep for the rest of the day and they should come back the next morning. Luke offered Adam a ride, but he said he could walk to his flat in Oxford and would catch a ride back to the worksite the next day.

At this point, it became necessary to explain some things to Roger, on the understanding that he would continue to keep his mother in the dark as long as possible. Emily told him first about their being paying guests and not friends of Allison's family, which he took easily in his stride; he only insisted they would not be charged for their stay because things had turned out so differently from what they had expected.

When Emily mentioned the building site, however, Roger said, 'Oh, I know all about that. Have done from the beginning. I go all over the estate, you know, hunting butterflies, so they could never have kept that from me. I didn't realize Adam was the architect, but that's neither here nor there. If Allison didn't think it was a problem to work with him, it certainly wouldn't have bothered me.'

'Well, in that case, since you know about the baby, I guess we're all on the up and up.'

'Good. I always prefer it that way, though Mother,

unfortunately, does make a certain amount of secrecy necessary.' He sighed. 'I suppose I'll have to tell her about the
miscarriage, though I hardly think she deserves to know, given
the way she reacted to the pregnancy. She may simply be
relieved – she'll see it as severing Allison's connection with
the family.'

His brow darkened in a way Emily had never seen on him.
'But I will have a thing or two to say about that. Allison
belongs to the Fitzhughs now. Nothing and no one can make
me turn her out unless she herself chooses to go.'

They picked at some cold lunch, then the afternoon
stretched before them, a blank none of them knew how to fill.
Roger eventually took refuge with his butterflies, but Emily
was too restless to simply sit in the house and read or knit.
It was Sunday, and she had missed church, although she
knew of a small Orthodox parish in Oxford she might have
visited; that only made her more discontented.

'Let's explore Binsey,' she suggested to Luke. 'We can check
out that pub, and maybe find something else interesting to
do. I can't sit in this house with Lady Margaret's disapproval
looming over me from the other wing.'

'Fine by me,' Luke said. 'I could do with a stroll.'

The village was only half a mile away and was contained
within a small radius, so it wasn't an onerous walk. They
went first to the Perch, which was as old and thatched and
full of history as Emily could desire. The inside of the pub
was overflowing with weekend trippers, so they got a pint for
Luke and a glass of wine for Emily and found a small table
in the extensive garden.

'How's the beer?' she asked him when he'd taken a few
sips.

Luke nodded noncommittally. 'Warm.' He smacked his lips,
ruminating. 'It's kinda strange, but I think I could develop a
taste for it. Yours?'

She shrugged. 'White wine is white wine. I don't suppose
this came from Washington or California like most of what I
drink, but in this price bracket it's probably pretty much the
same the world over.'

This was the first time they'd been alone (and awake) since

the tragedy, so as much as Emily would have liked to talk about something neutral, she found herself unable to keep off the subject. 'Are you convinced it was an accident?'

He shrugged. 'Till we hear more from Allison, I'm keeping an open mind. But on the face of it, it's hard to see how it could've been anything else.'

Emily frowned. 'I guess it's just my nasty suspicious mind, or else the fact that when we run up against a dead body, it generally turns out to be murder. I just find it a little hard to accept that with tensions at boiling point in that household, someone could die and it just be a random accident. You know?'

'Yeah, I know. Not entirely rational, but I feel kinda the same. Wouldn't have expected it to be James, though, if someone did get deliberately killed.'

'No. He was the one person holding the whole place together. I would have thought if anyone was going to get bumped off, it would have been Lady Margaret. She was in everybody's way.'

'Too tough to die,' Luke said with a wry grimace.

'Indeed. Not that anyone seems to have tried. Maybe they just knew it would be pointless and so they refrained.' She gave a short laugh. 'Look at us, reduced to absurdities. And our corpse-free honeymoon smashed to smithereens.'

He leaned forward and took her hand. 'We could just escape. After the inquest, that is. We have no real obligation to these folks. We could go to Scotland, or London, or even Paris. We're free agents.'

For one brief shining moment she was tempted. Leave the agony behind and have a proper honeymoon with nothing to focus on except each other. But that was what they'd expected in coming here, and look what had happened.

She sighed. 'I don't know, Luke. It's tempting, but I have this feeling that trouble would end up following us wherever we went. Like a Greek tragedy. You try to run from fate and you just end up running into it instead.' She downed the last of her wine. 'But we have this afternoon, anyway. Let's go see what else Binsey has to offer.'

They walked the circular drive that enclosed the village,

passing cottages that were picturesque enough but not particularly different from those they'd seen already. Then they rounded a bend and came upon a small church.

It was a stone church built in the simplest possible style, with no tower or transept. It looked ancient, deserted, and a little unkempt, with tall grass growing amongst the tilting headstones in the churchyard. But Emily was drawn to it somehow. Without much considering what she was doing, she approached the tiny porch and tried the door.

It was open.

The church was indeed deserted, not just at the moment but, she guessed, most of the time. It seemed to function more as a memorial of some kind than as an active parish church. But it had been active once – the pews and pulpit were timeworn, and the stone floor sagged slightly in the middle from centuries of treading feet. The beams that supported the ceiling were chipped and uneven, darkened with the smoke of countless candles – perhaps even incense, though few Anglicans used incense anymore. But if you went back far enough, before the Reformation, she felt sure incense would have been burned here. It had seeped into the walls, giving the church an ethereal, holy scent.

Emily stepped into a pew and knelt facing the undressed altar that stood against the far wall, on the other side of a pointed stone arch. Luke hung back near the door.

Her knees slid into depressions in the wooden kneeler made by generations of knees of supplicants before her, praying for she knew not what. But surely some of them had prayed for the resolution of uncertainty and conflict, for ease and comfort for the bereaved, for the souls of those who had departed before their natural time, as she was doing now.

Eventually, she surfaced from her prayer and turned to see Luke perusing a brochure he'd picked up from a small table. She went to see what he'd learned.

'Saint Margaret of Antioch,' he said.

'Of Antioch? She must be an Orthodox saint, then. Oh, I remember – we call her Marina. How old is this church?'

'Twelfth century. Built on the site of an even older church

dedicated to Saint Margaret by the patroness of Oxford, Saint
– I can't pronounce that, can you?'

Emily read the name *Frideswide*. 'Free-des-wee-duh?' She
shrugged.

'Says here Margaret's the patron of women in childbirth.
And something about a dragon? I don't get the connection.
Anyway, this says there's a holy well on the grounds. Must
be around the other side. Want to take a look?'

'Absolutely.'

They exited the nave and walked around the back of the
church to see some bricked steps dug into the ground,
surrounded by a low wall, with a band of 'caution' tape across
the entrance. At the end opposite the stairs, the wall was cut
by a triangular opening, far too small to admit a grown person.
'I guess if the well is really ancient, the ground would have
grown up around it,' she said. 'But it doesn't look like we can
access the well itself.'

'Too bad,' Luke said, but Emily knew he had no real
understanding of how much they were missing. Wells like
this had been the sites of many miracles in centuries past,
and although the faith of the people who visited them had
diminished, the wells' power had not. Miracles still waited
for those who truly believed.

Emily prayed for a miracle for Allison now. What kind of
miracle, she had no idea, but it would take no less to make
her life bearable again after her terrible loss.

Monday morning, Luke, Emily, and Roger went to visit Allison
again. Her condition had stabilized – physically, at least – so
she'd been moved to a regular room. She was awake, but they
had to wait because the chief constable was with her. He
emerged after a few minutes, frowning.

'Could she tell you anything?' Luke asked.

'Something,' Colonel Allan replied. 'Not much, but something. Can't talk about it now. You'll find out at the inquest.'
He held up a sheet of handwritten notes. 'Have to get this
down to the station, get a statement typed up, and get her to
sign it before fourteen hundred hours.' He nodded farewell
and strode off.

Roger and Emily were again allowed in, while Luke had to wait outside. Even on the regular ward, visitors were limited to two at a time. This time Luke had provided himself with something to read – and Emily had brought her knitting, though it appeared she might not need it. She followed Roger into Allison's room.

The bruising on Allison's face had begun to change color, but other than that she looked much the same as the day before – except her eyes. Yesterday they had been vague; today they were haunted. Emily's heart constricted at the sight.

'Hello,' Allison said wanly. 'Come to drop the other shoe? Never mind, they already told me. They had to say something to explain the blood.'

'Oh, Allison.' Emily hurried to the bedside and reached for Allison's hand, but she pulled it away. 'I'm so sorry. About everything. I just can't tell you how sorry.' She looked around as if some way to make herself useful might manifest itself among the bedclothes, equipment, and wires. 'Is there anything I can do?'

Allison gave a sound that might have been a laugh. 'Do? Yeah, you can tell me this is all a bad dream, and I'm going to wake up tomorrow and find James and our baby alive again.' A tear snaked its way down her cheek, and she angrily brushed it away. 'That's all anybody can do for me now.'

Emily felt any further words from her would only make matters worse. Roger tried in his turn. 'Allison, dear, have they given you any idea how long you'll be here?'

'I haven't asked. I don't think I care. It's not as if I had anywhere else to go. Not now.'

'Don't talk that way, please. You will always have a home at Fitzhugh Manor, as long as you want it – at least as long as I'm alive. I'm the baronet now, and Mother can't run you out. You still belong to us, regardless.'

Allison teared up again. 'That's so sweet of you, Roger. I suppose I will have to come back to recuperate – they won't let me stay here for six weeks till my ankle heals. But after that, I'll probably go back to the States. I don't think I could bear to live at Fitzhugh, or even in England, without James.'

Her eyes filled, and this time she let the tears overflow. 'Oh, James . . . Why? Just why? With all the terrible people in the world, why did the one perfect one have to die?'

Emily couldn't even try to answer that. Her faith taught that God always takes a person when he or she is most ready to meet eternity, but that thought would not comfort Allison in this moment. Eternity was nothing to her. She needed her husband *now*.

The two of them held her hands and mourned with her until she had cried herself back to sleep. Then they tiptoed out. The inquest would be soon enough for them to find out whatever she had been able to remember about the accident.

THIRTEEN

In the old days, Emily supposed, the inquest would have been held in the Perch, with one of the village tradesmen acting as coroner. Evidence would have been given by those directly concerned as to how the deceased met his death, and since that incident did not involve the immediate participation of any other human, a quick verdict of accidental death would have been returned.

As it was, the inquest was held at the coroner's court in Oxford, the coroner was a permanent government official, and evidence would be given by various doctors and policemen who had never known James in his lifetime, as well as by his family and friends. Emily had no reason to be nervous as she waited her turn to be called; she had nothing of any importance to contribute, no one to fear implicating, and certainly nothing to hide. But her stomach was nevertheless filled with butterflies – of a less attractive variety than those Roger was wont to pursue.

Luke was called first, since he had found the body. In addition to describing that event, he was asked to say where and when he had last seen the deceased. 'At breakfast in the dining room of the manor house, about eight a.m. on Saturday, June eighth.' It was obvious from his demeanor and precision that Luke had given evidence many times before.

'And what did you understand the deceased's plan to be after that?'

'He and his wife were going to go for a horseback ride.'

'Did they give you any specifics about where they planned to ride or for how long?'

'No, they did not. James did mention he wanted Allison to ride Buttercup because she was gentle, and Allison needed to be careful because she was pregnant.' A small buzz rippled through the courtroom at that. 'For that same reason, I assumed the ride would be short, but nothing was actually said to that effect.'

The coroner consulted his notes. 'I understand you were also the first to discover the body?'

'Yes, sir. I organized the search after Roger – Sir Roger Fitzhugh, as he is now – told me they were missing. I was riding ahead of Conan O'Donnell and Bunty – Penelope Fitzhugh – and was the first to spot Sir James's body.'

'And did you call the police immediately?'

'Yes, sir. As soon as I was sure he was dead. I did not interfere with the body or the scene any more than was unavoidable. I waited a short distance away for the police to arrive, while the others went on to search for Allison.'

The coroner nodded. 'Very commendable. Thank you. You may step down.'

Luke came to sit with Emily.

'Call Emily Richards to the stand.'

Her knees buckled as she stood, but she managed to walk calmly to the stand and be sworn in. 'Mrs Richards, I understand you are staying at Fitzhugh Manor with your husband?'

'That's correct.'

'And were you also present at breakfast with your husband and the Fitzhughs on Saturday the eighth of June?'

'I was.'

'Do you recall anything being said about the proposed direction or duration of the Fitzhughs' ride?'

'No. They only talked about the horses, as Luke said.'

'Do you have any other information pertinent to this inquiry?'

She might have said all kinds of things about the relationships and tensions in that house over the week of their stay. But what constituted information, and what could be considered pertinent? As far as she could tell, none of it. 'No, sir. I'm afraid I do not.'

'Thank you. You may step down.' She went back to her seat, grateful it was over. A representative of the police was called next – not the chief constable, but one of the uniformed officers who had answered Luke's call.

'Please state your name,' the coroner said.

'Constable Shefali Mohindra.'

'Constable Mohindra, please summarize for us your investigation of the scene of this death.'

The constable cleared her throat and read from her prepared statement. 'We received a call at seven-oh-three p.m. on Saturday the eighth of June from Mr Luke Richards, guest at Fitzhugh Manor, saying there had been an accident and Sir James Fitzhugh was dead. The call also requested an ambulance for Sir James's wife, Lady Fitzhugh, who had not yet been found but was presumed to be nearby. I and three other officers arrived at Fitzhugh Manor and followed Mr Richards's directions to the spot on the grounds where the body was located. This was on a grassy slope leading down to a small lake, next to a bridle path that bordered a wood. We were told the deceased had gone riding that morning. The position of the body was consistent with a fall from a horse. The head had been injured, and there was a large stone embedded in the ground nearby, which made it probable the deceased had been thrown from his horse and had hit his head on the stone, then bounced or rolled a short way off.'

'We'll get the attending physician's report on the condition of the body, Constable.'

'Yes, sir.'

'Please continue your account of your own activities at the scene.'

'Leaving the forensics team in charge, my partner and I joined the search for Lady Fitzhugh. We found her soon afterwards a short distance away inside the wood. She was alive but unconscious, so we alerted the ambulance and she was taken to hospital.'

'Were the horses in question found?'

'One of them, the one they call Buttercup, was found in the wood, a short distance from where Lady Fitzhugh lay. Its reins had become badly tangled in a bush and it was trapped. The other horse was not found at that time. We assumed it had returned to the stable after throwing Sir James.'

'We will verify that point shortly. Thank you, Constable. You may step down. Please call Doctor Charles Mortimer.'

A middle-aged man in a suit answered the call. He looked exactly like Emily's image of a British doctor – slightly pompous, slightly vague, but essentially kindly.

'Doctor Mortimer, you were the medical officer in charge of the forensics team that attended the scene of Sir James Fitzhugh's death?'

'That is correct.'

'Please summarize your findings with regard to the body itself.'

'As the constable mentioned, the body's position was consistent with having been thrown from a horse. There were a number of lacerations and contusions all over the body, but the fatal wound was to the right side of the skull, which was crushed. This wound was consistent with the head having struck a nearby large stone as it fell. We found traces of the deceased's blood and hair in the crevices of the stone in question.'

'What did you find as to time of death?'

'It's always difficult to be precise when a body has been outdoors for any length of time, especially in variable weather as we had that day. But I could certainly say the deceased had been dead for some hours – perhaps six to ten.'

'So the time of the death could be consistent with the time the Fitzhughs are known to have left for their morning ride?'

'I would say so, yes.'

'Did you find evidence of any sort of human intervention at the scene? Anything that could have caused the horse to throw its rider?'

'No, we did not. The body was in the open, so nothing in the nature of a tripwire could have been used. We saw nothing that should not have been there.' The doctor took off his glasses and applied his fingertips to the corners of his eyes. Emily wondered if James had been a friend. 'Nothing, that is, except the body itself.' He put his glasses back on.

'Was a post-mortem performed?'

'Yes, but not by me. The pathologist at the John Radcliffe performed the post-mortem.'

'Did your team examine the scene where Lady Fitzhugh was found?'

'Certainly. We found nothing untoward there either.'

'What is your conclusion as to the manner of death?'

'I would say it was accidental.'

'Thank you. You may step down. Call Doctor Sophie Mortimer to the stand.'

'Two Mortimers?' Emily whispered to Luke.

He shrugged. 'Maybe they're husband and wife.'

But the woman who now came to the stand was no more than thirty, with blond hair in a French twist, attractive in spite of the severe black suit she wore. 'Maybe father and daughter,' Luke amended.

'Doctor Mortimer, you performed the autopsy on Sir James Fitzhugh, is that correct?'

'Yes.'

'What did you find as to cause of death?'

'Just what my fa— what Doctor Charles Mortimer said. There were a number of minor injuries, but the cause of death was clearly the blunt trauma to the right side of the skull.'

'Can you give a more precise opinion on the time of death?'

'Yes, we are able to narrow that down a little better in the lab. I would say death most likely occurred between eight and ten a.m. on the day in question.'

'Did you perform a chemical analysis of the blood and organs?'

'We did. We found no evidence of intoxicants, drugs, or poison. The results were completely normal.'

'And your conclusion as to the manner of death?'

'Based on the autopsy, I would say it was accidental.' She gave a tiny grin. 'Unless you want to arraign the horse.'

Emily was surprised at the somewhat inappropriate humor from one who looked so straitlaced. But she supposed a pathologist would need a little humor to stay sane doing the work she did.

The coroner glared at her sternly over the tops of his glasses. 'We do not require levity in this court, Doctor Mortimer. You may step down.'

Looking sheepish, the young pathologist made way for the next witness.

'Call Mr Conan O'Donnell.'

When Conan was seated, the coroner said, 'What is your occupation, Mr O'Donnell?'

'I'm the stable manager at Fitzhugh Stables.'

'And are you responsible for preparing the horses for Sir James and Lady Fitzhugh to ride?'

'No, they always do that themselves. The grooms and I take care of the horses generally, but James and Allison always like to saddle up and put their horses away on their own. They're both – were both – very accomplished horsemen.'

'I see. On Saturday the eighth, were you present when Sir James and Lady Fitzhugh went out for their ride?'

'I was present when they arrived at the stables, yes.'

'But not when they rode out?'

'I was there, but I was busy inside one of the stalls. I heard them go, but I didn't see them.'

'Do you know which horses they were riding?'

'Allison – Lady Fitzhugh – was on Buttercup, and James was on Jackie.'

'Did you speak to the Fitzhughs at all?'

'Only to say hello and pass the time of day.'

'Did they mention where they intended to ride or how long they would be out?'

'Nary a word.'

The coroner frowned. 'Was anyone else present in the stables during the time the Fitzhughs were there?'

'As far as I know, only Bunty – Penelope Fitzhugh. She's the riding instructor. She was getting a horse ready for a lesson at the time. Over in the other wing, where we keep the riding-school horses.'

'Did anything at all out of the ordinary occur that morning, either before, during, or after the Fitzhughs' visit?'

'Not a thing, sir. Just a normal Saturday morning at Fitzhugh Stables.'

'What time did the Fitzhughs leave the stables?'

'I couldn't say for certain, sir, seeing as I don't wear a watch. But I would guess it was eight thirty or thereabouts.'

'How long would they typically ride?'

'Not more than an hour or two, as a rule.'

'At what point did you become concerned that they had not returned?'

'I thought it was odd they didn't come back by noon. They would have wanted to get the horses unsaddled and brushed down in time to change for lunch at one.'

'But you did not raise the alarm at that time?'

'It wasn't my place, sir. For all I knew, they might have decided to ride farther. James is – was – the boss. He could do as he liked.'

The coroner glared over his glasses. 'At what point *did* you raise the alarm?'

'Well, I didn't, as a matter of fact. I got busy with my duties and didn't think too much about it. It was Roger who came to me when they didn't show up for tea. I offered to go search for them then, but he wanted to ask around the rest of the staff first. Then Mr Richards came back, and he sort of took over. We all went out at that point.'

'And what about the horses they were riding? Did they ever return?'

'Buttercup came back with the searchers. She'd been trapped near Allison, as you know, sir. But we didn't see Jackie until near dark. She came back alone with her reins trailing, all lathered up and worn out. The Lord alone knows where she'd been wandering.'

'Did you put the horse away at that point?'

'No, Bunty did that. I mean Penelope.'

'Very well. We shall speak to her presently. You may step down. Call Sir Roger Fitzhugh to the stand.'

Roger was as nervous and discombobulated as Emily had ever seen him. He kept straightening his tie and trying to tame his wild hair with his shaking hands. Emily knew of no reason he should be nervous any more than herself; it was probably just the situation that flustered him.

'Sir Roger Fitzhugh, please tell us your relation to the deceased.'

'I'm his uncle.'

'The younger brother of his father?'

'That's correct.'

'And in the absence of male issue, the title and property revert to you?'

Roger cleared his throat. 'Yes.'

'Please tell the court when you last saw your nephew and his wife.'

'I–I hadn't seen them at all that day. Saturday, I mean. I breakfasted early and went out hunting butterflies. I'd seen a particularly fine specimen in the woods on Friday but hadn't been able to catch it, and I wanted to try again.'

'Would this be the same wood near which Sir James's body was found?'

Roger's eyes widened. 'It would. I mean, it was.'

'And were you there all day?'

'Most of the day. I nipped back in for a bit of lunch, but James and Allison weren't there. I thought nothing of it at the time. We had a cold spread since our guests were out for the day, so I assumed they'd been in before me or would come in later. I was only there for fifteen minutes or so.'

'And you then returned to the wood?'

'Yes.'

'Did you see or hear anything unusual in the course of the day? In the morning, particularly?'

Roger gave a nervous laugh. 'I get quite absorbed when I'm hunting. Someone could speak my name right in my ear and I might not hear them.' His brow furrowed. 'I think, though – I think I did hear something.' He thought for a moment, then his face cleared. 'Yes, that's it – I heard some gunshots.'

Luke and Emily exchanged a startled glance. 'It's not hunting season,' Luke whispered. Emily nodded – she remembered James had mentioned that. But maybe it was legal to shoot vermin at this time of year.

The coroner's impassive face registered interest. 'Indeed? Do you know what time that was?'

'I'm afraid not. I don't pay much attention to the time when I'm hunting, either. But somewhere around the middle of the morning, I suppose.'

'How many shots?'

'Two or three, I think.'

'Could you tell where they were coming from? How far away?'

'I'm sorry, no. Sound echoes around in a wood, and as I said, I wasn't paying particular attention.'

'Could you make a guess as to what type of gun?'

Roger gave an apologetic smile. 'I'm not good with guns, I'm afraid. One doesn't use a gun to hunt butterflies.' A quiet titter ran around the court, and the coroner frowned it down. 'But I do remember thinking it was odd because it wasn't the right time of year to shoot birds, so perhaps that means it sounded like a shotgun?' He shrugged one shoulder. 'I'm sorry, I'm afraid that's the best I can do.'

'Did you see any other person while you were in the wood? At any time during the day?'

'Not a soul. I did catch that butterfly, though.' He smiled in satisfaction.

The coroner closed his eyes for a moment, which Emily suspected he did to stop himself rolling them. 'You may step down.'

Roger scurried back to his seat in obvious relief.

'Call Lady Margaret Fitzhugh.'

The bailiff bustled up to the bench and handed the coroner a note. He frowned over it, then announced, 'Lady Margaret Fitzhugh is not well enough to appear. She informs the court that she has nothing to contribute as she did not see her grandson at all on the morning of Saturday the eighth, and only learned of his death after the searchers had returned to the house.'

Luke nudged Emily and whispered, 'Well, that's a howdy-do. What about her being so sure Adam had murdered him?'

Emily shook her head, as baffled as her husband. 'Maybe she knows it wouldn't stand up in court. Plus, think of the scandal if she accused Allison publicly of infidelity. She'd never want to wash that dirty linen in public.' Luke made a 'you've got a point there' face.

The coroner set the note aside with a look that suggested to Emily that had it come from any less august a personage than Lady Margaret Fitzhugh, the excuse would hardly have been accepted. 'Call Penelope Fitzhugh.'

Beyond clarifying her relation to the Fitzhughs, Bunty had nothing to add to Conan's testimony about the morning. She had not even spoken to James and Allison that morning but only heard them say hello to Conan.

'You were present when the horse' – the coroner consulted his notes – 'Jackie, returned?'

'Yes, sir.'

'What was your impression of the horse's condition?'

'I'd say she'd been seriously spooked. She looked as if she'd been running for hours, and there was a kind of wild light in her eye. But she was too exhausted to put up a fight.'

'Have you any idea what could have spooked her?'

'Well' – Bunty blinked and swallowed – 'if she saw James dead, that would certainly have spooked her. Most horses are terrified of blood.'

'Is the horse Jackie particularly highly strung?'

'No, not as a rule. She's quite gentle and even-tempered most of the time. It was a shock to see her that way.'

'Could you speculate at all about what could have caused such a gentle horse to throw its rider, as she also seems to have done?'

'The gunshots Roger mentioned might have done it, I suppose. Our horses are pretty well used to guns, but if it was close enough, it might have set her off.'

'When Jackie returned, was her saddle intact? Did you check to see that her girth was properly secured?'

'It was, and I did. There was nothing wrong with her tack.'

'Thank you. You may step down.'

Next, the groundskeepers were called. They had nothing to report except the fact that they had taken out no guns themselves on Saturday, nor were they aware of anyone else at the manor having done so. So much for the vermin-shooting idea.

Emily looked around the courtroom, wondering who might be called next. It seemed they had heard from everyone who had any knowledge of the events – except Allison.

'Call Chief Constable Colonel Henry Allan to the stand.'

The chief constable, now in full dress uniform, mounted the witness box, holding a sheet of typescript.

'Chief Constable, I believe you were able to obtain a statement from Lady Fitzhugh, who is not yet well enough to attend this court in person.'

'That is correct.'

'Will you please read the statement to the court.'

'Certainly.' He cleared his throat. '"On Saturday the eighth of June at approximately eight thirty a.m., I, Allison, Lady Fitzhugh, walked to the Fitzhugh Stables with my husband, Sir James Fitzhugh, to prepare for our morning ride. We said hello to Conan O'Donnell, the stable manager, saddled our own horses as usual, and set off. Because I was nearing the end of my first trimester of pregnancy, James insisted I ride Buttercup, the oldest and most placid horse in our stable. Jackie needed exercise, so James rode her instead of Lucky, his usual mount."'

Emily whispered to Luke, 'There's no way Allison was coherent enough to say all that in those exact words. And she wouldn't, anyway. "I, Allison, Lady Fitzhugh"? Give me a break.'

He shook his head. 'Statements don't have to be in the witness's own words. They take what the witness actually said, put it in logical order, and translate it into police-speak. The witness signs off that the content is materially true, not that it's their exact words.'

Emily humphed. 'I hope Allison was lucid enough to tell whether this was materially true.'

Luke only nodded.

The chief constable went on. '"We took one of our usual routes – down to the lake that lies on the estate, around it, and back up towards the house along the bridle path that runs between the lake and the wood. The day had turned fine, and

we were enjoying ourselves immensely. We had got as far as
the bridle path when something must have happened."

Colonel Allan stopped and cleared his throat again. "'I
remember nothing more until I awoke in the hospital. I do not
know how I came to be injured and my husband killed. Signed,
Allison, Lady Fitzhugh.'"

The coroner exerted what was clearly his greatest effort at
self-control yet. 'In other words, Chief Constable, Lady
Fitzhugh has been able to tell us nothing we did not already
know or could have surmised.'

'That's about the size of it, sir.'

'Under the circumstances, do you wish to request an
adjournment until such time as Lady Fitzhugh may recover
her full memory of the incident, or until further evidence may
come to light?'

The chief constable swallowed. 'No, sir. We feel the evidence
we have now clearly points to death by misadventure, and we
do not intend to pursue the matter further.'

Emily wondered whether a quiet word in his ear from
Lady Margaret had influenced that decision. Even the suggestion that her grandson might have been murdered, regardless
of who the culprit was, could count in her book as a scandal
to be avoided at all costs.

'Very well. You may stand down.'

The coroner shuffled the papers in front of him, which now
included Allison's statement.

'That concludes the evidence in this matter. Although it has
not been conclusively shown that no human agency was
involved in the death of Sir James Fitzhugh, neither have we
heard any evidence suggesting such agency did exist. The
police are satisfied that this death was accidental.'

He banged his gavel. 'We find that Sir James Fitzhugh met
with his death by misadventure.'

Lady Margaret still did not appear that evening, for which
Emily was grateful; she couldn't imagine trying to make polite
conversation with her after being told to her face she wasn't
welcome in the house anymore. Roger retired early, pleading
a headache, so Luke and Emily took their after-dinner coffee

up to their room and sat in front of the fireplace. It felt deca-
dent to light a fire in June, but the room was cool, and Emily
felt chilled on the inside as well.

'Were you satisfied with that verdict?' she asked Luke when
they were settled.

'Not entirely. You?'

She shook her head. 'Something doesn't sit right. I keep
thinking about that horse.'

'You mean Jackie?'

'Yes. Is it normal for a gentle horse to go crazy like that
just because of a gunshot?'

'Not really. I've had horses spook at a gunshot, sure, but
not so bad they threw me. James had about the best seat on
a horse I've seen. He wouldn't throw easy. And then for Jackie
to run off and not come home till sundown – that's downright
peculiar.'

'That's what I thought. This sounds crazy, but do you think
Jackie could have been . . . tampered with?'

'You mean drugs?'

'That's the general idea.'

Luke scratched his chin meditatively. 'I guess it's possible.
I don't know offhand what kind of drug could do that to a
horse, but there might be something. Have to ask a vet, I
suppose. But then we still come back to the question of *why*.
Why would anyone want to hurt James? And who?'

Emily sighed. 'Good questions. To which I have no answers.'
She sipped her coffee for a few minutes in silence.

Luke spoke up then. 'Come to think of it, I do know of one
fellow who doesn't seem to like James much.'

'Oh? Who's that?'

'Simon Braithwaite. He seems like a hot-headed kind of guy,
and he has access to the stables. And he's carrying a grudge.'

Emily sat forward. 'We should definitely check him out.
And I hate to say this, but Lady Margaret was right about
one thing.'

'What's that?'

'Adam had a motive to kill James, too. He's obviously still
very much in love with Allison. He could have hoped that
with James out of the way, he'd have a chance with her.'

'I guess. His reaction to the news seemed genuine. But if he'd meant to kill James, then thought he'd killed Allison instead, it might make some sense.'

Emily sat back with a sigh that was almost a laugh. 'Listen to us. Not only have we lost out on our corpse-free honeymoon, but now we're talking about taking over an investigation that not only is half a world away from your jurisdiction but officially is not even happening. Maybe we should just let it go – accept that it was a pure accident, and give everyone a chance to grieve and adjust and get on with their lives.'

Luke thumped his hands on the arms of his chair. 'You know what? You're right. We're grasping at straws here anyway. This case, if it even is a case, is none of our business. We're here to enjoy our honeymoon, and dagnabbit, that's just what we're going to do.'

He stood, took both her hands, and pulled her up and into his arms. 'And I vote we start doing that right now.'

Even if her lips had been free to protest, Emily wouldn't have dreamed of it.

FOURTEEN

The next day, Emily, Luke, and Roger returned to the John Radcliffe to visit Allison again. She was calmer – in fact, calm to the point of apathy, which concerned Emily. Perhaps this was one of the stages of grief she didn't know about. Or perhaps it was the effect of medication or of the concussion itself.

'How's everything at home?' Allison asked Roger, without seeming much to care. 'The dragon as fiery as ever?'

Roger opened his mouth without speaking, putting Emily in mind of that codfish again. He looked at her with a mixture of entreaty and confusion. She gave him an encouraging nod.

'Mother is devastated,' he said. 'She keeps to her own apartment. We've scarcely seen her since . . . it happened.'

Allison's eyes widened. 'She's that upset because I got hurt?

I would have thought she'd be dancing in the streets. Figuratively speaking, of course.'

Emily took a deep breath. Apparently, it was worse than she'd thought – Allison had either forgotten or refused to accept that James was dead.

'Or maybe she's upset that I didn't die,' Allison said lightly. 'Well, tough beans, Granny dear. We Bookers aren't that easy to kill. I'll be back, and James and I will make that estate pay for itself yet. We'll make sure little James Junior inherits a going concern he can be proud of.' She finished with a satisfied smile.

Roger and Emily exchanged horrified glances, then watched as Allison's smile faded and the blood drained from her face. 'James . . .' she whispered. 'Oh, James . . . our little son . . .' Her eyes welled and she turned her face to the wall.

'She's clearly remembered about the baby,' Emily whispered to Roger. 'But does she realize about James? I can't tell.'

Roger shook his head. 'I don't know. But I think she has as much reality as she can handle for now.'

Emily nodded. Allison seemed to be drifting back to sleep, most likely medication-induced, so they gently released her hands and slipped out.

In the hall, Emily and Roger encountered Dr Mirama, and Luke joined them to hear what she had to say. 'Doctor,' Emily asked her, 'Allison doesn't seem to be completely in touch with reality. When we first came in, she didn't even remember her husband and baby were killed. Is that something we should be concerned about at this point?'

Dr Mirama shook her head. 'It's quite normal with the type of concussion she had. She'll be foggy for some time. Memories and reality will come and go. And, of course, the medication doesn't help. Once her pain subsides to the point that we can discontinue that, she should begin to return to normal.'

'Were you able to get in touch with her parents?'

'Unfortunately, no. They're traveling somewhere in Asia, out of mobile range, and their house-sitter hasn't been able to get in touch with them yet. She said they're expected back at the end of the month.'

Luke and Emily exchanged glances. So much for their

carefree honeymoon – with the best intentions in the world, Roger would not be capable of looking after Allison and protecting her from his mother's wrath all on his own.

'Do you know when Allison will be able to come home?' Roger asked.

'We can't say with certainty. It will depend on how the concussion heals. As far as her other injuries are concerned, she could go home today, provided she has someone to look after her. But it could be tomorrow, or it could be two or three more days till her mind is clear.'

Roger bit his lip. 'Oh dear. I don't know if I can hold Mother off that long.'

'In terms of what?' Emily asked.

'The funeral. She wanted to have it today, as soon as the police released James's body, but I put my foot down as baronet and talked her out of it. But two or three more days . . .'

'But isn't it Allison's responsibility to arrange the funeral? She is James's wife, after all.'

'Yes, but clearly she's in no fit state. And you know Mother – she assumes she's in charge of everything unless someone stands up to her very firmly indeed.'

Emily linked her arm through Roger's. 'We'll stand up to her with you,' she said, glancing at Luke, who nodded. 'I've never yet met anyone who can beat Luke in a contest of wills.'

From the hospital, Luke and Emily wanted to go on to the Ashmolean Museum, since they were already in town. But they weren't sure what to do with Roger.

He solved the problem for them. 'Would you mind very much if I don't go back with you?' he said. 'I want to visit the Museum of Natural History. They've added to their lepidoptera collection recently, and I simply must see what they have. I won't have a chance for some time after Allison comes home. I'll catch a bus back.'

Emily brightened. 'We wanted to go to the Ashmolean, so we can meet up after that and take you home. Shall we say five o'clock?'

Roger beamed. 'Perfect.'

Street parking in the center of Oxford was impossible, so

Roger directed them to a central parking garage from which they could all walk or bus to their respective destinations. The Ashmolean turned out to be a little farther away than Emily wanted to walk, given how much walking they'd have to do inside the museum, so they caught one of the frequent double-decker buses that dominated the Oxford streets.

From the top of their bus, she got her first proper look at the quintessence of Oxford – the university. It was less cohesive than she'd imagined. Dozens of self-contained colleges were spread out over a wide area, with all the usual public spaces, businesses, and amenities of a small city mixed in between. The architecture spanned centuries, but the colleges here in the city center shared a medieval-to-Renaissance aesthetic and the unifying element of the weathered yellow Cotswold limestone she was coming to know and love. She was so enthralled with the architecture that surrounded her that she was tempted to forgo the Ashmolean and take a tour of the university instead.

'I vote we stick to the plan,' Luke said. 'These buildings have been here for centuries. They're not going anywhere. We've got the Bodleian reserved for Saturday, so let's add another tour or two on to that.'

'I suppose that would be best. The Ashmolean should be amazing in its own right.'

And amazing it was. The collection spanned all corners of the world and most of recorded history. Emily knew they'd never manage to see it all in one day, so she voted to stick to European art from the medieval period on. That in itself took them all the rest of the day and reduced Emily's feet to an aching pulp. Her favorite painting was of St Nicholas, depicted as flying through the air with his bishop's cape billowing behind him, saving a ship from being wrecked in a storm. And her favorite object by far was a statuette of an extremely sassy and skeptical-looking bird – possibly an owl, possibly an eagle, possibly a dodo – that looked as if it belonged in Alice's Wonderland.

They broke their wanderings with lunch, and later tea, in the museum café, and by a quarter to five Emily was more than ready to head back – despite the thousands of paintings and *objets d'art* that yet remained unseen. She wished she had made this trip when she was younger and had more endurance;

but then she would not have brought to it all the knowledge and perspective of a lifetime, so perhaps it was just as well she was doing it now.

That evening at dinner, Lady Margaret made her first appearance since her dramatic accusation of Adam. She looked as if she had died along with her beloved grandson. Her sunken, watery eyes were deeply shadowed, her whole face was haggard, and her figure was bent nearly double; she needed the support of Caddie as well as her cane to make her slow progress down the stairs and into the dining room. Emily had to wonder what could make the journey worth the effort.

She soon found out. They were barely into their first course when Lady Margaret laid down her knife and fork – with which she had been cutting her food into tiny pieces without eating it – and drew herself up to something like her former formidable stature.

'The funeral will be held tomorrow,' she announced.

'Mother, we discussed this,' Roger said, with more than his usual force but not, Emily feared, enough to withstand Lady Margaret. 'We have to wait until Allison gets out of the hospital.'

'The arrangements are already made.'

Roger shot a look of entreaty at Luke.

'Then you're going to have to unmake them,' Luke said. 'Allison will probably be ready to come home in a day or two. It won't hurt anything to wait that long. If she hadn't been injured, she'd be the one arranging the funeral, so you really have no right to go ahead without her.' His tone was polite but firm.

'I have the right of the only one who truly loved James.' Her voice wavered slightly, but not enough to suggest she was giving in.

'Mother!' Roger spoke with real energy now. 'How can you say that? I loved James dearly. So did lots of people. And Allison – love is an understatement. He was her whole world.'

Lady Margaret shook her head. 'She did not love him at all. It was a mere pretense.' She drew herself up even further. 'The verdict at the inquest was mistaken,' she pronounced. 'My grandson was murdered.'

Luke and Emily were too shocked to speak. Roger said in a tone that tried to be placating, 'Mother – please. There's no justification for that. The coroner looked at all the evidence, and it was clearly an accident.'

'It was not an accident. That woman killed my grandson. She and her lover, that Marshall person, conspired to kill him so they could marry and pass on the estate to their bastard.'

Luke said gently but firmly, 'Lady Margaret, I honestly don't see how that could be true. Everybody but you knows how much Allison loved James. We're all sure the baby was his, including James himself.'

'I cannot help that you have all been duped by her. She was a schemer and a gold-digger from the very beginning. You know she was still engaged to Marshall when she and James met? She saw a good thing and went for it, but her affections never changed. She and Marshall have been conspiring together ever since, and the pregnancy gave them the opportunity to gain possession of the whole estate in the child's name, rather than settling for a widow's portion. Thank God, the estate itself is entailed on the next natural heir – she can't get her claws into it now.'

Luke set down his fork and ran a hand over his head. 'What evidence do you have for this accusation?'

'I do not require what you call evidence. I *know*. I have seen them together, and I know.'

'Seen Allison and Adam?' Emily put in, startled. 'When? Where?'

'She thinks I am oblivious to what happens on my own estate. Simply because my apartment is in the far wing and I cannot walk across country, she supposes I am unaware of the spurious project she has begun on the other side of the copse. But I am still perfectly capable of mounting the stairs to the tower, and the tower windows provide an excellent view.'

'Still, you could hardly have made out their faces at that distance.'

'I have the aid of an excellent pair of binoculars. I have seen Allison go into the copse and emerge on the other side, and I have seen Marshall come to greet her.'

'But you can't have seen them . . . embrace or anything. I'll never believe that.'

Lady Margaret looked down her aristocratic nose at Emily. 'They are not so shameless as to display their affection in public. But I am not so naive as to doubt what goes on behind closed doors.'

'I'm afraid your belief is not evidence, Lady Margaret,' Luke said. 'And anyway, if you had all these suspicions, why didn't you come to the inquest and voice them? Or tell the chief constable? You must've known all the evidence pointed to an accident.'

Her eyes widened. 'And air my family's dirty linen in public? Only an American could imagine such a thing. No, I do not require the justice system to avenge me in this case. It is enough for me that the Jezebel has been hoist with her own petard. In her haste to dispatch James, she destroyed her bastard as well.' A smile of stomach-turning satisfaction spread over her wasted face. 'Her plan is foiled. She will never get Fitzhugh Manor now.'

Emily's appetite deserted her. That the dowager's hatred for Allison could be so strong as to overpower her love for her grandson, to render her grief for him as of naught in the shadow of her gloating revenge – Emily could not remember when she'd encountered such a depth of depravity. And all concealed by a mask of the utmost respectability and virtue.

Luke looked similarly revolted, but he recovered himself enough to say, 'What exactly are you suggesting Adam and Allison did? Pulled James off his horse right where he would smash his head against a rock?'

'Possibly. Or perhaps they simply arranged for the gunshots in the wood and left the rest to chance. I do not credit either of them with the intelligence to construct a foolproof plan.'

Roger finally had all he could take. 'Mother. You are being absurd. Allison is probably the most intelligent person I've ever met. If she had really wanted to kill James, she would have done it in a way that did not endanger herself and her child.' He drew himself up, and an unexpected fire came into his eyes. 'But all this is completely ridiculous and unfounded, and I will not hear another word of it at my table. I insist you either desist or return to your own apartment.'

Lady Margaret blinked as if attempting to bring her younger son into focus. She must have seen something of his father in him at that moment, because she rose without further protest. 'I find I am not hungry after all. I shall retire.' She looked around the table with an arrogance that reduced them all to inferior life forms. 'You will do as you like about the funeral, I have no doubt.' She tapped her way out of the room without Caddie's assistance.

Emily stared at her, temporarily dumbfounded. Then she said to Roger, 'Well done. I hate to ask this, but is there any insanity in the family?'

Roger sighed. 'I suppose it depends what you mean by insanity. Like all the great English families that haven't died out, we have our share of eccentrics.'

Emily suppressed a smile, knowing most people would put Roger himself in that category.

'And my mother's capacity for obsession and self-delusion is not unprecedented, either. But I do hope she has merely been temporarily deranged by her grief over James's death. I would hate to be left as the sole sane scion of this ancient family.'

Emily's estimate of Roger's strength of character had risen to the point that she thought he might be able to manage the role of baronet. But she also would hate to see the family reduced to him alone. He would wander in solitude about these ancient halls until he withered away, his life cut short like that of one of his butterflies, with no posterity to mourn or honor him. That would be a tragic fate indeed.

FIFTEEN

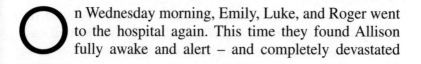On Wednesday morning, Emily, Luke, and Roger went to the hospital again. This time they found Allison fully awake and alert – and completely devastated

by her eventual complete realization that James and their baby were dead.

'I have to get out of here,' she told them, throwing off the bedclothes. 'I can't stand this place another minute.'

Emily understood that for Allison the hospital would forever be the place where she learned of her family's death, even though it was not the place where they died. But surely Fitzhugh Manor would hold even more painful associations.

'Are you sure?' she asked. 'Won't Fitzhugh be difficult as well?'

Allison stopped with her feet halfway off the bed. 'Yes. It will. But there is no place on earth that won't be difficult for me now. And at least Fitzhugh is home.'

Roger stopped her as she moved to yank out her IV. 'Not so fast, my dear. We have to do this through the proper channels. Sit tight and we'll ask the doctor to discharge you.'

Allison still looked determined, so Emily said, 'It really is the best way, you know. There are things they'll need to do to make sure your recovery at home goes smoothly.'

She sighed heavily. 'Oh, all right. Do what you have to do. Just get me out of here – *today*.'

Emily pressed the call button, and a nurse came in. 'Allison would like to be discharged today. Do you think that's possible?'

The nurse looked at her patient with raised eyebrows. 'That will be the doctor's call. I'll see if I can find her.'

A few minutes later, Dr Mirama appeared in the doorway. 'I'll need to be alone with my patient,' she said to Roger and Emily, so they waited in the hall with Luke. Emily got through a couple of rows of the cowl she had started with her new Shetland wool before Dr Mirama returned.

'All right, we're going to discharge her,' she said. 'Her condition is borderline, but when a patient wants to leave as badly as she does, it's usually best to let her go. It will take us an hour or so to get her ready and get the paperwork done, so sit tight.'

An hour and a half later, the nurse wheeled Allison out. Emily had brought some fresh clothes for her just in case, so she was dressed in a sweater and jeans with her lower right leg encased in a boot cast. She held a pair of crutches across her lap.

The nurse gave instructions, addressing herself to Emily since she must have been the most nurseish-looking person there. 'Here's her pain medication – it's to be taken as needed, but she mustn't exceed the maximum dose; this stuff can be addictive. She should stay off the ankle completely for the first week; after that, she can walk a little, as long as she doesn't overtire herself. She needs to rest as much as possible and eat a good, balanced diet – she has bones that need to mend, and her brain won't heal completely for a very long time. She'll likely have headaches and periods of dizziness or fogginess, with decreasing severity and frequency, for months. Personality changes are not uncommon with concussion as well – usually, they're temporary, but not always. She'll need to come back for a follow-up visit next week, and at that point she can probably be released to her regular physician's care.'

Emily felt overwhelmed. She wasn't prepared to take on the role of Allison's primary caregiver, and she didn't think Roger well suited to it either. Caddie was fully occupied with Lady Margaret, and besides, she was bound to share her mistress's prejudice against Allison.

'Would some home nursing help be a possibility?' she asked. 'My husband and I are only guests in the house – we're on our honeymoon, from America. Besides us, there's only Roger, and although he's willing enough, I'm not sure he can handle all her care.' He certainly wouldn't be up for the more intimate aspects, such as helping her dress and get to the bathroom.

The nurse nodded. 'Yes, that can be arranged. Sir Roger will need to initiate that as a member of the household.' She turned to Roger and gave him instructions about whom to call and what to ask for.

They had some difficulty getting Allison into the rental car with her boot cast and crutches. The front seat had to be pushed all the way back, and Emily, sitting behind her, was afraid by the time they reached Fitzhugh Manor she might have lost all feeling in her legs and be in need of crutches herself. If only they'd been anticipating her discharge today, they could have brought one of the larger cars from the estate. But she and Allison both survived the journey, and Emily was able to stagger unaided from the car after Luke had helped Allison out.

Luke was ready to carry Allison into the house and up to her bedroom, but she insisted on trying out her crutches. After a couple of false starts on the stairs, she got into a rhythm and managed fairly well.

But at the top of the first flight, where the stairs split to go to the different wings, Lady Margaret was waiting. With her blazing eyes and outstretched pointing finger, Emily expected her to bellow, 'You shall not pass!'

But Lady Margaret had probably never read Tolkien, so she did not have the image of Gandalf confronting the Balrog to draw on. Instead, she uttered in a voice that echoed all through the house, 'Murderer! That woman shall never enter my home!'

Roger scurried up the stairs to confront her, blocking her from Allison's view. 'Mother! We've discussed this. Remember? I am the baronet now, and I say she can stay. Allison is a Fitzhugh, she is not a murderer or anything like it, and this is her home for as long as she condescends to grace us with her presence. Now go back to your room!'

When Roger drew himself up, he had a couple of inches on his mother's withered form, and now he loomed over her, looking more impressive than Emily had ever seen him. Lady Margaret faltered, then put her hand out to Caddie, who hovered nearby. 'Caddie, I am weary. I believe I shall retire.'

Caddie hurried to her side and supported her up the stairs to her own wing.

Allison's route would take her up the opposite staircase. But she stood dumbstruck halfway up the first flight, Luke and Emily ready on either side to catch her in case she should stumble.

Allison finally found her voice. 'I knew she hated me. But does she seriously think I had something to do with James's death?' She looked from one face to another, her own drained of color except for the bruising that stood out purple and yellow around her eyes. 'Is she really that insane?'

Roger hastened back down to stand before her. 'I'm so sorry you had to witness that, my dear. I'm afraid Mother is temporarily a bit . . . deranged by her grief for James. I'm sure if she were completely rational, she'd realize her charges are unfounded. But I did hope you wouldn't have to know what she's been saying.'

'You mean she's said this before?' Again she surveyed their faces. 'Just to you three, or does the whole world know?'

'Only us, my dear. And I'm sure Caddie has had to listen to her ravings at length. But no one else. The coroner declared James's death accidental, and everyone but Mother knows that's true. No one else would ever dream you had anything to do with it.'

Allison started to shake her head, then winced. 'I don't believe it,' she said faintly. 'I just don't believe it. As if losing James wasn't bad enough.' She squared her shoulders. 'Well, she won't have to put up with me much longer. As soon as I've recovered, I'll be moving out. God knows where to, but I certainly can't stay here. I'm sorry, Roger, but that's the way it has to be.'

They got Allison settled and had some lunch, then Roger went off to attend to funeral arrangements. Lingering in the dining room, Luke and Emily looked at each other and knew they were both having the same thought.

'We can't let this go on,' Emily said. 'Allison has to be vindicated to Lady Margaret's satisfaction. Otherwise, her life will be more intolerable than it already is.'

'And the only way to do that is to prove how it really happened. I know,' Luke replied. 'Looks like we're in for an investigation after all. The police sure as heck aren't going to contest the inquest verdict and reopen the case with no hard evidence to go on.'

'Roger's arranging the funeral for tomorrow. That will get everyone together in one place. On TV the police always learn something important at a funeral.'

'Let's hope the magic works for us. Meanwhile, I don't want to sit around here all afternoon, do you?'

'No,' Emily said. 'But it's a bit late to get started on any of the other things we've planned.'

'Tell you what – I'm curious to see this famous building site. Want to show me around?'

'Sure. Maybe we can talk to Adam while we're there – see if there's anything in Lady Margaret's fantasies as far as he's concerned.'

Emily changed into walking clothes, and they set off across the lawn toward the copse. The day was fine, the view was lovely, they held hands as they walked, and Emily could almost imagine they were simply out for a stroll like any normal honeymooning couple.

When they reached the building site, Emily could see the progress that had been made in the last week, especially on the one house that would serve as a model. The roof was on, and the holes in the façade no longer gaped; they were filled with white-framed multipaned windows and a solid oak door. What had once resembled a skull was now a welcoming, if slightly sleepy-looking, face.

'I guess we should let Adam know we're here before we just poke around uninvited,' Luke said.

Emily agreed and led the way to the office. She knocked on the open door. 'Adam? It's Emily and Luke. May we come in?'

Adam came to the door, his eyes deeply shadowed, hair and clothes disheveled as if he hadn't slept. 'Hi. Sure, come in. How's Allison?'

'Better. She came home this morning. Her head is clear, though still a little painful, and she's getting around on crutches. But the doctor said she needs to rest as much as possible.'

Adam closed his eyes and sagged in relief. 'Thank God.' His mouth quirked. 'I don't really believe in God, but I've been praying for her. Funny how we'll grasp at any straw when we get desperate.'

Emily laid a hand on his arm. 'Well, I believe in God, and I also believe He hears prayers, even when they're said more in desperation than in faith. Don't stop just because she's feeling a little better. She still has a long road of recovery ahead of her – emotional as well as physical.'

A spasm of pain crossed his face. Was it purely sympathy for Allison's pain, or was there an element of resentment that her emotional suffering was caused by grief for another man? Emily reminded herself that was not for her to judge. The only thing that mattered, as far as James's death was concerned, was whether Adam's suffering was caused by his having injured his beloved Allison in the process of murdering her husband.

'Luke was hoping to get a look at the building project. Do you mind if we poke around?'

Before Adam could answer, Luke put in, 'Or maybe you'd like to show us around yourself. If you have time.'

Of course, Emily thought. That would give them an opportunity to question him – in a subtle way, so that he wouldn't know he was being questioned.

Adam hesitated. 'I, uh – sorry, but I don't really have time right now. I'm supposed to meet with a supplier in a few minutes. But feel free to have a look on your own. Just stay on the main road and don't go too close to where the guys are working. For your own safety, you understand.'

'Of course.' Emily was a little disappointed, but they could make an opportunity to question him another time. And this way, Luke would be able to concentrate on the cottages instead of being distracted by playing detective.

First she showed him the model and floor plans there in the office. 'Now, this is more like it,' he said. 'Wouldn't you rather have one of these nice new places where the walls are straight and true and everything works? With decent closets and more than one bathroom? And ceilings I won't bump my head on?'

Emily hemmed. 'I do see the appeal. In fact, when I first looked at these, I kind of fell in love with them. But Rose Cottage has the history I'm looking for. I just love the idea of living in a place where generations of people have lived before me. Rose Cottage made me feel – I don't know – embraced somehow.'

'You think the people of Lower Gloaming would embrace you? Little places like that tend to be pretty insular. You think an outsider, and an American to boot, would just naturally be welcome? I wouldn't count on it. I think you'd have a better chance of fitting in here in this little community, where everybody will be new.'

Emily didn't want to admit it, but a part of her suspected

he was right. 'Let's table this for now and go look at the actual houses.'

'Fine by me.'

All the units had advanced in the past week, but the model was the only one that already looked like a house. Emily approached a workman as he was coming out of the front door. 'Excuse me,' she said. 'I was here last week with Allison, and Adam gave us permission to look around today. Is there any chance we could see inside?'

The man hesitated, looking over his shoulder. 'I suppose you could. We're all about to take a tea break, anyway. But you'd better put these on.' He grabbed a couple of hard hats that were lying on the ground by the door.

Emily and Luke put them on and stepped gingerly over the threshold. The interior was barely framed, with plywood laid over the floor joists. From the entryway they could see between the studs clear to the far corners of the house, which made the interior seem immense. They moved through what would one day be rooms, but Emily had a hard time picturing how the house would feel and function, what it would be like to live in when it was finished. Her mind kept superimposing the beamed ceilings, crooked walls, and well-trodden floors of Rose Cottage on the studs and plywood before her.

Luke was more interested in the workmanship – what there was of it so far. 'This place looks pretty solid,' he pronounced. 'They're not skimping on quality. I could sleep well at night in a place like this.'

'Yes, but will it last five hundred years?'

'Maybe not, but neither will we. Unless you've got some secret elixir of life hidden up your sleeve.'

'And no one to hand it down to, either.' She sighed. 'Well, the middle of an investigation probably isn't the best time to make a big decision like this. We don't even know for sure that Roger will go forward with the project. I mean, assuming this all technically belongs to him now, along with the rest of the estate.'

'Yeah, that's an interesting question. I guess Allison would know. I'd hate to put it to her right now, though. Could be just one more thing to worry about at a time when her whole life's been turned upside down.'

'True. I imagine Adam would have some idea.'

They turned to leave the model house and saw Adam coming up the road toward them. They went to meet him.

'Pretty nice houses you're building here,' Luke said. 'Good and solid. I like that.'

'Thanks,' Adam said a bit absently. 'Allison always insists on the best.'

'We were just wondering – not really our business, except we were thinking of maybe buying in here – but what does James's death mean for this project?'

'That's the sixty-four-dollar question, isn't it?' Adam shot a glance toward the canteen across the road. 'Look, I was just going to get a snack. You want to join me?'

They followed him. Luke got a soda and Emily a cup of tea, and they sat down at one of the small tables.

'I don't suppose you two know anything about how the inheritance works?' Adam asked. 'Does Allison get any part of the estate?'

Emily shook her head. 'My understanding is the estate is entailed on Roger, along with the title. Allison might get some money or personal property according to James's will, but not real property.'

'So it's up to Roger.' Adam raked a hand through his hair. 'I don't know him very well. What do you think he'll do?'

'I'd imagine he'd let the project go ahead, as long as he didn't have to be personally involved in it,' Luke said. 'He's not much of a businessman, but if Allison decides to stay, I expect he'll let her go ahead with whatever she wants to do on the estate.'

Emily nodded agreement. 'Did all the funding for the project come out of the estate? As well as the land?'

Adam shook his head. 'Allison had a little money of her own that she put into it. And I put some in, too. The rest is loans. So if we get closed down, we're all in big trouble. Really big.'

'Once Roger understands the situation, I'm sure he won't let that happen. He's a very kind man.'

'He won't let that dragon mother of his bully him? He seems like a pushover to me.'

'So far, he's shown a remarkable amount of backbone where his mother is concerned,' Emily said. 'I'd say it all depends on whether Allison stays or goes.'

Adam clutched his head with both hands. 'Everything depends on whether Allison stays or goes. Absolutely everything.'

SIXTEEN

The funeral was held at St Margaret's, by special dispensation since it was no longer a fully functioning parish church; the Fitzhughs had been buried in its ancient churchyard time out of mind, and James could be no exception. The tiny fetus, encased in a three-inch-long vial wrapped in white silk, was placed under its father's crossed hands – an unusual benefit for one that was lost so young. Emily had put up a fight on Allison's behalf to prevent the hospital from simply putting the fetus out with the biological waste, and Allison had been touchingly grateful.

The funeral seemed lightning-quick to Emily, who was accustomed to Orthodox funerals that ran for several hours. Before she had time to catch her breath, the coffin was in the ground, the final prayers were said, and Allison, helped to her feet by Luke, was leading the mourners in casting a handful of dirt into the grave. This part at least was familiar. Emily cast her handful in the shape of a cross and said a final prayer for James's soul. The minuscule innocent that shared his grave needed no intercession.

Emily had kept a watchful eye on all the attendees throughout the service but observed nothing unusual or untoward in their demeanor. Lady Margaret kept her black handkerchief to her lips behind her heavy black veil and uttered no sound. Allison sat erect in her wheelchair, composed but looking as if she might break at any moment. She attempted to sing the first hymn, but her voice broke and she was silent thereafter.

Roger gave the eulogy in broken tones. He was not terribly articulate, but it didn't seem to matter; everyone present knew what sort of man James had been, how much he was loved, and how much he would be missed. This was particularly manifest among the estate staff, whose reserve was not as perfect as that of their stiff-upper-lipped employers. More than one sob and sniff was heard from the back of the church as Roger spoke.

Conan and Bunty sat together, red-eyed, holding hands in despite of Lady Margaret, who had no attention to spare for them anyway. Emily supposed that with James's death had died any hope the dowager might have cherished of one day seeing the Fitzhugh line continue untainted by alien blood. Bunty was exercising the iron self-control of her class, but Conan, as a working man and an Irishman to boot, could be seen to wipe away a tear now and then, and his face occasionally contorted in pain.

The person who surprised Emily the most was Simon Braithwaite. He sat erect and stony-faced, but several times she caught him, too, dashing away a rebellious tear. Was it possible he had cared for James more than he let on? Or were these tears of guilt for having enacted his violent revenge?

Adam, unsurprisingly, was not present. He could find an excuse to attend the wedding of his rival but not his funeral. Nor was he missed, except by Luke and Emily, who had originally placed him near the top of their list of people to watch. After the previous day's revelations, though, Emily thought it less likely he would have endangered his own livelihood as well as Allison's safety by doing away with James.

She and Luke had higher hopes for the reception back at the manor, where a glass or two of wine might be expected to loosen people up a bit. But the atmosphere there proved to be rather oppressive, the inherent somberness of a funeral intensified by the awkwardness of the dual hostesses. Lady Margaret sat in state near the drawing-room fireplace, graciously receiving guests with a beringed hand outstretched for them to kiss, while Allison held a similar post in the dining room – which proved the more popular room due to the presence of food. The younger people congregated around Allison, extending their sincere condolences and wishes for her recovery, while the old retainers and family friends paid court to Lady Margaret.

Luke strolled through the drawing room occasionally, but he and Emily both concentrated their observations on the dining room, where the people most involved in James's day-to-day life had ended up. They each made a circuit of the room and then met in a window bay to compare notes.

'I don't see anyone acting guilty, do you?' Luke asked Emily in an undertone.

'Not really. Not even Simon – did you see he actually cried during the service?'

'Could've been from guilt, I guess. But that's not the reaction you'd expect.'

'I do wish Adam had some reason to be here. He doesn't seem to be one for hiding his emotions. He might have given himself away.'

'Mmm,' Luke said noncommittally. 'We've been looking at the people with a grudge against James, but when it comes to people in his social position, especially, the truism is always "follow the money." Where does the money lead?'

'Well, Roger, first, but we've ruled him out, haven't we?'

'*Oh* yeah. Never saw anyone less interested in wealth and position than Roger.'

'Allison probably gets some sort of legacy, but we've ruled her out *a priori*.'

'Right. Wouldn't be investigating otherwise.'

'So who's the next heir after Roger? Even if the title dies, the property has to go somewhere.'

Luke scratched his chin. 'You know, I think it might be Bunty. I heard her and James joking around in the stables. She was threatening to bump him off so she could tear down the house and build a huge stable, and he reminded her that Roger stood in the way. They weren't remotely serious, but that could still be the actual line of succession.'

'And if Bunty inherited, Conan would be right in there with her.'

'Indeed he would. Nothing would stand in the way of their marrying then. And the fact that he's having trouble making the payments on his partnership wouldn't matter one little bit.'

'Plus they both know all about horses and were on the scene when James and Allison went out for their ride. Motive, means, and opportunity – isn't that the holy trinity of detection?'

Luke nodded solemnly. They both gazed at Conan and Bunty, who were standing together a little apart from the main group. Behind their obvious grief for James, Emily could detect in both a subtle glow that kept threatening to break through their somber demeanor. Was it just that they now felt free to let people see their relationship? Or was there something more?

The food-laden table stood between the two couples, so Luke and Emily casually strolled toward the table, put a few hors d'oeuvres on their plates, and then meandered in Conan and Bunty's direction.

'How're you folks holding up?' Luke asked.

'We've been better,' Bunty said with a shaky smile. 'I'm sorry you two have been caught up in this. What a shame your honeymoon should be ruined.'

'Oh, that's the least of our worries,' Emily replied. 'I'm just so terribly sorry for poor Allison. To lose everything at one blow like that – husband, baby, home. I'm not sure I could survive it.'

'I know what you mean,' Bunty said. 'I'm not sure I could either. Losing James as my cousin-slash-substitute-big-brother is bad enough. But Allison's tough; she's had to be to share a house with Lady Margaret. She'll weather the storm where others might go under.'

'I see you two are being a little less furtive these days.' Emily glanced significantly at Bunty and Conan's clasped hands.

Bunty blushed. 'I don't know how much our situation has actually changed with regard to Lady Margaret, but honestly, I wouldn't be able to get through this without Conan by my side. Openly by my side, that is. And it's tough for him, too – he and James were very close. He needs me now as much as I need him.' She and Conan exchanged a look of deep emotion.

Emily allowed a minute for Bunty to regain her self-possession. 'What happens for you now? Will James's death change anything, other than allowing you to really be together?'

Bunty shrugged. 'I honestly don't know. Roger hasn't said anything. My guess is he'll want us to go on as we have been, though we'll have to scale back a bit; James won't be easy to replace, even in his role in the stables. He had all the connections that got us our clients. You'd be surprised how much the family name still talks in the county.'

'You have the name, too. And aren't you the next heir, after Roger?' Emily said this with every appearance of innocence, but she watched Bunty closely as she replied.

Bunty's eyebrows rose. 'Highly unlikely. The estate follows the title – it's entailed on the male line. I'm not aware of any close relatives other than myself, but there would have to be no remotely connected Fitzhugh male anywhere in the world – and even then I'm not sure it wouldn't just revert to the crown.' She gave a wry smile. 'Britain has seen a lot of reform over the last century or so, but it still doesn't extend to letting women inherit a title.'

So Bunty had no financial motive to kill James. And from what Emily had seen of their relationship, no personal one either.

Meanwhile, Luke had been chatting with Conan, asking many of the same questions. Now their conversation came to the fore.

'Does James's death mean your partnership in the stables is safe?' Luke asked.

That question went a bit beyond the limits of what was socially acceptable from a mere acquaintance. Conan drew back slightly, his brow furrowing. 'I don't know what it means. I suppose Roger inherits my debt along with everything else. He could probably pitch me out on my ear if he so chose.'

Bunty stroked his arm reassuringly. 'Roger would never do that. Not only is he not that cruel, he's not that proactive. He'll want as little trouble as possible, and that will mean keeping everything status quo.'

Conan gave her a tiny smile, but his face remained troubled.

Emily felt they'd learned all they could from the pair, and Luke's expression suggested he agreed. They made their excuses and moved on, now in search of Simon. But he had apparently left early, no doubt to make some meeting or close some deal. As a venue for detection, the funeral had proven a disappointment.

Luke and Emily spent Thursday afternoon after the funeral with Allison, who badly needed their support. Being with all those people, having to appear strong for their benefit, had drained her and sent her back into the worst spiral of her grief. A funeral is meant to provide some measure of closure for loved ones, but Allison had spent so much of the intervening time unconscious, drugged, and cooped up in the hospital that she had not had the opportunity to go through the intermediate rituals of planning the funeral, choosing a casket, holding vigil with the body – rituals that can seem like a burden to the bereaved but in fact provide them with way stations in their early grief. Allison had missed all that, and it was as if she had gone directly from hearing of her husband's death to saying goodbye to his body forever. She needed time to absorb it all.

By the time Allison had dropped off into much-needed sleep, it was dinnertime. Luke and Emily shared a cold collation of leftovers from the funeral with a mostly silent Roger, then took their coffee and retreated to their room for the evening.

'What do you think about Conan?' Emily asked Luke as they sipped their coffee in front of the fireplace.

'As a murderer? Hard to say. He's got some kind of dark edge to him, but if he's right about Roger inheriting his debt, it's tough to see his motive, unless he plans to kill Roger too – wipe out the debt entirely. He did take a hell of a time to raise the alarm about James and Allison, though. That's hard to figure unless he was actually hoping they weren't OK. What did you think about Bunty?'

Emily shook her head. 'I think she was genuinely fond of James. And the entail is pretty solid, apparently – if no remotely connected male heir could be found, she thinks the estate might revert to the crown.'

'Roger would know about any remote connections, wouldn't he?'

'I'm not sure, actually. He knew he was James's heir, but that was fairly obvious. I get the impression the bloodline isn't straightforward after Roger, and he's not the type to spend a lot of time puzzling it out. He would have just assumed James would have a son and the line would go on in the usual way.'

'Yeah, you're probably right about that.' Luke stretched his arms over his head. 'We're not going to be able to trace the Fitzhugh bloodline tonight. Maybe tomorrow we can get in touch with a lawyer or something.'

'If they'll talk to us. We have absolutely no right to interfere, remember. And it's my impression British solicitors tend to be pretty tight-lipped about their clients' affairs.'

'True. We might have to dig another way. And meanwhile, we've also got to follow up on Simon. And consult a vet about what somebody might have done to Jackie. But for now, what say we just be honeymooners for an hour or two?'

Emily couldn't argue with that.

SEVENTEEN

On Friday morning, Luke set off for the stables, ostensibly to go for a ride, but actually to quiz Conan and Bunty further. He'd had the feeling when they spoke at the funeral that there was something Conan wasn't telling him – that he was withholding not necessarily guilty knowledge but some knowledge that could be of use to the investigation. At the very least, he could give Luke the name and number of the family vet.

He found Conan and Bunty in the courtyard with another man, who was leading a palomino pony in a wide circle as they looked on. Conan caught sight of Luke and called, 'Be with you in a minute.'

Luke came up to them. 'Is this Blossom's replacement, by any chance?'

Conan blinked. 'You know about that?'

Luke gave a wry grin. 'I happened to encounter Simon on his way out after he complained to James about the price. Nearly a way-too-close encounter. Then James gave me the scoop.'

'I see. Yeah, we're considering this girl. She looks pretty good. I wish we had a child around to try her out, though. With kids, the pony's attitude is everything.'

'She's gentle as a lamb, I keep telling you,' the palomino's American-accented owner said. 'I guarantee you'll be completely satisfied.'

Bunty glanced at her watch. 'As a matter of fact, Lily's due any moment. We could get her to give Patty a try.' She spoke to the other man. 'If you don't mind waiting, that is.'

He gave a patient sigh. 'Me? I've got all day.'

Just then Luke heard an engine in the lane. 'That sounds like Simon now.'

In another moment Simon's Porsche screeched on to the gravel courtyard. Simon and Lily got out.

'Where's Blossom? Why isn't she ready?' growled Simon. 'Price I pay, you'd think I could get some decent service around here.'

At the same moment, Lily ran toward the palomino and put out a hand to pat her neck. 'Oh, you beauty! Can I ride her?'

Bunty smiled. 'We were hoping you might do just that. We need someone your size to test her out before we buy her.' Then to Simon, 'I'll go get Blossom now. She's ready; I just didn't want to bring her out while the new pony's here in case of complications.'

Conan helped Lily on to Patty's ready-saddled back and they set off in a circle of the courtyard. 'Can I take her into the paddock?'

'Sure thing, little lady.' Patty's owner kept hold of the reins as they walked into the paddock, then handed the reins to Lily and allowed her to put the pony through her paces.

Simon fumed as his daughter jumped the palomino over the low hurdles in the paddock. 'And how much are you going to pay for this one?' he asked Conan. 'Half the price I paid for Blossom, I shouldn't wonder.'

Conan said coolly, 'That's really none of your concern. We try to run this business at a profit, just as you run yours. You can't fault us for that.'

Simon continued to glare in Lily's direction until she walked the palomino back into the courtyard, glowing. 'This is a lovely pony. She isn't Blossom, of course, but I'm sure the other children will get along with her just fine.' She dismounted and gave the palomino a parting pat before going over to the waiting Blossom. 'Don't worry, Blossom old girl, I still love you best.' She mounted with Bunty's help and walked Blossom toward the paddock.

Conan and Bunty looked at each other and nodded. 'Right then,' Conan said to the pony's owner. 'If you'll come into the office for a moment, we'll get everything squared away. Luke, would you look after Patty in the meantime?'

'Glad to.' Luke gave the pony a once-over, stroking her mane. She reminded him of a pony his son Aaron used to ride, back when he was a carefree boy before his parents' divorce.

Simon, however, continued to fume, glancing at his watch every few seconds. 'While they're in the office, what am I supposed to do? Twiddle my thumbs for an hour? I can't work in my car. I need internet.'

'Well, it won't earn you a penny, but I'd like to talk to you for a minute, if you don't mind.'

Simon crossed his arms over his chest. 'Oh, very well, it seems I have nothing better to do. What do you want? I don't give free investment advice, if that's what you're looking for.'

Luke held up his hands. 'I wouldn't dream of it. I've got my little nest egg right where I want it. No, I just wanted to ask you if you were around here at all last Saturday morning.'

Simon's eyebrows rose. 'Saturday? You mean the day James' – he swallowed visibly – 'was killed?'

Luke nodded. 'That's the day.'

Simon ran a finger under his collar. 'Well, Lily did have a lesson that morning, as she always does on Saturdays. But it wasn't till nine o'clock. I understand James and Allison went out around eight thirty.'

'I believe that's correct. You didn't happen to come early for any reason?'

'Wh–why no. At least, not that I remember.'

Luke raised a skeptical eyebrow. A guy as obsessed with time as Simon, not remembering whether he'd come early to an appointment? He both looked and sounded like a man who was hiding something.

'I think maybe you did. And I think maybe you had some reason you don't want to tell me about.' He fixed Simon with the stare that had caused many a petty criminal's palms to sweat.

Simon stood the stare for about ten seconds, then relented. 'Oh, all right. I did come a bit early. I wanted to check on Blossom. A vet I know had told me a trick to make sure the pony was the age James claimed she was. I thought he was cheating me.'

Simon was so embarrassed that Luke felt ninety percent sure he was telling the truth. He was torn between amusement and disgust. 'I see. And did you make that determination?'

Simon rolled his eyes. 'As far as I could tell, the damned pony is exactly the age James said.'

'So did you see anyone else on that occasion? Any of the grooms – Winky, for instance?'

'Winky? Oh, you mean that horrible old geezer with the eyepatch. Not him – he would have been in the other wing. I did catch a glimpse of the other groom, that young girl, mucking out the other stalls, but she didn't see me.'

'Surely Bunty was around, getting ready for the lesson?'

'Again, I saw her, but she didn't see me. I parked in the lane and waited till she went into the office, then I slipped into the stall. It only took me a minute to do what I needed to do. Then I went back to the car and waited till nine o'clock.'

'And what was Lily doing all this time?'

'I gave her my phone to play her favorite game. She was so absorbed she had no idea what was going on or how much time had passed.'

'I see. So you never saw James or Allison? Never went near their horses?'

'What? No, of course not. Their horses are kept in the other wing.' Simon's eyes narrowed. 'What exactly are you getting at?'

'Nothing special. Just trying to get a full picture, is all.' Luke gave him an innocent-American grin. 'I'm a lawman back home, see, so whenever I come up against something that doesn't quite make sense, I can't resist trying to get to the bottom of it. And James's death doesn't quite make sense to me.'

Simon's expression changed instantly. 'Do you know, I feel the same way. I can't tell you why, but that verdict of misadventure doesn't sit right with me. James was too good a horseman to go that way.' He paused, and when he spoke again, his voice cracked. 'Too good a man.'

Luke didn't press his questions any further. Not only did Simon seem sincere, but it wasn't likely a man who couldn't tell the age of a horse without help would have the knowledge and resources necessary to tamper with one.

Simon went to sit in his car, and a girl of about sixteen, with a brown ponytail and dressed in jeans, came out of Bunty's wing of the stables. She reminded Luke a bit of Katie, Emily's young housekeeper. 'I'll take care of Patty now, if you like,' she said to Luke.

'Sure, thanks.' He searched his excellent memory for the name of the female groom Bunty had mentioned when she was talking to Lady Margaret the previous week. 'You must be Jenny. All over your cold now?'

'Yes, thank you.' She looked a little bewildered at his knowing about the state of her health.

Luke shook her hand. 'Luke Richards. I'm a guest at the manor.'

'Yes, I've seen you around. Did you want to go for a ride? I could rustle up Winky to help you.'

'That's all right, thanks. I'm just here to make a nuisance of myself.' He grinned, and she grinned back. 'I'm trying to get a picture of what went on here Saturday morning.'

The girl's eyes widened. 'You mean the day Sir James was killed?'

'That's right.'

'But . . . why? It was an accident, wasn't it?'

'Officially, yeah. But I'm a lawman back home, and I have

kind of a nose for things that don't seem to add up. I just want to make sure nothing important was overlooked.'

Her brows drew together. 'I see. I thought it was strange that Sir James could go like that. If there's anything I can do to help—'

'I would like to ask you a couple of questions, if you don't mind.'

'Anything.'

'I understand you were here in the stables Saturday morning around the time Sir James and Allison rode out.'

'I suppose so. I didn't see them, but I was here from eight o'clock on.'

'You stayed in the riding school wing the whole time?'

'Yes. I was busy mucking out the stalls and feeding the horses.'

'Did you see anybody else at all?'

'Only Bunty. She was back and forth between the stalls and the office.'

'Hear anything unusual?'

Her mouth twitched as if suppressing a smile. 'Not exactly unusual, but I heard Winky snoring in an empty stall in the other wing.'

'You know for sure it was Winky?'

'He has a very distinctive snore. And weekends especially, he ends up sleeping it off here more often than not. The stable's closer to the pub than his hovel is, so he just staggers in here and falls into the first pile of straw he sees.'

'I see. Anything else at all strike you about that morning?'

She screwed up her eyes, remembering. 'I heard Conan and some woman talking – far off, you know. I couldn't hear what they were saying.'

'Sure it wasn't Bunty?'

'I don't think so. Bunty was in the office at that point. The voices were coming from the other wing. And anyway, it didn't sound like her.'

Luke made a mental note and underlined it in red. Conan hadn't mentioned such a person at the inquest. If he had some kind of dealings with a woman that he didn't want Bunty to know about, that definitely deserved looking into. Though what it could have to do with James's death, Luke had no idea.

'Anything else? Normal or otherwise?'

She shrugged. 'Just an ordinary Saturday morning at Fitzhugh Stables. I heard people and horses moving about in the other wing and the courtyard – I suppose that must have been Sir James and Allison – but I didn't pay much attention. I'm sorry I can't be more help.'

'You've been great. Thanks for your time. I'll let you get back to work now.'

She led the new pony off toward its stall. Conan and the new pony's seller emerged from the office, shaking hands, then the other fellow got into his pickup with its now-empty horse trailer and drove off.

Conan came over to Luke. 'Did Jenny take Patty?' he asked.

'Yep, just now. Nice girl.'

'She's all right. Better worker than some we've had. You wouldn't believe how many horse-crazy teenaged girls think they want to work in a stable, then they find out it's mostly shoveling horseshit and push off after a week.'

Luke chuckled. 'I can imagine.'

'Did you want to ride today?' Conan asked. So far Luke had offered him no real reason for his presence in the stables.

'Maybe later. I actually wanted to talk to you, if I could.'

'Oh? What about?'

'I'm trying to get a clearer picture of what happened in the stable Saturday morning.'

Conan swallowed and turned his gaze off toward the paddock, where Lily was putting Blossom through her paces. 'Really? What for?'

'Just incurably curious, that's all. Seems to me the police were a little hasty pushing through that misadventure verdict. I feel like James's death deserves more scrutiny.'

Conan cleared his throat and kept his gaze on the paddock. 'What do you want to know?'

'Did you tell the coroner absolutely everything you know about that morning? Did you mention every person you know to have been on the premises?'

Now Conan turned startled eyes on Luke. 'What do you mean? What have you heard?'

Not 'What are you talking about?' as any innocent person might say, but 'What have you heard?' Very interesting.

'You were overheard in conversation with a woman in one of the stalls. And it wasn't Bunty or Jenny.'

Conan closed his eyes and took a deep breath. 'Bloody hell. I was afraid that would get out.' He looked around to see if anyone else was in earshot and lowered his voice. 'Listen, there's a perfectly innocent explanation for that, but I don't want it to get back to Bunty until it's all a done deal. I was negotiating with Lady Winthrop, one of the people who board horses with us, for the sale of my own horse, Fionn.'

Luke was taken aback. He didn't know what he'd been expecting, but it wasn't that. 'Sell Fionn? Why?'

'To help pay off my partnership with James. My mam could go on for years in that home. I can't stand being here on sufferance. I'll do anything to get that debt cleared.'

Luke impaled him with his gaze. 'Anything?'

Conan blinked and took a step back. 'Anything, you know, within the bounds of law and common humanity. Not harm James, if that's what you're suggesting. Good God, man, he was my best friend. Practically my brother.' Conan's eyes filled and he spoke in a strangled voice. 'I'd do anything – and this time I do mean *anything* – to get him back.'

'Then why wait so long without getting up a search party? That's what I keep coming back to. If you cared about him so much, why weren't you more worried?'

Conan threw up his hands. 'You think I wouldn't replay that whole day if I could? Lady Winthrop decided to pass, and I had a couple of other people come in and look Fionn over. I was so focused on getting them in and out without Bunty noticing that I honestly didn't have a thought to spare for James and Allison. I'm ashamed to say it, but that is the God's own truth, and I'd give my life to be able to make it different.' He turned away, his face working.

Luke couldn't doubt the man's sincerity now. He clapped a hand to Conan's shoulder. 'It wouldn't have changed anything, Conan. James was dead as soon as his head hit that rock. I doubt quick action could've saved the baby, either. And Allison's going to be fine, despite lying out there injured for hours. You can't blame yourself.'

Conan wiped his arm across his face and turned back to Luke. 'Just watch me. But was there anything else you wanted to know?'

'Just curious why you don't want Bunty to know about selling Fionn.'

Conan threw up his hands. 'Only because she'd try to talk me out of it. And she'd probably succeed, and then I'd be miserable and I'd take it out on her. She's always been comfortably off – she doesn't understand about a poor man's pride when it comes to money. That's the long and the short of it, detective.' He gave a wry grin.

Luke nodded. 'I can understand that. I'm married to a woman who has more money than I ever dreamed of. She wants to buy me everything I look twice at, but all I want is to pay my own way.' He clapped Conan on the shoulder again. 'Good luck selling your horse.'

EIGHTEEN

When Luke returned to the house, Emily was in the dining room getting another cup of coffee after checking on Allison. He helped himself to a cup, then they sat down and he gave her a rundown of what he'd seen and heard in the stables.

'So you think Simon is innocent?' she asked him.

'It appears that way. I wouldn't absolutely rule him out, but there are a few points in his favor. One, he doesn't seem all that knowledgeable about horses; he had to ask somebody how to judge a pony's age. Whoever interfered with Jackie, if that is what happened, had to know what they were doing.'

'That's a fair point. I, for example, would have no idea what to do or how to do it. But conceivably he could have recruited or paid someone else to do it for him.'

'True. Hadn't thought of that. But who? I mean, we have to consider Conan and Bunty in their own right, but I don't see them acting against James on Simon's instructions. Jenny's obviously in the clear, and on her showing, Winky was dead to the world. Who else could it be?'

'Aren't there some other grooms?' Emily asked. In fact, she had no idea how many people were needed to run a stable that size.

'Maybe, but not that I've seen.'

'OK, what's your number-two point in Simon's favor?'

'His grudge against James seems to be kind of on the surface. Underneath, I think he actually liked and respected him. And he had nothing to gain except vengeance, which doesn't seem that compelling in this case.'

'Hmm. I don't know. You remember Alexander Hamilton and Aaron Burr?' They had recently seen the show *Hamilton*, and Emily had become curious enough to read the book on which it was based. 'Burr had no motive to challenge Hamilton to a duel other than years of festering resentment. Hamilton was the man he wanted to be, and he couldn't stand that anymore. Couldn't it be the same with James and Simon?'

'Huh. I guess you got me there. Simon's reaction to James's death could come from guilt as much as grief, now that I think about it. Like "I'm the damn fool that shot him."'

Emily nodded. 'I'd keep him on the back burner for that reason. But did you have another point in his favor?'

'Yeah. Point three, he admitted the accident verdict seemed off to him, too. Course, if he were guilty, he would know it was off, but to admit that to me doesn't sound like a guilty man. Especially since he doesn't have anything to fear from me – I don't have any authority here, and the case is officially closed.'

'That could just be his wily way of throwing you off the scent.'

Luke smiled at her. 'You have a devious mind, you know that? You've got an answer for everything. Do you really want it to be Simon that bad?'

'It's more that I don't want it to be anyone else we've

considered. I like Conan and Bunty, and even Adam. He's obsessed, but at least he's sincere. His argument that he would never risk harming Allison seems convincing to me. If he wanted to get rid of James, he'd have chosen some other way.'

'You're just a crazy romantic at heart, aren't you?' He leaned across the corner of the table and kissed her. 'Can't stand the thought that anyone in love could be a murderer.'

'You're one to talk. Who held on to a locket for thirty-five years with no expectation of ever being able to deliver the gift? Hmm?' The locket in question now hung around Emily's neck.

This promising moment was interrupted by the sound of the front-door knocker. Emily knew Roger was out butterfly hunting and the cleaners were busy upstairs, so she went to answer it.

Once again Adam stood on the doorstep, looking calmer than she had yet seen him. 'Sorry to barge in on you again. I just wanted to ask how Allison's doing. I tried calling her but she didn't answer.'

'She's still resting a lot,' Emily replied. 'And still on pain meds. But she's improving. There's no reason to fear any permanent damage.'

'Thank God for that.' He hesitated as if unwilling to leave. Emily hated to send him away, but she also didn't dare invite him into the house in case Lady Margaret should come down and stage a repeat performance of her dramatic role as oracle and avenger of her grandson's death.

'Hold on a minute, Adam.'

Emily went back into the dining room to consult Luke. 'I feel like we should talk to Adam some more, but not here. Any suggestions?'

'How about the pub? That's neutral ground.'

Emily checked her watch. 'It's almost eleven. It should be open by the time we get there.'

She returned to the hall and said to Adam, 'Luke and I would like to talk to you, if you have some time. We could go to the Perch?'

His eyes widened in relief and surprise. 'Yeah, I'd like that. It's been kind of lonely since . . . since it happened.'

Luke emerged right behind Emily. He grabbed light jackets for them both, since the day was cool and cloudy. It seemed one could never rule out rain in this part of the world.

They set off, and Luke began the conversation. 'So what brought you to England?'

Adam's answer was uttered with single-minded simplicity. 'Allison. We were high school and college sweethearts, and when she won the Rhodes, I just naturally tagged along. I wanted to share the experience with her.'

Emily read into this that he was insecure in their relationship and wanted to make sure Allison didn't get seduced away from him – which in the event was exactly what happened.

'If you don't mind me asking,' she said, 'when she got engaged to James, why did you stay?'

He shrugged. 'I was studying to be an architect. I didn't want to interrupt that.' He grimaced. 'I was shattered at first. But after a while I began to think I might be able to exist without her. By then, though, I had a job and I'd kind of fallen in love with the country. There wasn't much waiting for me back home. Then Allison hired me for her project, and seeing her every day – well, I realized my love for her wasn't dead; it was only sleeping. I kind of got addicted to being around her again. She's the only woman I've ever really loved.' His voice dropped until it was hardly audible. 'Even if she'll never love me.'

Emily's heart went out to him even as she felt he was not doing himself any favors by giving in to that kind of thinking.

Luke voiced her thoughts, as gently as only a man once disappointed in love himself could do. 'Don't you think you might be better off going home? Giving yourself a chance to get over her? I know it won't be easy, but as long as you're here, working for her and seeing her every day, how can you ever get on with your life?'

He put a hand on Adam's shoulder as they walked to the pub. 'Look, buddy, I know whereof I speak. I lost the woman I loved when I was young, but I went on with my life, and eventually I built something I could at least be proud of, if not a hundred percent satisfied with.' He shot a glance at Emily, confirming it would be best not to mention that he had eventually gotten that woman back. No such final result seemed likely in Adam's case.

Adam heaved a deep and heavy sigh. 'I suppose you're right. But now that James is gone – I mean, for her sake I'm sorry he's gone – I can't help hoping there may yet be a chance for me. I mean, she needs time to grieve and reevaluate, of course, but' – he swallowed and blinked back tears – 'maybe one day I can be worthy of her.'

Emily and Luke exchanged glances. Those didn't sound like the words of a man who would murder to get back the woman he loved.

They had a drink at the Perch, talking neutrally about the experience of being an American in England. Emily exchanged phone numbers with Adam, promising to update him on any significant change in Allison's condition, so he wouldn't have to brave Lady Margaret's wrath in future. At the entrance to the estate, they parted ways, with Adam heading off to the building site. The completion of the project now seemed in jeopardy, but there were materials to use and workers to pay, and Adam wasn't willing to call a halt until he was ordered to.

Emily decided it was time she checked on Allison again. She'd looked into her room earlier in the morning, but Allison had still been asleep. A nurse was on duty to look after her physical needs; Emily's job was only to offer emotional support and companionship as wanted.

She found Allison sitting up on a chaise longue drawn up to her bedroom window, her ankle elevated on a stack of pillows.

'Good morning,' Emily said. 'This looks like progress. Are you feeling better?'

'My head's a little clearer, if that's what you mean. The ankle pain has subsided, and my ribs only hurt when I take a really deep breath. Or probably if I laughed.' She winced. 'Not much chance of that, fortunately.'

Emily pulled up a small chair from the vanity table to sit facing her. 'That day will come. Eventually. But I imagine your ribs will be well healed by then.'

Emily had experience of grief – her parents and her brother,

Geoff, had died young, and her first husband, Philip, had passed away unexpectedly three years before – but she knew her grief could not compare with what Allison was feeling now. Emily's love for Philip had been genuine but of the quiet, domestic, contented kind rather than anything passionate. And when he died, she had lost only him, not the entire life they had planned and built together. Not her home. And not her child. That last, however, was a grief Emily could empathize with fully, though her own loss was now in the distant past.

Allison stared out of the window, her face a desolate land-scape juxtaposed against the lush greenery of the grounds and the blue sparkle of the lake in the distance. 'Why did I survive?' she said in a low voice. 'What is the point of me now? Everything I was depended on James, on the family we were going to have together. I've never seen myself as one of those helpless women who can't do without a man, but I'd built my life around him, around this estate. Now I'm here only on Roger's sufferance. Everything we hoped to accomplish . . . Who will it be for?' A solitary tear escaped her eye and trickled down her cheek. Her voice dropped to an anguished whisper. 'Why couldn't I have died along with them?'

Emily took her hand. 'I don't know if you believe in any kind of God, but I do, and I know He spared you for a reason. What that reason is, I have no idea, but I do know you'll find out in time. You have a purpose. You just need to find it again.'

Allison gave a deep sigh. 'Maybe you're right. I'll have to hope so, anyway.'

Emily chose her next words carefully. She didn't want to make things worse for Allison, but she did need to know whether she'd remembered anything more about the accident.

'Would it help at all if we could clear up exactly what happened? It wouldn't provide a philosophical answer to why you survived, but we might at least be able to come to a factual explanation.'

Allison nodded. 'Yes, I think it might help a little. Then at least I could stop going over and over it in my mind.'

'So have you remembered more about the accident?'

She rubbed her brow below the bandage that wrapped her head like a hairband. 'A little. I'm still not clear on how we both got thrown, but I do remember Jackie was . . . well, weird. Not her normal self. Skittish, jumping at shadows. From the beginning of the ride. James remarked on it, said how fortunate it was that I wasn't riding her.' She gave an ironic snort, followed by a grimace of pain. 'I wish it had been me.'

Emily squeezed her hand and gave her a moment. 'At the inquest, it came out that someone heard gunshots that morning. Do you remember anything like that?'

Allison gazed into the distance. 'Gunshots . . . Yeah, I think I do. From inside the wood.'

'Was that what spooked Jackie? Made her throw James and bolt?'

'I don't know . . .' Allison covered her eyes as if trying to see into the past. 'Maybe . . . I think it was. I have this vague picture of Jackie rearing, James in trouble, and then . . . Yes, that was when Buttercup bolted, too. The gunshot alone would never have fazed her, but having Jackie go wild right next to her set her off. After that, I needed all my attention to try to stay on and calm her down.'

'But you weren't able to stay on?'

Allison shook her head. 'She bolted into the wood and ran too close to a tree. It swiped me right off.' She screwed up her eyes in one final effort. 'I must have hit my head against the trunk, or a low branch, or something. And I think maybe my foot got caught in the stirrup for a minute – that must be how my ankle broke. Then I guess the fall itself did the rest of the mischief. That's just speculation, though. Once my head hit the tree, I was out. It's all black until I woke up in hospital.' A great sob racked her. 'Oh, James . . . Why wasn't I with you at the last? I could have done something, saved you . . . Oh, James . . .'

Allison curled in on herself, abandoned to her grief. Emily knew there was nothing more she could do for now except sit with her and share her pain.

By the time the gong sounded for lunch, Allison had cried herself to sleep.

*   *   *

At lunch – where Roger did not appear, having taken a packet of sandwiches with him to the far end of the estate – Luke got the lowdown from Emily about what Allison had remembered.

'Yup,' he said, hearing about Jackie's erratic behavior. 'That sounds like drugs, all right. Some kind of amphetamine, maybe. To wind her up. I'm gonna have to talk to a vet.'

'But how will you do that without involving Conan or Bunty? We haven't completely ruled them out yet, have we?'

'Nope. I'll have to be tricky.' He winked at her. 'I can be tricky when I need to.'

He could be tricky, but he was also going to have to rely a fair bit on luck.

After they finished eating, he headed back to the stables. He could have used wanting a ride of his own as a pretext that morning, but with all the business with the new pony and Simon, it hadn't been necessary. The sky had cleared and the weather was fine for riding, so he could use that pretext now.

He found Conan and Bunty just returning from lunch themselves. 'Hey there,' he called to them. 'Any chance I could take out a horse?'

'Sure,' Conan said. 'In fact, you can take your pick of the estate horses. Not much going on today – we've had several lessons canceled for today and tomorrow.'

'Out of respect for James?'

'I hope that's all it is,' Bunty put in. 'But since horses were involved in his death – *our* horses – it's conceivable some people may be put off Fitzhugh Stables entirely.'

'As if we needed one more thing to worry about right now,' Conan added.

'I'm sure it'll be all right,' Luke said meaninglessly, as he could be sure of no such thing. But the situation did add one more checkmark on the side of Conan and Bunty both being innocent – that is, if they could have foreseen this effect from James's death. 'Sounds like you've got some horses needing exercise, then. Which one would you most like me to take out?'

'I'd say Ginger,' Conan replied. 'He hasn't been out for a couple of days.'

'OK by me. Ginger and I get along just fine.'

Conan led the way to Ginger's stall and began to saddle him. Luke heard noises in the next stall, Lucky's, and soon a man's head appeared over the partition.

Luke and the other man eyed each other, a bit warily on both sides. Conan said, 'Luke, I don't believe you've met Mr Granger, our vet. Anthony, this is Luke Richards, a guest at the manor.'

Luke grinned widely. Lady Luck was on his side today. 'Pleased to meet you,' he said, shaking hands. He glanced at Lucky. 'Something wrong with the old boy today?'

Anthony Granger shook his head. 'Conan called me in because he seemed to be favoring the foreleg again. But it was only a pebble lodged under his shoe.' He cocked an eyebrow at Conan. 'You should have found that yourself. You must be slipping.'

'I am that. My head's all over the place these last few days.'

'Of course it is. My apologies; I wasn't thinking.' Granger addressed Luke. 'Were you acquainted with Sir James?'

'Just a little. We arrived about a week before the accident – hadn't met him before that. But he seemed like a fine man. Great loss to his family.'

'And to the community, I can assure you. He will be sorely missed.' Granger turned to Conan. 'I'll be going, then, unless you have any more little jobs for me?'

'No, that was all. Sorry I called you out for nothing, Anthony.'

'Think nothing of it. And there's no charge.' The two men shook hands, and Granger headed out.

Luke said hastily to Conan, 'I'll meet you in the yard,' and hurried to catch up with the vet.

'Say, Mr Granger,' he said, walking alongside the vet toward his car. 'Mind if I ask you something? A professional question, I mean.'

'As long as it's theoretical. That is to say, I can't diagnose a horse long-distance.'

'No, nothing like that. I've just been thinking about what

happened to James and Allison. I'm a lawman at home, see, so when something like this doesn't feel right, I can't resist looking into it.'

Granger stopped and turned to face him. 'And James's death doesn't feel right to you?'

Luke shook his head. 'Jackie's a gentle, steady horse by all accounts, and James was an excellent rider. It just doesn't make sense that she would react to a gunshot so violently as to throw him.' Luke sized up the vet – he looked like a sensible, impartial kind of guy. 'And now that Allison's remembering more about the accident, she says Jackie was acting strange from the beginning of the ride. Skittish. Not her usual self.'

Granger's brows drew together. 'You think she may have been interfered with?'

'Seems possible, to me at least. But you're the expert. Does it sound like drugs to you?'

Granger's frown deepened. 'If this were any other stables, I'd say yes. But who do you imagine could, or would, do such a thing here?'

'I have no idea. I figure I need to nail down the *how* first, and then I can think about the *who*. Doesn't have to have been anybody who works here. I'd be as reluctant to accuse them as you are.'

Granger shifted the weight of his medical bag to his other hand. 'I could make some excuse to examine Jackie. She hasn't had a going-over since the accident, and from what Bunty said, she was in quite a state afterwards. If she had been drugged, there wouldn't be any trace of it left in her system by now, but still I might be able to learn something.'

'I'd appreciate that.' Luke dug a business card out of his wallet and handed it to the vet. 'Call me if you come up with anything. Not sure I can justify hanging around here much longer.'

Granger put the card in his jacket pocket. 'I have more calls to make this afternoon, and I'm taking my family to the seaside for the weekend, so I may not be able to get back to you till Monday.'

'No problem. This isn't even an official case, so it sure

doesn't come with any deadline. Just want to put my mind at rest.'

'I share that sentiment. If there was anything untoward about James's death, I'd want to get it out in the open, too. He was a good man. His family deserve the truth.'

They both turned back, Luke toward Ginger's stall and Granger toward the corner between the two wings, where Bunty was just leading out a horse. They spoke for a moment, then Bunty looped the horse's reins over a rail and led Granger inside.

Winky limped out of the stable block, leading Ginger. ''Ere ya go, guv'nor. 'E's all ready for ya.' He handed Luke the reins, squinting at him with his one good eye.

'Thanks.' Luke took the reins and mounted, giving Ginger a welcoming pat. He didn't really regret that he'd have to wait to hear what the vet had to say. It was a beautiful day for a ride.

NINETEEN

The next day, Saturday, was the day for which Emily had reserved their spots on a tour of the Bodleian Library in Oxford. The tour was scheduled for early afternoon, so they had the morning to wander around the university. Emily was enthralled by the grand medieval architecture, which seemed to exude not only history but nearly a millennium of accumulated learning and culture.

She knew that in terms of its human element, Oxford was not fundamentally different from her own Reed College or any other institution of learning: it had its politics, its petty rivalries and jealousies, its share of students (and even professors) who cared nothing for tradition or scholarship but only wanted to use the prestige of the university to further their careers. But here, within the shadows of these ancient yellow limestone walls that reached their dreaming spires toward heaven, she could idealize the place to her heart's content.

Oxford held a magic deeper than the fictional wizardry of

the Harry Potter films, which had been largely filmed here. Something closer to the 'deep magic' of Narnia permeated these walls. Narnia's creator, C.S. Lewis, had walked these hallowed lanes with his friends, J.R.R. Tolkien and Charles Williams. Dorothy L. Sayers had created Lord Peter Wimsey to haunt the halls of Balliol forever. Charles Dodgson had pursued his career in mathematics here while creating the immortal Alice in the person of his alter ego, Lewis Carroll. And these were only a few of the more recent exemplars of Oxford's literary tradition – a tradition it would take another lifetime to explore.

Some of the larger colleges required reservations, which they did not have, but they explored Balliol, where Emily imagined she could see the ghost of the young Lord Peter flying, cap clutched to head and gown flapping, down a staircase and across the quad, late for a lecture. From there they walked down the famous Broad Street, lined on one side by college buildings and on the other by shops; cut across between the Clarendon and the Sheldonian Theatre, which Emily recognized from innumerable episodes of the Morse-based trilogy of detective shows; and found them-selves confronting the pedestrian bridge that spanned New College Lane – patterned after the Bridge of Sighs in Venice and often called by its name.

They passed under the bridge, and Emily stopped Luke just on the other side. 'This spot is where Harriet Vane finally accepted Lord Peter Wimsey's repeated proposals of marriage. They embarrassed the proctor by embracing – in their academic robes, no less – right here in the street, under the warden's windows.'

Luke took the cue, pulled her a little out of the foot traffic, and took her in his arms. 'Bit late for a proposal, but it is our two-week anniversary. That excuse enough for you?'

Emily smiled her acquiescence and they kissed, oblivious to the murmurs and titters of the passers-by.

'Now Oxford is part of *our* history,' she whispered.

They joined a tour on its way to New College ('new' only in the sense of being a century or two less ancient than the other central colleges) and saw, among other things, the tree under which Draco Malfoy had been transfigured into a ferret. New College also boasted a familiar-looking cloister walk, a fine dining hall, and a beautiful church.

In the course of the day, they saw many fine churches, as each college had its own in addition to the immense main university church; but it saddened Emily to realize that the deep love and devotion, as well as the painstaking skill and care, with which these structures had been built were now almost completely absent in the people who used them. The churches had become mere *objets d'art* to be gawked at by tourists and catalogued by architects and historians, their soul-exalting acoustics lending themselves to the odd concert but rarely if ever to the worship of God. At least she could say a brief prayer and cross herself before each altar they visited.

They stopped for lunch at the Eagle and Child, fondly dubbed the Bird and Baby by the Inklings, who had once haunted it. Emily had to admit the lingering spirits of Tolkien and Lewis were the pub's most attractive feature. Then it was on to the Bodleian.

The main building enclosed a central courtyard, which Emily found unexpectedly forbidding with its limited windows and vertical stone ridges like bars leading up to narrow, spiky spires that punctuated the battlements along the roofline. It felt more like a prison than a library. But once they were inside, where rows upon rows of beautiful leather bindings competed with carved arched ceilings for her awed attention, Emily realized this was a prison she would gladly be immured in for life. Her remaining days on earth could hardly be suffi-cient to exhaust the treasures of a single room.

Although he admired the architecture, Luke was clearly less entranced than Emily was, but he gamely nodded and smiled at her raptures. He perked up a bit when they got to Duke Humphrey's library, which had stood in for the Hogwarts library in some of the films, and to the Divinity School, a single large hall which had housed variously the Hogwarts infirmary and the dancing lesson in *Goblet of Fire*.

The tour led out through a side arched passageway on to a large green dominated by the graceful octagonal bulk of the Radcliffe Camera, past which Lewis and Hathaway had strolled at the ending of nearly every episode of their series. 'I love all those mystery series set in Oxford,' she said to Luke. 'But I have to say I'm glad we're not in one of them.'

'Except we kind of are,' he replied. 'At least, we've got a mystery of our own to solve. With no police resources to back us up.'

Emily came back to earth with a thud. 'True. We can only escape for so long.' She sighed. 'Sometimes I wonder what it would be like to lack curiosity, to just go through the world taking things at face value with no urge to look underneath the surface.'

'Pretty boring, I'd guess,' Luke said. 'And if everybody was like that, this whole place would never have been built.'

'Very true. And that would be a tragedy.' She took his arm and braced herself emotionally. 'We are among the curious, and a mystery has dropped into our laps. I guess we'd better get back and do our best to solve it.'

Emily and Luke had seen little of Roger since the funeral; he'd flitted in and out of the dining room like a butterfly and eaten about as much as one, spending the rest of his time around the estate or in his workshop, or occasionally checking on Allison. But tonight he finally sat down with them for a meal.

Since the accident, they'd dispensed with Witherspoon's services, given that Lady Margaret kept to her room and they preferred to serve themselves. The cook had not gone out of her way either, providing cold spreads or (relatively speaking) barebones meals of simply cooked meat, potatoes, and vegetables. Emily and Luke didn't mind; at home, they had Katie to cook gourmet meals for them, and if they'd wanted a food-focused honeymoon, they could have gone to France or Italy.

Tonight the meal consisted of mutton, boiled potatoes, and roasted mixed vegetables. Emily hadn't eaten mutton before and had to confess she preferred lamb, but Mrs Terwilliger was not capable of cooking anything badly. It was a good thing the dinner was satisfying, because conversation was nearly non-existent.

At last Emily could stand the silence no longer. 'How are you holding up, Roger?' she asked.

He blinked as if he'd forgotten anyone else was in the room. 'Me? I'm all right, I suppose. My butterflies keep me sane.' He gave a self-deprecating smile, acknowledging that in his case 'sane' was a relative term.

'Haven't you had a lot of business to deal with since James's death?' Emily and Luke had been too busy investigating to pay much attention, but she had noticed a gray-haired man in a suit who might have been a solicitor coming and going on several occasions.

Roger ran a hand over his flyaway hair. 'Oh, yes, quite a lot of business. Thank the Lord James didn't make any of the family an executor; that job would be completely beyond me. But I've had plenty of papers to sign and decisions to make or at least think about.' He pushed the vegetables around on his plate. 'I hate making decisions.'

'I suppose that would include things like whether to let all James and Allison's projects go on – like the stables and the housing development?'

He nodded. 'The stables are an easy yes; with Bunty and Conan as both investors and managers, there's really nothing for me to do except give them my blessing. But the building project is more complicated.' He grimaced. 'I hate to force Allison into any kind of decision right now – not only because it would be cruel, but because I'm afraid she'd make the wrong one. But without knowing her plans, I simply can't go either forward or back. I'd hate to leave things half finished, but I'm certainly not capable of taking over for her if she decides to leave us.' His face crumpled as if he could barely hold back tears.

Emily reached over and pressed his hand. 'I wish there was something we could do to help.'

He took out his handkerchief and buried his face in it, then emerged blinking. 'You're terribly kind, but there's really nothing. Having you here to talk to has been an enormous relief. I can't burden Allison with my troubles, and I don't dare go near Mother.' He shuddered.

Emily and Luke exchanged glances. 'Have you *tried* going near her?'

'Every morning I go to her door and ask Caddie how she's

doing. The answer is always "Her Ladyship is as well as can be expected and does not wish to be disturbed." Spoken in the firmest possible tone with the door open the merest crack. Thank goodness I don't need to consult Mother about anything, because it would clearly be impossible.'

Poor Roger. The mouse might have become a man, but it would take a superman to penetrate the combined barrier of Caddie and Lady Margaret. For her part, Emily was glad the dowager had chosen to seclude herself. More scenes like the one she'd staged when Allison came home from the hospital must be avoided at all costs if this household were ever to return to anything like normality.

On Sunday morning they escaped to Oxford again to attend church – not in any of the vast, ornate, empty edifices of the university but in a tiny Orthodox church tucked away in a residential neighborhood. Emily's spirit relaxed and expanded under the influence of the familiar incense, icons, and hymns. She was especially taken with an icon of St Margaret, whose ancient church they had visited in Binsey. Margaret was shown smilingly trampling on a dragon as she speared it with a long-stemmed cross. If only Lady Margaret could have had more in common with the saint she was named for rather than resembling the grisly foe the saint had conquered.

Nearby was an icon of St Frideswide, founder of St Margaret's Church and patroness of Oxford. Emily asked a nearby parishioner how to pronounce the name and got the answer 'Frieds-wide,' which made her think of thick-cut French fries (or chips, as the Brits would call them). She preferred her own version.

As the worshipers milled about the crowded narthex after the service, drinking coffee or tea and munching goodies prepared by the older Russian ladies who made up much of the congregation, Emily spotted the former student who had told her about this parish. 'Alex!' she called across the room.

'Emily!' the young woman responded, making her way through the crowd to meet them. 'You made it! It's so good to see you!'

They embraced, and Emily introduced Luke. The words 'my husband, Luke' still tasted new and tingly on her tongue.

They chatted for a while until Emily's feet grew tired of standing, and she suggested they all go out to lunch. Alex took them to a snug little café nearby, then offered to give them a personal tour of Magdalen College (pronounced 'Maudlen'), where she was working on her doctorate. Magdalen was one of the larger colleges, remarkable for its extensive grounds bordering the river Cherwell as well as for its majestic buildings.

After the tour, Alex took them punting on the Char, as the river was affectionately known. Luke insisted on poling once Alex had shown him how. Emily reclined in the punt and imagined she was Harriet Vane seeing Lord Peter, as he poled the boat along the river, for the first time as a physical male rather than merely an embodied mind. For Emily, though, Luke had always been a physical male; her appreciation of his mind had come later.

Emily felt her Oxford experience was complete. Or nearly so. She insisted on treating Alex to dinner at the Randolph Hotel, where Lord Peter had stayed when he visited Harriet in Oxford, and then it was complete indeed.

All in all, the day was a lovely respite from the situation they had embroiled themselves in at Fitzhugh Manor. But they couldn't stay away forever. As they drove back after dinner, Luke said, 'I don't know about you, but I want to wrap this thing up and move on. Maybe Scotland or the Lake District. Someplace with more sheep than people.'

'Yes,' Emily said sleepily. 'Someplace peaceful sounds very nice indeed.'

TWENTY

On Monday after breakfast, Emily felt guilty for neglecting Allison for so long and went up to spend some time with her. Seeing her sitting on the chaise longue, dressed and eager for company, she called Luke in to join them.

Emily started by telling Allison about their adventures in Oxford over the weekend.

'Oh, you went to Magdalen?' Allison said, brightening. 'That's my old college. I'm so glad you got to see it. Isn't it lovely?'

'It certainly is. Almost makes me want to pursue another degree myself.' Luke's eyes widened, and she hastened to add, 'Not quite, though. I think my brain may be a bit past it at this point. The book on Dostoevsky I've recently finished is my swansong as far as academia is concerned.'

Allison looked out over the Fitzhugh lawn as if she were seeing her old college herself.

'What about you?' Emily asked. 'Would you ever want to return to the ivory tower?'

Allison heaved a deep sigh. 'I don't know. I honestly have no idea what I want to do now.'

'Of course. And you shouldn't rush it. Decisions made in the first throes of grief tend to be bad decisions. But it could be one option.'

'I suppose so. Along with crawling back to my parents in Boston, or finding a job somewhere in England, or – I don't know, going zip-lining in Zimbabwe. James left me enough money that my options are pretty much open.' A wry smile touched her lips. 'Or I could marry Adam. That would at least make somebody happy. Though that somebody wouldn't be me.'

Emily and Luke exchanged glances. 'Allison – I know Lady Margaret is far from rational on the subject of you and Adam. But I couldn't help wondering – do you think there's any chance he could have been involved in James's death?'

Allison's brow furrowed. 'Involved? How could anyone have been involved? It was an accident.'

'Yes, but – well, you mentioned Jackie had been acting strangely, and we just wondered . . .' Emily looked to Luke for help.

He spoke gently. 'We wondered if somebody might have . . . well, done something to Jackie. To make her skittish. Not necessarily thinking to kill James, but . . .'

Allison sat up, her face a study in disbelief. 'You mean you think it might not have been a pure accident? But how? Why? Who would do such a thing? Everybody loved James.' She slumped back against the chaise. 'Almost everybody . . . And even Adam would never do a thing like that. *Could* never. For one thing, he knows nothing about horses, and for another – well, Jackie is *my* horse. Nobody knew ahead of time James would be the one riding her that day. And Adam would certainly never do anything to harm *me*.'

Emily and Luke gaped at each other. Emily could only blame the stress of the last couple of weeks for preventing them from considering this from the beginning. Allison could easily have been the intended victim – in fact, it all made much more sense that way. And that meant they had to look at all their suspects in a new light.

Emily and Luke retired to their room to mull over this new angle in front of the fireplace.

'All right,' Emily said. 'Let's assume for the moment that Allison was the intended victim. Who knew she was riding Buttercup that day? We can rule them out.'

'Well, us, of course. And Conan. Possibly Bunty – she was in the stable when they rode out, but she said at the inquest she didn't actually see them.'

'On the other hand, suppose Conan had tampered with Jackie before James and Allison arrived. When he saw James getting ready to ride Jackie, would he have said "Oh, no, James, you mustn't ride that horse, she's fixed"?'

'Not likely. But he could've made some excuse. Pretended she was ill or something. Unless he didn't much care who got hurt.'

Emily drummed her fingers on the arm of her chair. 'You've seen more of Conan and Bunty than I have. Have you picked up on any kind of bad feeling between them and Allison? Either of them?'

Luke shook his head. 'Not a bit. She wasn't interfering in the stable or with their romance; she didn't have anything they wanted. I'd say the four of them – James included – all got along just fine.'

'What about the baby? We have to allow for the baby as the possible target, too. A fall from a horse would be much more likely to cause a miscarriage than to kill an adult rider.'

'True, but if we didn't like Bunty as a suspect for James, why would we consider her for the baby? Killing it wouldn't put her any closer to inheriting, given the entail. If she was gonna bump anybody off, it'd be Lady Margaret, so she and Conan could marry in peace.'

Emily's eyebrows rose. 'Lady Margaret. If we're looking for someone who hates Allison, she has to top the list.'

'Yeah, but she was bedridden, remember? The doctor confined her to her room after that turn she had.'

'Oh, right. Even if she did slip out, she would have been too frail to get to the stable and do whatever someone did.' Emily frowned in thought. 'So what about Simon? We know he was in the stable that morning, but he didn't stick around to see James and Allison, so he wouldn't have known which horses they were riding.'

'True. But I like Simon better for James than for Allison and/or the baby.'

'Unless he wanted to hurt James by hurting them?'

Luke screwed up his eyes. 'I don't know. It's possible, I guess, but it seems kinda convoluted. Simon's resentment of James went way back, before James even knew Allison. And James had never done anything to hurt Simon's family. I don't see the psychological consistency.'

'No, I don't either. And from what you've said, it doesn't sound like he knows enough about horses to have pulled it off.'

'Nope. Not without help.'

'And Allison as the target would definitely rule out Adam.'

'Definitely. Unless . . .' Luke rubbed the back of his neck. 'Like you said a minute ago, a fall from a horse is way more likely to hurt a fetus than its mother. If Adam knew Allison was pregnant, he might've wanted to get rid of the baby because it would tie her even tighter to James.'

'Ooh . . . Talk about convoluted, though. It's true Adam is obsessed with Allison, but do you think he's as far gone as that? I mean, it's at least bordering on irrational to think you could control the outcome to that extent – to get rid of the baby without seriously injuring Allison herself.'

'Yeah. It's a long shot, for sure. And there again, at least according to Allison, Adam doesn't know enough about horses to have pulled it off.'

'So we're back to someone associated with the stable.'

'In other words, we're back to square one.' Luke banged his hands on the arms of his chair. 'Maybe this whole thing is a wild goose chase after all. Maybe it was just an accident – Jackie was having an off day, the gunshots spooked her, James was distracted and lost his seat. It could've happened that way.'

Emily fixed him with her gaze. 'You don't believe that any more than I do.'

Luke blew out a long breath. 'No, dagnabbit, I don't. Y'know, sometimes I think instinct is a detective's worst enemy.'

He stood and paced around their two chairs. 'We've still got one ace in the hole – the vet, Granger. He should be getting back to me today.'

'Did he hold out any real hope of evidence?'

'Not much, but he did think there was cause for suspicion. At least it's one door that hasn't shut in our faces. Yet.'

Luke went off to the stables, hoping to dig further. But before he got past the terrace at the back of the house, his phone rang.

'Richards? Granger here.'

'Thanks for getting back to me. Did you find out anything?'

'I examined Jackie and took a blood sample, but I couldn't find anything untoward. Too much time had elapsed – anything that might have been in her system would have been long gone, and it wasn't anything that would cause lasting observable effects.'

Luke's hopes plummeted. Even if he did somehow manage to ascertain that foul play had occurred and who was responsible, without this kind of physical evidence, he'd never get the chief constable to contest the coroner's verdict.

'Thanks for trying, Doc. I guess that's all we can do.'

The vet cleared his throat. 'Not quite. I did find something – not on the mare herself, but in her stall.'

Luke was all ears. 'Not a hypodermic?'

'No, nothing as obvious as that. Keep in mind, the stall has no doubt been mucked out every day for over a week since the accident. But I did find something stuck in a crack in the floor underneath the horse's head.'

The vet paused, no doubt for dramatic effect. Luke held his breath.

'A tiny yellow flower. A flower I have identified as belonging to the ephedra plant.'

'Ephedra. That anything to do with pseudoephedrine?'

'Everything to do with it. The plant is a natural source of ephedrine, which acts similarly to amphetamines. It's illegal to prescribe it for horses or to give it to them for competition, but it's been done on the sly for ages. And the really interesting thing is that ephedra does not grow naturally in England – it needs an arid climate – so there is no possibility that this flower got into Jackie's stall by accident.'

The vet cleared his throat again. 'In my professional opinion, this flower is a very strong indication that Jackie was given ephedra deliberately in the hope of causing injury or death to her rider. And I would be willing to testify to that in court.'

After Luke left for the stables, Emily decided to revisit the library. She had an intuition bordering on conviction that this murder, if murder it was, hinged on issues of family and property. Maybe the Fitzhugh historical records in the library would provide some clue.

The books had been meticulously catalogued – in a previous generation, Emily guessed, since the cataloguer had used a card file system. A search under *History, Fitzhugh* quickly yielded a volume penned in the late nineteenth century by some studious offshoot of the family.

She tugged the ponderous tome from its place on a shelf and lugged it to the large, scratched and pitted oak table in the middle of the room. Starting from the beginning, when the Fitzhughs came over from France in the army of William the Conqueror, she skimmed over nine hundred years of births, marriages, and deaths; of wars at home and abroad, skirmishes with neighboring lordlings, changes of

religion as the Fitzhughs held firmly to the side in power
– from Catholic to Anglican under Henry VIII, back to
Catholic under Mary Tudor, then permanently to Anglican
under Elizabeth I.

The family had its share of black sheep, some even blacker
than Sir Percival the Prodigal, and more than one strong, ruthless woman like Lady Letitia. One medieval baronet had
attained his title by murdering his slightly older twin brother
as soon as their father died. A fifteenth-century baronet with
predilections similar to Percival's had died without legitimate
issue – in a fall from a horse, strangely enough – and one of
his infant bastards had been quietly retrieved from its peasant
mother to be raised in the manor as the heir, the whole thing
being efficiently hushed up by the baronet's widow. The author
of the present chronicle had unearthed the stolen page of
the parish registry that listed the child's birth.

But the Fitzhugh history contained some admirable
characters as well. In more recent times they had grown
more respectable. Under the early Georges through Victoria,
they had been statesmen, philanthropists, equitable landowners,
just and merciful magistrates. The history ended on a note of
praise almost amounting to a panegyric of the then-baronet,
another Sir James. No doubt the author had been a dependent
who hoped to earn the lord's favor by his work.

One or two oddities appeared, however. Here and there a
birth was recorded with no corresponding death date. Setting
aside the fanciful idea of immortality as a family character-
istic, Emily wondered if these might have been offspring
who were considered 'defective' in some way – severely
disabled or mentally ill. In an old aristocratic family that
often intermarried with cousins, distant or not, such cases
were pretty much inevitable. If these unfortunates had been
quietly secreted away in some institution – or in a secluded
cottage with a caretaker – and forgotten, it was reasonable
to suppose their deaths might not have made it into the
family records.

Emily put that volume away and found another that brought
the family history up to the turn of the millennium. Here she
read about Fitzhughs who bravely fought for their country in

two world wars while their womenfolk turned the manor into a temporary hospital. Between and after the wars, the survivors had become shrewd businessmen, investing the proceeds of the estate wisely enough to offset the effects of higher twentieth-century taxes. The family, once large, had dwindled, mainly as a result of many of its young offshoots being claimed by the two wars, until only Bunty's family and the family currently at the manor were left. James's father, Sir William, and his wife, Elizabeth, had been killed in a plane crash, leaving only Roger and James.

This volume included photographs, and Emily was startled to see one of what looked like a young Roger standing next to – himself. The caption read: *William and Roger Fitzhugh, born May 23, 1961.* The well-beloved of his mother, William, and the derisively dismissed Roger had been identical twins.

Emily knew it was not uncommon for identical twins to have radically different personalities. One twin would often be dominant even in the womb, taking the lion's share of the nourishment and ending up the taller and stronger of the two throughout their lives. This twin, who usually pushed his way out first, would likely also have the more extroverted and dominant personality, while the younger tended to be quieter and more retiring. That certainly would apply to Roger. Fascinating.

But not particularly relevant to the current inquiry. Emily would not even entertain the notion that Roger might have followed in the footsteps of his twin-murdering ancestor – in that prior case, no doubt, the birth order had been reversed, with the less aggressive twin exiting the womb ahead of his dominant brother. If Roger had been so eager to get his hands on the title, why wait until James was in his thirties with a baby on the way? Why not get rid of him as a child? No, that horse wasn't even in the race.

But had she found anything useful at all in this dive into Fitzhugh history? She'd learned that the family had had its share of ruthless and determined men and women. Even among the more recent respectable ones, she suspected a drive to maintain that outward respectability at all costs, up to and including the discreet suppression of unacceptable offshoots. Lady Letitia might be the most notorious of the Fitzhughs of this ilk, but she was far from being the only one. And the family pride most definitely rested on the property as well as the title. Though a few of the more extravagant lords had sold off bits of the estate here and there, others had reclaimed and extended it. Unlike so many of its counterparts throughout the country, the Fitzhugh estate appeared to be larger today than it had been when originally granted.

Emily was also able to find an explanation of how inheritance worked in the family. The title of baronet descended according to general English law, from father to son, or to brother if there was no legitimate issue. Various convoluted provisions existed for the title passing to a cousin in default of any male in the direct line. The Fitzhugh estate was entailed on the holder of the title. Only if the males of the family completely died out could the estate pass to a daughter or wife. So Bunty's claim was remote indeed – it depended not only on the deaths of Roger, James, and James's possible son, but on the failure of the courts to discover any remote male connection who might have the right to become the next baronet. Bunty would have had to be absurdly optimistic as well as ruthless to attempt to claim the estate for herself.

Emily put her books away with one dominant impression: the Fitzhughs as a whole (with some happy exceptions) had been a proud and powerful clan whose position in the world mattered to them more than anything else. In this context, Lady Margaret was no anomaly but the last representative of a long and, by some definitions, glorious tradition. It was little wonder that she could not bear to see the pride of the Fitzhughs degraded by vulgar commerce.

Once again, Emily saw all the players on this little stage as characters in a Forster novel: Bunty and Conan, James and Allison, Adam, even Roger in his unassuming way, all attempting to lead authentic lives, acting according to a moral code and pursuing goals that they personally found compelling; all set against Lady Margaret and her small cadre of old retainers, whose lives were completely defined by the increasingly desperate attempt to keep up appearances. Simon, despite his resentment of the aristocracy – or perhaps as the cause of it – belonged in this latter camp as well.

On the whole, Emily had to regard this situation as an instance of Tolkien's dictum that the best stories to read are not the best stories to be in. But she had been written into this one, and she would have to make the best of it.

TWENTY-ONE

L uke thanked the vet profusely and continued on the path to the stables. The day was gloomy and drizzly, not very attractive for riding but not prohibitive either. The stable staff were present in force.

He found Conan and Bunty in the office, both working on their computers. He closed the door behind him. 'Can I talk to you two for a minute?'

Conan's eyebrows rose. 'Sure, what's up?'

Luke looked from Conan to Bunty and back. Their expressions were open, surprised but not wary or secretive. He made a snap decision to trust them both.

He pulled up a straight chair and sat on it backwards, leaning his elbows on its back. 'I've come to a conclusion. Two conclusions, in fact. One, Jackie was drugged on the morning of James's death, most likely by someone working here in the stables. And two, that person acted in the belief that Allison would be the one riding Jackie that day.'

Bunty and Conan exchanged looks of shocked disbelief. 'How on earth did you conclude that?' Bunty asked.

'Well, for starters, besides myself and Emily, on your own showing you, Conan, and maybe you, Bunty, were the only ones who knew which horses James and Allison would be riding that day. We couldn't figure out any reason either of you would want to harm James, so the logical conclusion was that the person responsible thought he was sabotaging Allison's ride instead of James's.'

'But what makes you think Jackie was drugged?' Conan said.

'I asked Granger to take a look at her. He couldn't find anything on her or in a blood test, 'cause too much time had passed. But he did find evidence of the drug itself. Well, not technically a drug, but an herb. Ephedra.'

'Ephedra!' Conan exclaimed. 'We don't allow that in this stable. I don't allow any herbal remedies – too risky, too difficult to determine the correct dose. We don't give our horses anything except what Anthony Granger prescribes.'

'That just makes what he found all the more suspicious, then. Whoever brought ephedra into the stable had to have had some nefarious purpose in mind.'

'Well, it wasn't one of us,' Bunty said indignantly. 'I'm as much opposed to that sort of folk medicine as Conan is. And I can vouch for Jenny, too. I know she uses some sorts of herbal remedies for herself, but she would never give anything to the horses that we hadn't authorized.'

Conan cleared his throat and twisted a ring he wore on his right hand.

Luke impaled him with his gaze. 'What about Winky?'

Conan heaved a sigh. 'I hate to say it – even though the old boy is useless – but that sounds like precisely the sort of thing he would do. He knows all the tricks from his time as a jockey – where to get the stuff, how to give it, and how much, depending on the effect you want – and he's not above going behind my back. He doesn't think he needs to answer to me, ultimately, since I'm not one of the *family*. On top of that, he's none too fond of Allison.'

Luke remembered the encounter he had overheard from Ginger's stall early in their stay at Fitzhugh. 'Yeah, I got that impression. But you think he'd actually try to hurt her?'

'He probably wouldn't have thought of it in those terms. After all, Allison is an excellent horsewoman, so he would most likely have told himself she would just have a bit of a bumpy ride.'

'But with her being pregnant, even a bumpy ride would be dangerous.'

'Oh, I can't imagine he knew about that,' Bunty put in.

'Conan and I didn't know until the inquest. James and Allison were keeping that pregnancy very close to their chests. Besides, the gunshots were apparently what set Jackie off in a big way. Winky wouldn't have expected those at this time of year. And I'm sure he wasn't responsible for them; he doesn't know one end of a gun from the other.'

Luke pondered. It all seemed to fit, except for one thing. 'When I talked to Jenny the other day, she said she heard Winky snoring in a stall that morning.'

'No doubt he was,' Conan said. 'He could easily have spent the night in one of the stalls. And he could just as easily have woken up, given the stuff to Jackie, and gone back to snoring – whether he was really asleep or not.'

Luke had to admit the logic of that. 'Is he around?'

Bunty, who had a view into the courtyard from where she sat, said, 'Here he comes now. And it looks as though he saw you come in – he's got Ginger all ready for you.'

Luke had only half thought of riding that day, the weather being what it was; he had no fondness for getting cold and damp if he didn't have to. But since Winky had gone to all the trouble of saddling a horse for him, he figured he might as well go out for a little while.

'You folks got a rain poncho I can borrow?' he asked.

Bunty grabbed one off the coatrack in the office. 'Here you go.'

'Better wear a helmet, too,' Conan added. 'The bridle paths will be slippery.' In fact, Luke had worn a helmet for all his rides at the manor. He had no wish to end up like James. Or, for that matter, like Allison.

Luke donned both helmet and poncho and went out to meet Winky. 'Got him all saddled up for me, eh? How'd you know I was even planning to ride today?'

Winky gave him an ingratiating grin. 'Why else would ya be 'ere, guv'nor, if not to exercise this fine lad? All part o' the service. "Anticipate the client's needs" – ain't that what those marketin' blokes say?'

Luke raised one eyebrow. 'I guess they do.' He gave Ginger a careful going-over before mounting. The saddle was cinched tightly, harness snug as it ought to be, and the horse stood quietly, merely huffing and nodding his head in greeting as Luke stroked his muzzle. 'I won't stay out long, though. It'll be lunchtime soon.'

He mounted Ginger and set off for the paddock, out of which led several bridle paths. He avoided the one James and Allison had taken on the fateful day, as well as their other favorite, the path that wound through the copse. Instead, he chose a shorter loop of only a mile or two that stayed on relatively flat ground in the open.

At first Ginger was his normal self, gentle and biddable. Luke kept him to a walk since the ground was slippery. But after about fifteen minutes, the horse showed an inclination to break into a trot unbidden. Luke pulled him back, but he did it again. Finally, Luke decided to give Ginger his head, figuring the horse knew what he could handle in terms of terrain. Now Ginger took his pace up to a canter. Luke began to wonder if Winky might have done something to him, after all – this wasn't his typical behavior.

The sky had been growing darker and more threatening since shortly after they set out. Now, quite suddenly, the clouds burst and let loose a torrent accompanied by a crash of thunder that sounded unnervingly close. Ginger screamed, reared, and plunged off down the path at a gallop. It was all Luke could do to keep his seat. At this point, his only thought was to stay alive.

They'd passed the midpoint of the loop, and the stables were in sight. Ginger set his nose toward them in a straight line across the lawn and ran hell for leather, Luke leaning forward until he was practically hugging the horse's neck. Ginger didn't slow until they entered the courtyard, where he circled a few times, gradually losing speed until Luke was able to slide off his back. Then he continued to trot, a wild fire in his eyes.

Conan ran out of the office, a poncho thrown hastily over his head. 'Are you all right? What's the matter with Ginger?'

'I'm fine, just a little shook up. Thunder spooked him, but he was jittery before that. I think Winky fixed him up for me. Must have heard part of our conversation, knew I was on to him. If I were you, I'd get that little bastard under lock and key before he can do any more damage. I'm calling the police.'

Conan got hold of Ginger's reins and talked him down as only someone who has a special bond with horses can do. He led him into the stable while Bunty pulled Luke into the office.

'Good heavens, you're soaked through. Let's get you out of those wet things.' She pulled off his helmet and poncho, sat him down, and tugged off his boots. Then she tucked a rough blanket around him and stuck a steaming mug of coffee in his hand. He started to sip, but she held up a hand to stop him and added a glug of brandy to the mug. 'There. That should do you.'

Luke sipped the hot brew gratefully until he felt more like himself again. 'Listen, Bunty, I'm morally certain Winky did something to that horse just now. Probably the same thing he did to Jackie. I've got to call the police.'

Bunty closed her eyes for a minute, then nodded. 'I understand. It's shocking to think anyone could have caused that terrible accident on purpose, but if he did, he'll have to pay for it. We can't have the lives of our horses, let alone our riders, left in the hands of a man like that.'

Luke pulled out his phone, then hesitated. 'What do you think? Regular emergency number – nine-nine-nine, is it? Or go straight to the chief constable?'

Bunty grimaced. 'I would say Colonel Allan, but he's more or less in Granny's pocket, and Granny would no doubt want the whole thing hushed up – Winky is a favorite of hers, God knows why. Better call nine-nine-nine.'

'Right.' Luke hit the buttons, waited for someone to pick up, and said, 'Police. Fitzhugh Stables, Binsey. We've got an attempted murder. Maybe two.'

Conan had found Winky going about his usual business and locked him in a stall while he took care of Ginger. At Luke's insistence, he also called Anthony Granger to come and look the horse over. Luke hoped the vet would be able to find the positive evidence in Ginger that he had been too late to find in Jackie.

When the police arrived, the detective inspector, whose name, by weird coincidence with TV drama, was Hathaway, set a constable to guard Winky, then interviewed Luke in the stable office while his sergeant, Milner, talked to Conan and Bunty in the courtyard. The rain had stopped shortly after Luke got back.

Luke introduced himself as an American sheriff and watched Hathaway's estimation of him go up a notch. A cautious notch, though – he was still American, after all.

Having heard the course of the morning's events, Hathaway fixed Luke with a skeptical eye. 'Isn't it normal for a horse to be spooked by an electrical storm?'

'Most horses don't pay much attention. And anyway, he was acting weird before that. And he didn't calm down for some time, even though the storm passed over pretty quick.'

'Hmm. What makes you think this groom – what's his real name? Pollard? – would have it in for you personally?'

'I think he overheard me talking to Conan and Bunty.' Luke gestured toward a Dutch door that led directly from the office into the stables. 'That top part of the door is ajar. I didn't notice it before, but if it was ajar when we were talking, Winky could easily have heard without us noticing.'

'And what would he have heard that would have put the wind up him?'

'At the very least, he would've heard me say that I was sure somebody had doped Allison's – Lady Fitzhugh's – horse on the day she was injured and Sir James was killed. Only it was her own horse, Jackie, not the horse she was actually riding that day. James rode Jackie, but nobody knew that except Conan and Bunty.' Luke realized that from Hathaway's perspective he was probably talking gibberish. But he could go into the details later. 'Anyway, if he stuck around long enough, Winky could've heard us come to the conclusion that he must've been the one responsible.'

Hathaway screwed up his eyes. 'Suppose you go through that whole argument for me the way you put it to them.'

Luke took a deep breath and put himself into witness mode. Then he spelled out the whole course of events as he had reconstructed it in his mind, beginning with breakfast on the day of the accident.

Hathaway listened intently. 'So you have no direct evidence either that the horse was drugged – Jackie, I mean – or that this groom Pollard was responsible?'

'Not direct, no. Combination of circumstantial evidence, process of elimination, good guess at motive, and pure hunch.'

Unexpectedly, Hathaway grinned. 'Just the kind of case I like. An almost impossible one.' He glanced out the window, where Luke could see Granger striding across the courtyard, medical bag in hand. 'Is that the vet? If he can verify your horse today was interfered with, that'll be a pretty strong indication. Without that, we won't have enough to hold Pollard beyond twenty-four hours for questioning. But who knows, maybe we'll get lucky and the old boy will give himself away.'

'He might at that. He's cunning, but I don't think he's actually very smart. If he was, he'd have realized going after me wouldn't do him any good in the long run.'

'True.' Hathaway stood. 'I'm going to see what the vet has to say. Come along if you like.'

Luke did like. He followed Hathaway and Granger to Ginger's stall.

Granger greeted Luke and was introduced to Hathaway. 'Are you thinking this is another case like Jackie?' he asked Luke.

Hathaway cut in before Luke could answer. 'Let's just have your unbiased opinion, please.'

'Of course.' He turned to the horse.

Ginger was still restless and wild-eyed, pawing at his straw and waving his head around. Granger approached him cautiously and crooned to him. 'There, there, old boy, only me. Let's see what's got into you, shall we?'

He listened to the horse's heart and shook his head. 'Much too fast,' he muttered. 'Irregular, too. And he's obviously as nervous as a thoroughbred. Breathing heavy.' He glanced up at Luke. 'How long since you got back? I take it he was galloping?'

'Forty-five minutes or more. Yeah, he galloped for about half a mile.'

Granger shook his head. 'His breathing should have calmed down long ago. Definite signs of a stimulant. I'll have to analyze a blood sample to be sure, but I'd put my money on ephedra.'

Hathaway gave a brisk nod. 'Right. Thank you, Mr Granger. If you'll just get the sample for me, we'll take it from there.'

Granger met that with a raised eyebrow and proceeded to take two vials of blood. He handed one to Hathaway and tucked the other into his bag. 'This horse is my patient,' he said, as Hathaway seemed about to protest. 'I must know what has been done to him so I can treat him properly – and I need to know sooner than a police lab is likely to provide an answer.'

Hathaway grinned. 'Fair enough.' He turned to Luke. 'Let's see what Pollard has to say.'

The detective led the way down the row of stalls to the one where Winky was being held. At a nod from Hathaway, the constable unlocked the stall door and stood aside.

The old man was huddled in a corner of the stall, head on his knees, but he scrambled to his feet when he heard the door scrape open.

'William Pollard?' Hathaway said, for form's sake.

Winky blinked his one eye as if unaccustomed to hearing his own true name. 'That's right, guv'nor. Winky, they calls me.' He winked again for emphasis.

Hathaway ignored this. 'I understand you saddled the horse Ginger this morning for Mr Richards to ride.'

'That's right, guv'nor. Brushed 'im and combed 'im and saddled 'im up. That's me job, takin' care of the 'osses and gettin' 'em ready to ride.' He gave an ingratiating semi-toothless grin.

'But no one had asked you to prepare Ginger specifically, is that right? You did that on your own initiative.'

Winky's grin flickered. 'Saw 'im come in, like – Mr Richards, that is. 'E always rides Ginger, 'e does, so I got Ginger ready for 'im.'

Hathaway fixed him with a skeptical eye, and Winky began to fidget.

'Did you give the horse anything to eat or drink during this process?'

'Only 'is oats and water, guv'nor. God's truth.'

Hathaway turned to the constable. 'Search Ginger's stall, especially his food trough. The vet will tell you what to look for. And take a sample of his water.'

The constable registered alarm, and Hathaway said, 'Oh, buck up, Nelson. They can move the horse to another stall while you work.' The constable nodded, looking relieved, and strode off.

Hathaway called to another constable in the courtyard. 'Jones! Come in here.' Jones loped in, and the detective said, 'Search this man and then search the stall. And I mean sift through every piece of straw, starting with that corner.' He pointed to where Winky had been sitting before they came in.

'We'll get out of their way,' he said to Luke, and they walked into the courtyard. 'This could take a while. I won't keep you – you must have missed lunch some time ago.'

Luke checked his watch. Two o'clock. He'd already let Emily know he'd be delayed, so she would have had them save him some food.

'Let me know what you find?'

'Absolutely. I have your number.' Hathaway shook Luke's hand. 'And thanks. Just between us, I was never all that comfortable with the coroner's verdict on Sir James. Couldn't understand why the chief constable let it go so easily.'

Luke rubbed the back of his neck. 'I don't know if I should say this, but according to Bunty, Allan's in Lady Margaret's pocket. No doubt she wanted to avoid the scandal of a full investigation.'

Hathaway sighed. 'That's the worst of these old toffs serving on the force. The county folk are all their personal friends. They take it for granted that class privilege extends to not being subject to the same law as the rest of us. Allan may try to shut us down on this, too, but I'll fight it as hard as I can.'

TWENTY-TWO

Emily got Luke's call as she was finishing up her reading in the library. She was hungry – her stomach had never quite adjusted to the later mealtimes in England – and she needed to be sure food was saved for Luke. So she took a book with her – *Where Angels Fear to Tread* seemed appropriate reading for the situation – and went to the dining room.

The book, however, proved superfluous, as Roger came in while she was still helping herself at the buffet. 'Good afternoon,' he said with a shy smile. 'I'm afraid we haven't seen much of each other lately. You must think me a terrible host.'

'Not at all,' Emily replied. 'Luke and I have been pretty busy ourselves.' She hesitated, wondering whether she should let Roger in on the fact that they had been investigating James's death. Best consult Luke before doing that. Not that Roger was a suspect himself, but she didn't want to upset him or risk his dropping a careless word in the wrong ear. Especially since they weren't yet sure whose the wrong ear would be.

So she made small talk, telling Roger about their tourist activities instead. He listened avidly, and Emily got the impression that although he lived within a few miles of Oxford, he had seen very little of it. He must have always been more comfortable outdoors amidst the flora and fauna than among crowds of people.

Roger seemed tired, in no hurry to return to his butterfly hunting, or classifying, or whatever he'd been up to in the morning. They lingered over tea until Luke came in at last, looking exhausted and bedraggled.

Emily shoved back her chair and hurried to meet him. 'Are you all right? You look like you've been through the wars.'

He gave a pale smile and kissed her on the cheek, no doubt to avoid embarrassing Roger. 'No, just a cloudburst. And a possible attempt on my life.'

'*What?*' She pulled back and looked him in the eye. 'Please tell me you're joking.'

'Unfortunately, no.' He glanced at Roger, who was pretending to be completely absorbed in drinking his tea. 'You might as well hear this, Roger. Now that it's all pretty much out in the open.'

'Hear what?' Roger started, sloshing tea into his saucer. 'What's in the open?' He stared wide-eyed from Luke to Emily.

'You get started while I get some food,' Luke said to Emily.

'I'm starved.' He went to the buffet and piled meat and cheese high between two slices of bread. He sat down and attacked the sandwich ravenously as Emily talked.

She smiled sympathetically at Roger. 'I'm afraid this may be difficult for you to hear. I hardly know where to start.'

'"Begin at the beginning, go on till the end, and then stop,"' Roger said, quoting one of Oxford's most famous authors.

'Yes . . . Well, I suppose it began with the inquest. Luke and I were never quite comfortable with the verdict of misadventure. We just had a feeling there must be more involved.'

Roger sighed, ruffling his flyaway hair. 'So did I. Only I had no idea what could be done about it.'

'Well, we're kind of accustomed to investigating things. It's Luke's job, and he puts up with me sticking my oar in.' She smiled at Luke, and he grinned back around a bite of sandwich. 'At first we thought – since it was really none of our business – we ought to let sleeping dogs lie. But then when Lady Margaret started throwing accusations around, we decided to step in just to vindicate Allison in her eyes. If anyone was responsible for James's death, we were certain it couldn't be Allison.'

'No, no, of course not!' Roger spoke quite emphatically, for Roger. 'Do go on. What, or whom, did you suspect?'

'We suspected Jackie had been tampered with somehow, but at first we had no idea by whom. We eliminated Conan and Bunty fairly quickly, since they had really nothing to gain by James's death and seemed genuinely fond of him. Then we eliminated Simon Braithwaite – you probably don't know him; he's an old school acquaintance of James whose daughter takes lessons with Bunty – and also Adam, because he wouldn't have risked hurting Allison.'

Luke had finished half his sandwich and was ready to add his contribution. 'I talked to Anthony Granger, the vet, about whether he thought Jackie might've been doped. He found some evidence to that effect. And meanwhile, Allison helped us figure out what we should've seen all along – that whatever had been done was probably aimed at her, since only a couple of people knew she wouldn't be riding her own horse that day.'

He took another bite and went on. 'Finally, just this morning, I talked to Conan and Bunty again and figured out the only person who could possibly have done anything to Jackie was Winky. And then Winky confirmed it himself – not in words, but sure as death and taxes he doped up Ginger the same way and saddled him up for me to ride before I even said I wanted to ride at all.'

Emily fought down a feeling of panic – obviously nothing terrible had happened, since Luke was sitting right in front of her, in full possession of his limbs and faculties. 'Oh my God! What happened? Did you figure it out before you got on?'

'Nope. I checked him over and couldn't see anything wrong – I guess the stuff takes a few minutes to take effect. But I took him out on one of the easy paths just in case. And sure enough, he started acting jumpy almost right away. Then when the thunder hit, he went crazy. He reared and ran back to the stable like the devil was on his heels.'

'But you stayed on? You weren't hurt?'

'I stayed on. Hung on by my fingernails, practically. I think Winky must've given Ginger a lower dose than he gave Jackie. Probably just wanted to scare me off rather than actually kill me.'

Roger had been listening to all of this with mouth agape. 'You don't think he intended to kill James, do you?'

'Not James – remember, he thought Allison would be riding Jackie that day. And no, I don't suppose he meant to kill her, necessarily. I don't think he has the guts for outright murder. I imagine it was just a bit of mischief in his eyes, trying to get his own back on somebody he didn't like.'

Roger cradled his head in his hands, moaning softly. 'Oh dear . . . Oh, poor Allison . . . Poor James. I simply can't take it in.' He raised his head and stared at Luke. 'Is he still at large? Winky, I mean.'

Luke shook his head. 'That's what took me so long. I called the police. Granger came and examined Ginger, confirmed he'd been doped. They took Winky in for questioning – for what he did to me and for James and Allison. We won't be seeing Winky again any time soon.'

'But do they have enough evidence to hold him?' Emily said.

'For his attempt on me, they do, assuming Ginger's blood test comes back positive. James is more speculative, but they might be able to make it stick. The detective's a pretty smart guy.' Luke grinned at Emily. 'You'd like him. Name of Hathaway.'

Emily almost laughed, but Roger wouldn't have gotten the joke. 'He isn't tall and blond, by any chance? Cambridge theology graduate? Plays the guitar?'

'Not that I know of. Average height, brown hair. But I think he's got some of the other Hathaway's brains.'

'I look forward to meeting him, then.' Emily was thrilled in spite of the gravity of the overall situation. Not only had she seen the backdrops of several of her favorite mystery shows on this trip, but she could go home and tell her friends she'd met Inspector Hathaway. She needn't mention he wasn't actually the Hathaway of *Lewis* fame.

Meanwhile, Roger had tottered over to the liquor cabinet and poured himself a glass of brandy. 'Mother would be shocked at me drinking in the middle of the day. But this is medicinal.' He downed it all in one shot, then staggered back to his chair. 'Mother. Oh Lord. I suppose she'll have to be told.'

Emily and Luke exchanged glances. 'I don't think *you* need to tell her,' Luke said. 'We can let the police do that. Once everything's settled.'

Roger nodded, breathing deeply. 'Yes. Yes, the police. By all means. Let the police do it.'

A new thought struck Emily. 'What about Allison? Should we tell her?'

Luke hesitated. 'Maybe not just yet. It'll be a lot for her to take in. Maybe wait till it's all settled for her, too.'

Roger pushed unsteadily to his feet. 'I think I need to lie down.'

Emily and Luke watched Roger leave the dining room. Then Emily turned to her husband. 'I think you might need to lie down, too,' she said. 'You've had quite an ordeal today.'

He stretched and winced. 'You have a point there,' he said.

'But first I think I'll take advantage of that nice big tub of ours. Want to join me?'

She did, then tucked him up for a nap and sat down with her knitting. The gold Shetland cowl was nearly finished. Once again, she went over in her mind everything that had happened since that fateful Saturday of James's death. From a purely logical point of view, it all fit and made sense. From what Luke said, Winky stood at least a fair chance of being convicted of something – though she wasn't entirely sure of what, since Luke had not been harmed and the evidence for the previous crime might prove insufficient. Malicious mischief, perhaps? She had no idea what sort of sentence that would carry. But Winky was old and decrepit enough that even a few years could prove a life sentence for him.

So why did she not feel satisfied? Was it simply the feeling that James's death had been a terrible waste? In a sense, it could still be considered accidental, since he was not the intended victim. But why should she feel any better if he'd been killed with malice aforethought? A good man was still dead, whichever way you looked at it. Allison was still a widow and a mother bereaved of her unborn child.

No, what was bothering Emily was something else. Her instincts – whether detective or literary or ordinary feminine intuition – were still on the alert, still searching for some missing piece that would make this puzzle complete. This death wasn't a proper Forster death, for one thing. It lacked his perfect sense of dramatic irony. And Winky wasn't a proper murderer – he lacked force of character and firm intention. He was a bit player, not a star.

She revolved these ideas along with her circular knitting until Luke awoke, just in time for dinner. Emily stole down to the dining room and loaded their plates on a tray so they could eat in their room. She wanted to share her thoughts with Luke in privacy.

He listened in silence, then sighed. 'I don't know, Em. I think maybe you just want this case to be all neat and tidy like a novel or a *Midsomer* episode. Life isn't always like that. Sometimes what's behind a tragedy really is stupid and point-less and commonplace and boring. Sometimes a bit player does kill a star, maybe without even meaning to. I think it's time to let this thing go.'

He reached across to her chair and stroked her cheek. 'What about that corpse-free honeymoon we keep talking about? I for one am ready to get started on it.'

Emily knew he wasn't talking about packing their bags for Scotland – at least not right this minute. She set her niggling doubts aside and became a proper newlywed bride for the next few hours.

But later that night, when Luke was snoring gently beside her, she lay awake, the doubts having returned in full force. She was too restless to lie in bed, and she didn't want to disturb Luke by turning on a light and puttering about the room. She got up, put on her robe, lit the candle Allison had left in their room for emergencies, and set off for the dining room in search of the book she'd left there.

She had gotten as far as the landing where the stairs divided, to go up to each of the two wings and down to the main hall, when she felt a sudden chill. An old house like this was full of drafts, of course, so she thought nothing of it until she realized her candle flame had not flickered; it burned steady and high.

She heard a faint sound as if of the wind whistling far overhead, and then out of the corner of her eye she caught movement. Her first thought was that it might be Caddie, since she seemed to prowl about the house at all hours while being constantly attendant on her lady at the same time. But when Emily turned to look full on where the movement had been, she saw only the still and motionless hall, dimly illuminated by a low-wattage lamp next to the front door. Then she turned her head back toward the opposite staircase, and she sensed the movement again. It came up the stairs from the hall toward her, then moved past her and up the stairs that led to Lady Margaret's wing.

Emily could never explain afterward how it was that she perceived this movement. She seemed to feel it more with her soul than her senses. It petrified her, and yet she felt compelled to follow it.

When she reached the upper gallery, the light from the hall

was no longer visible, and no light had been left burning here. The brave flame of her candle alone showed her where to put her next step. Still, she could sense the presence moving ahead of her, leading her inexorably onward.

She turned the corner into Lady Margaret's wing, and suddenly her candle went out – as if caught by a breeze. But there was no breeze; only closed doors met her on either side of the corridor.

She looked around, trying to get her bearings in the dark, and then she saw it. Standing in front of Lady Margaret's door was the faint outline of a woman, with the full sleeves, slightly raised waistline, and skirt falling wide from the hips typical of seventeenth-century dress. Emily could not discern her features, but she knew, in the same way she'd known of the presence all along, that this was Lady Letitia Fitzhugh, exactly as if she'd stepped out of her portrait to bring Emily some kind of sign.

The apparition turned its face full on Emily and raised its right arm straight out at its side. A ghostly finger pointed at Lady Margaret's door.

TWENTY-THREE

Emily dropped her flameless candle, crossed herself, and fled the way she'd come, hands wide to warn her of obstacles in the darkness. Down the short stretch of corridor, turn the corner into the gallery, stumble along that for seeming miles, down the stairs to the landing and up the other side, another gallery, another corridor, and finally to the door of her own sweet room with her own dear, strong, sensible husband sleeping inside. She darted into the bed and snuggled up to his back. She was much too keyed up to sleep, but nothing in heaven or earth – or hell, for that matter – could make her depart from his reassuring presence again tonight.

She did sleep eventually, but her dreams were still haunted

by dozens of Fitzhugh ghosts, brought to life by her imagination to play out once more the comedies and tragedies of their earthly lives. Perhaps there was something to be said, after all, for knowing little of one's family history; at least it left one free to choose a life unfettered by the need either to repeat or to redeem the past.

The morning light was streaming full in through their east-facing windows by the time she woke. She turned to see Luke coming in the door bearing a tray laden with coffee, scones, bacon, eggs, and fruit.

He set the tray down on the table by the fireplace, came up to the bed, and leaned over to kiss her. 'Morning, beautiful,' he said. 'Are you ready to get up, or would you prefer your breakfast in bed?'

Emily was still groggy, but she preferred to put some distance between herself and the night's phantasms. 'I'll get up. Thank you for bringing breakfast. I may not be ready to face the world for some time.'

Something in her tone must have told him she wasn't referring to simple exhaustion. 'What's up? You not feeling well?' He smiled slyly. 'I kind of hoped I'd made you feel pretty good last night.'

She kissed him. 'Oh, you definitely did. It was after that.'

'After! What, bad dreams?'

'Give me a chance to drink some coffee and I'll tell you.'

She sat by the table and helped herself to coffee and strawberries. The heavier food would have to wait until her stomach was fully awake.

When she felt somewhat fortified, she told him about her midnight adventure.

His expression grew from concerned to skeptical. 'Emily, you're not seriously going to sit there and tell me you believe you saw a ghost?'

She'd had some lingering uncertainty herself as to what she'd actually seen, or imagined, but his skepticism made her defensive. 'And why not? As a Christian, I believe in life after death. I don't think souls commonly hang around on earth for centuries, but I have heard stories from reliable sources about people being visited by loved ones after death, either to offer comfort or to give some kind of warning. Not that Lady Letitia was my loved one, but this is her house and her family. And it definitely felt like some sort of warning.'

She finished her coffee and poured another cup. 'And besides, every old English manor house has a ghost. It's an absolute requirement, along with the old retainers and the paintings and the silver.'

Luke sat back in his chair with a sigh. 'Em, we've got to look at this rationally. Don't you think you might have been dreaming? Or imagining things in the dark? You wanted some kind of further development in the case – maybe your subconscious manufactured one for you.'

She shook her head stubbornly. 'No. I had dreams about Fitzhugh ancestors after I came back to bed and finally got to sleep, and they felt completely different – all mixed-up and nonsensical, the way dreams usually are. This was a clear, coherent, waking experience – if a terrifying and inexplicable one.'

She sat forward. 'In fact, I can prove I went to Lady Margaret's wing last night. I took the candle Allison left for us, and I dropped it when I ran away. It's probably still there.'

Luke blew out a long breath. 'All right, if it'll make you happy, we'll go look for it. But you should probably get dressed first.' He held up a restraining hand. 'Not that it would prove anything you think you saw – only that you were there.'

'And that I was terrified. Why else would I drop the candle?'

'Mmm. Maybe I'll allow that. We'll see.'

Emily threw on some clothes, and they hurried over to the other wing. One of the cleaners from the village was vacuuming the carpet in the corridor. Emily glanced around but didn't see a candle.

'Excuse me,' she said to the girl. 'Did you happen to see a candle on the floor here? A taper in a small brass holder with a handle?'

The girl's eyebrows rose. 'No, ma'am. Nothing like that, ma'am.'

'You're absolutely certain?'

'Yes, ma'am. I'd remember a thing like that – not the kind of thing we usually find lying around on a corridor floor.'

'No, I suppose not.' Emily was crestfallen, but she put on a smile for the cleaner's benefit. 'Thanks anyway,' she said. 'I must have dropped it somewhere else.'

The girl gave a small smile, and Emily caught a dismissive shrug out of the corner of her eye as she turned away.

Once they were back in the main gallery, Emily said, 'I'll bet Caddie already found it and cleared it away. That's just the sort of thing she would do.'

'Because she's a conscientious maid? Yeah, I guess she would.'

'Well, that, but also because she'd do anything to protect Lady Margaret.'

Luke stopped and turned her to face him. 'You lost me. How could clearing away a candle protect Lady Margaret?'

'Don't you see? Lady Letitia's ghost, or whatever it was, was accusing her. The fact that I was here and saw the ghost proves that. And the candle proves I was here.'

Luke put up both hands. 'Whoa, Nelly. Slow down a minute. Even supposing what you just said was true – which I am not admitting for a second, logically or otherwise – how would Caddie know all that? Even if she happened to be lurking in the corridor or peeking out a door and saw you, how would she know what you thought you saw, or what it meant? Sometimes a candle is just a candle, Em – just a mess on the floor that needs cleaning up.'

'She could have seen the ghost, too. As far as what it meant, I think that's pretty obvious.'

'It's not obvious to me.'

Emily stared at him as if he'd just flunked first-grade math. 'It means Lady Margaret is responsible for James's death.'

Something dawned in Luke's eyes that was not the skepticism and confusion he'd shown up to now. 'Let's get back to our room,' he said, taking her by the elbow. 'We shouldn't talk about this here.'

When they reached their room, Luke locked the door, then pulled Emily to sit with him by the fire. 'Now. Tell me how you see this playing out.' He held up a palm. 'Still not saying I believe in the ghost, mind. But your subconscious could've worked something out and sent you the message in that weird form.'

Emily rolled her eyes. 'That was not my subconscious. And I haven't had time to completely work it out. But we know Lady Margaret hates Allison.'

'Right.'

'And we know she didn't believe the baby was James's.'

'Right.'

'And we know she had no way of knowing James would be riding Allison's horse that day.'

'That's all true, but you're forgetting one thing. Lady Margaret was in bed that morning. She hadn't been out of bed for two days. At least, nobody had seen her leave her room.'

Emily deflated. 'Well, I don't know exactly *how* she did it, but she did it. I'm certain of it.'

'I don't share your certainty, but I do see another way she could be involved.' Luke got to his feet and started circling the little group of chairs. 'Lady Margaret and Winky are thick as thieves.'

'Oh! They are? He hardly seems like her type.'

'I grant you, they're about as far apart on the social scale as two people can get. But Winky was jockey to her favorite racehorse back in the day. Rode him to all kinds of prizes. She's had a soft spot for him ever since. And he'd do just about anything for her. I heard them whispering in the stable one day, and Allison was sure Winky was neglecting Jackie – on Lady Margaret's instructions.'

Light dawned. 'So she got Winky to dope Jackie for her.'

'Right. She probably told him she just wanted Allison shaken up a little, which he would've been happy to do; he resents Allison anyway. But secretly she may have been hoping for something more serious to happen – injury, miscarriage, whatever. I doubt even she would have consciously intended Allison's death, though on some level she must've recognized the possibility.'

'But what about the gunshots?'

'I don't know for sure. I don't think that was Winky, 'cause he has no experience with guns. But what about Caddie or

Witherspoon? In the old days, they probably would have acted as loaders for shooting parties – Witherspoon, at least. They're old, but I'd bet either one of them is still spry enough to get to the wood and back, and fire off a few shots in between.'

'But wouldn't someone have seen them?'

'Not necessarily. We know Roger was in the wood but oblivious to anything but his butterflies. The groundskeepers could've been working in a different part of the estate where they wouldn't see somebody walking from the house to the woods. And there's no view of that path from the stables. Pick your moment, and Bob's your uncle, as they say over here.'

'And if either Caddie or Witherspoon had happened to see James and Allison – and I imagine they must have been on the lookout for them – they wouldn't have known the horses well enough to know Allison was on the wrong one.'

'Correct.'

Emily's breath caught as the full implications dawned on her. 'Oh, Luke . . . Just think of how Lady Margaret must have felt when she found out what really happened. When she realized her plan had backfired, and instead of getting rid of a hated in-law, she'd actually killed her own grandson. The only person she had left in the world to love.'

Talk about dramatic irony worthy of a Forster novel. In trying to save the family line, Lady Margaret had destroyed it instead. There was nothing trivial or commonplace about this case now. It was a full-blown Greek tragedy.

'What should we do?' Emily asked. 'Call the police?'

Luke slowly shook his head. 'We don't have any proof. All we've done is figure out it makes sense. There's not one shred of evidence. Besides, calling them on Lady Margaret would be sure to get the chief constable involved, and he'd never listen to an idea like that. We'd have to have overwhelming proof to get him even to question her.'

'What about her minions? There must be some proof against them. And maybe they'd talk if they got frightened enough on their own account.'

'Well, the police already have Winky. His loyalty seems

pretty strong, but I'd be willing to bet it's not as strong as his sense of self-preservation. It's possible they might get it out of him.'

'But they'd have to know to try, right?'

'It would sure help.' Luke glanced at his watch. 'I could call Hathaway directly. He might listen. Bit early yet, though.'

Emily had been pondering. 'The police never followed up on the gunshots, did they? Look for cartridges in the wood, check the guns in the house for fingerprints, that sort of thing?'

'No, I don't believe so. The gunshots didn't come up till the inquest, and then the death was declared accidental, so there would've been no reason to pursue it.'

'Could we do that?'

Luke grimaced. 'Better I just suggest it to Hathaway. If we get involved, we might compromise the chain of custody of evidence or something. We don't want to create any more loopholes the culprits might squeeze through than we have to.'

Emily had never properly breakfasted, and now she found herself ravenous. She addressed herself to her breakfast, which was rather cold by this time but still satisfying. Then she groomed herself properly, having thrown on the first clothes that came to hand in order to search for her lost candle.

When she emerged from the bathroom, Luke was talking on his phone. 'OK, thanks, Inspector,' he said. 'Keep in touch.'

He ended the call and looked up at Emily. 'Hathaway's in,' he said. 'He thinks we're on to something. Winky's being cagey, but he did drop a hint he wasn't working alone. Hathaway'll be over shortly to check things out.'

'He will have the sense to get some kind of evidence before he confronts Lady Margaret, won't he?'

'Oh, yeah. He's gonna start by examining the guns, then he'll interview Caddie and Witherspoon. Then we'll see where we are.'

Emily stood with arms crossed, drumming her fingers on her opposite arm. 'I just have this feeling she's going to slip away from us. Lady Margaret, that is. She can't be a flight risk in her physical condition – I guess I'm just afraid she'll slip through some loophole in the law.'

'I know what you mean, but I don't see there's anything more we can do. The house'll be swarming with police in a few minutes, so Caddie won't be able to spirit her away.'

'True.' A new thought struck her. 'Should we warn Allison? And Roger?'

Luke rubbed the back of his neck. 'I guess we'd better. But let's keep it vague – the police are looking for further evidence with regard to the gunshots, but that's all.'

'Right.'

Luke loaded up the breakfast tray, and they went down to the dining room. To their surprise, Allison and Roger were both there, finishing their breakfast. Allison sat at one end of the table with her injured leg propped up on a second chair, a pair of crutches leaning against the arm.

'Morning, Roger,' Luke said. 'Bit late for you, isn't it?'

'I, uh . . . I didn't sleep well last night. Besides, it isn't good weather for hunting.' He nodded toward the window, which revealed an iron-gray sky and a settled rain.

Emily went up to Allison and bent down to kiss her cheek. 'Allison! You've come down! It's so good to see you up and around.'

Allison gave a pale smile. 'I couldn't stand that room a minute longer. My head feels fine most of the time now, and I can't lie on a chaise for five more weeks till my ribs and ankle are healed. I'll go mad. In fact, I'm already starting to invent imaginary complaints, as if the real ones weren't enough. I've been having weird feelings in my abdomen. I think my system is suffering from lack of activity.'

Emily nodded. 'That makes sense. I'm sorry I haven't spent more time with you up to now. Luke and I have been – kind of busy.'

Luke brought two cups of fresh coffee from the sideboard, and they sat on either side of Allison.

'Of course,' Allison said. 'You're on your honeymoon – I never expected you to spend it hovering over an invalid. It's bad enough you got caught up in our . . .' She couldn't finish her sentence.

Emily exchanged glances with Luke. 'As a matter of fact, we did get caught up in it, kind of by choice. We haven't been spending all our time sightseeing. I'm afraid the two of us can't resist a mystery, and what happened to you and James seemed like something of a mystery to us.'

Allison looked puzzled and opened her mouth to speak. Luke forestalled her.

'We've been poking around a little, and there are some things we think would bear a little more scrutiny. I called the police over to the stables yesterday, and today they're coming to the house.'

'Coming to the house? Whatever for?' Roger spoke for the first time since greeting them. Emily had almost forgotten he was there.

Luke acknowledged Roger with a glance but continued speaking to Allison. 'We, uh . . . We think those gunshots in the wood that day may not have been random coincidence. Somebody might've been trying to spook the horses on purpose. It's probably too late to get any real evidence, but the police are gonna examine the guns in the gun room anyway.' He turned to Roger. 'Is that all right with you?'

Roger fluttered his hands, which seemed like an affirmative.

'Are they going to want to talk to me again?' Allison asked.

'If you're up to it, I think it'd be good for you to tell them everything you've remembered about the ac— the incident.' Emily noticed the hesitation – Luke couldn't bring himself to call it an accident anymore.

She nodded. 'All right. I think I can handle that.'

Emily still felt uncomfortable. 'Allison, I hope you don't feel we've overstepped by looking into this. The police could turn up something that would – well, at the very least reopen the wound. Possibly make things worse for you.'

Allison shook her head. 'The wound hasn't even begun to close. It can't be any worse than it already is. Maybe knowing what really happened – *why* it happened – will be the first step on the road to healing.'

TWENTY-FOUR

The doorbell rang, and Luke said, 'I'll get that. It's probably the police.'

Hathaway and his sergeant, Milner, stood at the door at the head of a whole line of uniforms and bunny-suited forensics people. Hathaway held a sheet of paper in his hand.

'Come on in,' Luke said. 'The family – well, Allison and Roger, anyway – know you're coming. I don't think you need to bother with your warrant.'

Hathaway nodded and stowed the paper in his inside breast pocket. 'Good. I always prefer to do this with consent.' He spoke to his sergeant. 'Milner, take some constables and search the wood for cartridges. Start with a fifty-yard radius from where Lady Fitzhugh was found and move outward.'

Milner looked as though he'd rather be marooned on a desert island, but he picked out half a dozen constables and moved off toward the back of the house. Luke felt for him. The rain was letting up, but he'd still be looking for a needle in a haystack.

Hathaway stepped in, then stood aside and motioned the bunny suits through. 'Can you point these folks to the gun room? I'd like to talk to the family if I may.'

Luke showed Hathaway to the dining room, then led the forensics people to the gun room on the ground floor. By the time he returned to the dining room, the pleasantries were over and Hathaway was questioning Allison.

'Lady Fitzhugh—'

'Please, call me Allison.'

'Allison – have you been able to remember anything more about the incident since the inquest?'

Luke noticed Hathaway was avoiding the word 'accident' as well.

She nodded. 'It's all come back to me, more or less.' She

repeated what she had told Luke and Emily a few days before: Jackie's strange behavior, the gunshots, Jackie throwing James, Buttercup bolting with Allison into the wood and her getting thrown herself.

'Do you have any idea what time this happened?'

She cocked an eyebrow at him. 'I wasn't exactly thinking about the time. I was trying to stay alive.'

'I understand that, but since this was a favorite route of yours, do you have an idea how long it would usually take you to reach that spot?'

She blew out a long breath. 'I don't usually keep track of time even on a normal ride. But it's about an hour total, and that spot is maybe . . . two-thirds of the way through? Three-quarters?' She screwed up her eyes to do the mental math. 'We left the stable around nine, I think, so maybe nine forty, nine forty-five? But that's just a guess. I wouldn't want to swear to it.'

Hathaway nodded and made a note. 'That's very helpful, Lady— Allison.' He looked back up at her. 'Can you tell me how many gunshots you heard?'

She ran a hand over her hair. 'Oh, goodness. That's trickier. It's all a bit of a blur.' She stared into the distance. 'More than one, I'm pretty sure. Two? Maybe three?' She shrugged apologetically. 'I'm sorry, I'm afraid that's the best I can do.'

'I understand. Thank you.' He stood, moved to the window, and pulled out his cell phone. Luke heard him tell someone – presumably Milner – to look for at least two cartridges, possibly more.

Luke moved to join him as he put his phone away. 'Anything I can do to help?'

Hathaway glanced toward the chair-bound Allison and the fluttering Roger. 'Perhaps you could sort of represent the family. I don't think those two will be much use on a practical level. I need someone to gather the staff and introduce me.' His gaze rested on Emily, deep in conversation with Allison. 'Your wife seems to be doing a pretty good job as a stand-in family liaison officer. I'd like to have brought one of my own, but since this case is officially closed, it was all

I could do to come up with the people I've got.' He gave a wry smile. 'I do feel sorry for poor Milner. He ought to have four times the men I could give him to comb through that wood.'

'Yeah.' Luke shook his head. 'That's a long shot, all right. You think the cartridges'll be key?'

'If they have fingerprints, they could be. And they could help identify the gun that was fired, which might have prints or DNA itself. But that's trickier, because anyone in the household could claim they'd touched any of the guns in the ordinary course of things.'

Luke scratched his chin. 'Not absolutely anyone. The family, sure. And I guess Witherspoon might be responsible for cleaning them, though he's technically retired. I don't see any reason for the cook or the cleaners to touch the guns – a cleaner might dust the cabinet, but not open it – and it'd be a heck of a stretch for Caddie. She's personal maid to Lady Margaret – she doesn't do anything in the house outside her lady's apartment.'

Hathaway nodded and made a note. 'That's useful, thank you. Now, do you think you could gather the staff in the kitchen for me? Meanwhile, I'll see how the team in the gunroom is getting on.'

'I'll do my best.' Luke led the inspector to the gunroom and then headed to the kitchen.

Gathering the staff was not a simple task, as only the cook was actually present in the kitchen, tidying up from breakfast. The cleaners were off on their lawful rounds and had to be tracked down. Witherspoon wasn't even on the premises; Luke had to call him to come up from his cottage on the estate.

But the real challenge was Caddie. Luke was not an easy person to intimidate by any means, but even he found Caddie formidable.

Standing in front of Lady Margaret's door, for a moment he could almost believe in Emily's vision of the night before. There was an atmosphere about this place that could make anyone imagine evil taking visible shape. He had to force himself to knock.

Caddie opened the door, her skeletal figure in its somber black dress somehow filling the frame, denying entry to any who might threaten to disturb her Ladyship. She stared at him without speaking.

Luke cleared his throat. 'You're wanted in the kitchen, Caddie.' His impulse was to call her 'Miss Cadwallader,' but he'd tried that once and been frozen in his tracks by her glare.

'In the *kitchen*?' He might as well have said 'in the salt mines.'

Luke didn't want to mention the police in Lady Margaret's hearing. He couldn't see her, but he was sure she must be in the room Caddie was so zealously guarding. 'Sir Roger's orders' was the best he could come up with.

She continued to stare at him for another second or two, then Lady Margaret's voice issued from the room behind her. 'What is it, Caddie?'

Caddie answered without turning, her eyes still fixed on Luke. 'Mr Richards says Sir Roger wants me in the kitchen.' She'd tuned her voice to its usual deferential note, but it still held a tinge of astonishment.

Lady Margaret sighed audibly. 'Oh, very well. You'd best go and see what he wants. You can fetch me more tea and a biscuit while you're there.'

'Very good, milady.' Caddie shut the door behind her without taking her eyes off Luke, as if she half expected him to try to breach the fortress in spite of her. She didn't move until he set off down the corridor. When he turned to see if she was following him, he saw her heading in the opposite direction – presumably toward the back stairs. He half wished he could take that route himself – it was probably shorter.

By the time he got back to the kitchen, everyone he'd summoned was assembled there, along with Hathaway and a constable taking notes in a corner. Luke leaned against a back wall to be as inconspicuous as possible.

Hathaway smiled to include the group and said in his least threatening voice, 'Now, there's nothing to be alarmed about. I realize it's a nuisance to have the police in the house, and we'll try to inconvenience you as little as possible. But there are a few things we need to clear up about the day Sir James died.'

Caddie spoke out, loudly and with less deference than Luke had ever heard her show. 'The coroner declared Sir James's death an accident.'

Hathaway turned to her with a less conciliatory light in his eye. 'Yes, he did, but some facts have come to light since then that have compelled us to investigate further.' He turned back to the group. 'Now, I just need to know all your movements on the morning of Saturday the eighth. Cook – Mrs Terwilliger – let's start with you.'

The cook was a large, elderly red-faced woman who spoke defensively, in an accent Luke hadn't heard before. He'd have to ask Emily about it – the r's sounded almost American. 'I was here in the kitchen all mornin'. Had the breakfast to get and clean up from, then my bit of a sit-down, and then the lunch to see to. I've no time or energy for gallivantin'.'

'That's fine, Mrs Terwilliger, thank you. Was anyone with you? Did anyone come in or out while you were working?'

'Not that I saw or heard. They gets on with their work and I gets on with mine.'

'Right.' He turned to the cleaner Luke and Emily had met in Lady Margaret's corridor earlier that morning. 'Miss Munson? What about you?'

'I don't come in on the weekends, sir, not as a rule. Only if there's a big party or something. I was in Oxford shopping that morning. Me and Julie both.' She nodded toward her coworker.

Hathaway turned to the other girl. 'Miss Cartwright? You confirm that?'

The second girl, a wide-eyed blonde, nodded vigorously. 'Oh, yes, sir. We were shopping together, sir. All morning.'

'You caught the bus into town together?'

'Yes, sir. The nine-oh-six. We had a coffee while we waited for the shops to open.'

The inspector nodded. 'Thank you, girls.' He turned to Witherspoon, who seemed slightly tottery on his feet. 'Mr Witherspoon. Please sit down if you like.'

'No thank you, sir. I prefer to stand.' Witherspoon's voice was reedy but refined.

'If you say so. Now, where were you on Saturday morning?'

'I was at my cottage, tidying up and working in my little garden. I was not required at the house until near dinnertime.'

'Anyone vouch for you?'

Witherspoon's eyes widened. 'I live alone, sir. The grounds-keepers may have caught sight of me in my garden – I did glimpse them from time to time working in the formal gardens, which my cottage faces on the south side, near the gate.'

'Any idea what time you saw them?'

'I really couldn't say, sir. I was in my garden for at least an hour – roughly nine to ten, I believe – and I saw them off and on during that time.'

So they would all alibi each other, Luke thought. Hathaway didn't say that – no doubt he didn't want to alarm anyone by using official words like 'alibi.'

That left only Caddie. 'Miss Cadwallader,' Hathaway said.

He got the frozen treatment. 'I am called Caddie, sir,' she said through barely moving lips, her chin high.

'Caddie, then. What were you doing Saturday morning?'

'I was in attendance on her Ladyship, sir, as I am every day.'

'Did you stay in her rooms the whole time?'

'I came down to the kitchen to get her breakfast and again to return the tray, as I do every day. I may have done other small errands about the house – I really can't remember. That was some time ago, and one day is much like another.'

'Not that day, I wouldn't have thought. The day Sir James was killed.' Hathaway put a cruel emphasis on the final word.

Caddie blinked rapidly but otherwise did not react. 'We did not know that until the evening, sir. The morning was just like any other day.'

Hathaway's brows drew together. 'Would you happen to remember if you saw anyone going in or out of the gunroom in your trips through the kitchen?'

'No, sir. That is, I don't remember, sir. That would be unusual, sir, since it is not the season for shooting.' Her face continued to resemble flint, but Luke, who was watching her intently, thought he could detect an additional tightness around her eyes and mouth. He suspected Hathaway picked it up, too.

'You did not enter the gunroom for any reason?'

'I, sir? Why would I do that, sir?'

'You tell me.'

Up to now, Caddie had said nothing that would be an outright lie if she had indeed been the one to take out a gun. With this question, Hathaway had her backed up to the wall. Luke saw her swallow, and the pointed end of her tongue flicked out to moisten her lips.

'No, sir. I did not.'

Luke would have bet his badge she was lying. Hathaway's expression as he glanced at Luke told him he was thinking the same.

'I'll have to ask you all to give me your fingerprints,' the inspector said, addressing the group. 'Nelson, will you do the honors?'

The constable in the corner came forward with a finger-print kit. Caddie's already pale face turned several shades paler, but she held her ground. She submitted to being fingerprinted in her turn.

'Thank you,' Hathaway said when they had finished. 'You may return to your duties – except you, Caddie.'

She blinked rapidly. 'Her Ladyship will be needing me, sir. She asked me to bring her tea and a biscuit.'

'I'm afraid her Ladyship will have to wait.'

Caddie opened her mouth to protest, then shut it again.

'Sit down, Caddie. You're going to be here a while.' Hathaway turned to Nelson. 'Keep an eye on her. I'll be back in a minute.'

With his eyes, he invited Luke to accompany him as he moved down the corridor to the gunroom. 'Anything?' he asked the forensics officer in charge.

'Yes, sir,' she replied. One of the shotguns was lying on the table. 'This one hasn't been cleaned since it was fired last.'

'Any way to tell how long ago that was?'

'I'm afraid not. More than twenty-four hours – that's all I can say for sure.'

'Prints?'

'Loads. It'll take some time to process them all.'

'Right. Nelson's just printed all the staff, so we'll have something to compare them with.' Hathaway turned to Luke. 'I think it's time for a little creative interpretation of the facts.'

He led the way back to the kitchen and strode up to where Caddie was sitting. He loomed over her. 'All right, Caddie. Suppose you tell me the truth.'

She drew herself up in her chair. 'That's just what I have done, sir.'

'I don't think so. I think you went into the gunroom on the morning of Saturday the eighth. I think you took out a shotgun, walked down to the wood, and took two or three shots into the air in order to frighten your master's horses. I've got your fingerprints on the gun to prove it.'

Just then a very soggy and breathless Milner burst into the room, holding aloft an evidence bag containing three cartridges. 'Got 'em!' he cried.

Caddie fainted.

Emily, Allison, and Roger were lingering over second or third cups of coffee when Luke and Hathaway returned to the dining room. Luke briefly summed up for them what had happened.

'I'd say Caddie fainting is as good as a confession,' Hathaway said. 'At least for now.'

'Caddie?' Allison turned astonished eyes from Hathaway to Luke as if expecting Luke to say 'Just kidding.' 'But why on earth would she do such a thing?'

'We can't be sure quite yet,' Hathaway said cautiously. 'We need to talk to Lady Margaret.'

'Lady Margaret?' Her words held just as much astonishment as before, but her expression gradually shifted to dismay. 'Oh. I see.'

Hathaway turned to Emily. 'Mrs Richards, I'd like you to come along, if you don't mind. I need a woman present in case . . . well, in case she reacts as Caddie did. And I don't have a female constable available.'

'Of course.' Emily rose, pressing Allison's hand in

reassurance. 'Roger, do you think you could fill Allison in on what we were talking about last night?'

Roger, who had been blending into the background like one of his camouflage-patterned moths, started and blinked. 'Oh, you mean about what happened in the stables?'

Emily nodded. 'That's right. I think it's time she knew.' Emily would have felt better about telling Allison herself, but she also felt compelled on her own account to comply with Hathaway's request.

Roger came over to sit next to Allison, and Emily left them talking as she followed Hathaway and Luke upstairs.

'What about Caddie?' she said as she closed the breakfast door behind her. 'Will she be all right?'

'She's fine,' Hathaway replied. 'I left the cook tending to her and Nelson guarding her. Once Lady Margaret cracks, Caddie will talk. She may be naturally secretive, but she isn't a natural liar.'

Emily wondered silently at a loyalty so intense that it would extend to participating in conspiracy to murder. Caddie seemed almost an echo, an appendage of Lady Margaret herself. Was she capable of independent action or thought? Would either of them survive being separated, as the arrest of both would inevitably bring about? The idea of Lady Margaret in a police holding cell was so incongruous that Emily couldn't entertain it; the image refused to form in her mind.

These thoughts took her all the way to Lady Margaret's door, where the shadow of the previous night's horror still remained to shake her composure. She swallowed, wishing she had the authority of a police uniform to bolster her nerve. How could one fragile, elderly woman have such power to frighten her?

Hathaway knocked, and a querulous voice called back, 'Come in, Caddie, for goodness' sake. Whatever are you knocking for?'

Hathaway opened the door. 'It isn't Caddie, Lady Margaret. It's the police.'

He pushed between the velvet curtains with Luke and Emily in his wake. Lady Margaret, in a gray brocade dressing gown over a high-necked white nightdress, stood in front of her chair, upright, with eyes blazing.

'How dare you enter my apartment without permission!' she cried. 'Leave this room at once!'

Emily had to give Hathaway points for the unflappable composure with which he met this outburst.

'I'm afraid I can't do that, Lady Margaret,' he said, showing his warrant card, which she ignored. 'I need to speak with you urgently.'

Emily moved to the old woman's side. 'Why don't you sit down, Lady Margaret?' she said. 'This may be a little difficult.'

The dowager wrenched her arm away from Emily's light touch. 'I will stand when I wish to stand. Leave me alone. I don't know what you people are doing here, anyway. You should have been gone a week ago.'

Hathaway spoke, still calmly. 'I asked Mr and Mrs Richards to come with me, Lady Margaret. They're witnesses to what I have to say.'

'Witnesses! What on earth can you mean? This is not a court, and it is certainly not a wedding. Nor am I about to revise my will.'

'I'm speaking of witnesses to an investigation. Into the attempted murder of Lady Fitzhugh and the unlawful killing of Sir James Fitzhugh.' Hathaway speared her with his eyes. 'By you.'

At this, Lady Margaret swayed on her feet. Emily moved to support her, but the old woman's knees buckled under her and she fell into the chair, her eyes fixed on Hathaway's face.

'You, my good man, are either entirely deluded or insane. I never left this room on the day of' – she choked out the words – 'of my grandson's death.'

'I'm not disputing that, Lady Margaret. But you didn't need to leave this room. You had loyal servants to do your work for you.'

'More nonsense. I have no idea what you're talking about.'

'You employed the groom Pollard to drug the horse you expected Allison to ride. Then you ordered your maid, Caddie, to take a gun into the wood and fire several shots in order to spook the horse. Only your plan backfired.'

The old woman shook under Hathaway's gaze as if he were the devil accusing her before the judgment seat of God. But her eyes never left his face.

'What you didn't know at the time was that James had insisted Allison ride a more placid horse that day, while he himself rode the one Pollard had drugged. Maybe you didn't mean to kill Allison; maybe you only intended her to be injured and lose her baby. But when Caddie fired those shots in the wood, it was James who was thrown and killed.'

Lady Margaret now cowered back in her chair, having seemingly shrunk to half her former size. Her voice came out as a harsh whisper. 'You have no proof of any of this. You can't possibly have any proof.'

Hathaway smiled a small, pitying smile. 'I'm afraid we do, Lady Margaret. It isn't much, but I think it will suffice. We have Pollard and Caddie in custody, and I don't think their loyalty will extend to taking the full blame on your behalf. And we have physical evidence as well – thanks mostly to Mr and Mrs Richards here. That's why I called them witnesses.'

He paused and squared his shoulders. 'Lady Margaret Fitzhugh, I'm arresting you on suspicion of causing the death of Sir James Fitzhugh and the attempted murder of Lady Fitzhugh.' He continued with the full statement of rights.

By the time he finished, Lady Margaret had pulled herself together – visibly so, as if she were a reinflating balloon. She first sat straight in her chair, then with the aid of her cane rose to her feet.

'You will give me time to dress, I presume?'

'Of course.'

'Then I will need Caddie to help me.'

'I'm afraid that won't be possible. Caddie is in custody. Mrs Richards can help you.'

Emily quailed at the idea of being left alone with this woman, still formidable even in her ruin. But she nodded. She would do her duty.

The two men retreated behind the curtain, and Emily helped

Lady Margaret remove her dressing gown. 'You will find my clothes in that wardrobe,' she said, pointing to the far end of the room. 'The black coat and skirt, I think, with the gray silk blouse, and, of course, the appropriate underthings.' She spoke as if to a servant but absent the trust and affection she held for Caddie.

Emily went to the wardrobe, which was vast and full of small drawers and compartments. It took her a few minutes of opening drawers and rustling through garments to find everything. She laid the clothes out on the bed, then turned back to Lady Margaret.

She was just in time to see the old woman crumple to the floor, gasping, a beringed hand clutching her chest, her voluminous nightgown pooling around her. As Emily watched, frozen in horror, the last breath rattled from her throat and her eyes glazed in death.

TWENTY-FIVE

A sober and shaken party assembled at dinner that night. Hathaway had immediately suspected a heart attack, and the pathologist had concurred. Her own physician confirmed that the 'turns' Lady Margaret had been having from time to time had actually been minor heart attacks, so the fact that she should have a fatal one under the extreme circumstances came as no surprise.

Caddie was in police custody, and Lady Margaret was in the morgue. Their absence should have lightened the house, made it possible for the remaining inhabitants to breathe more freely, talk in normal voices, roam wherever they chose about the rooms and corridors. And eventually, Emily supposed, that would in fact happen. But for now, the four of them sat subdued, with only an occasional question or speculation from Roger or Allison about how it had all come to pass, and a brief response from Emily or Luke.

Emily did not mention Lady Letitia's ghost. She hoped

that august phantom would never again feel the need to appear.

Over coffee in the drawing room, Allison heaved a heavy sigh. 'I've come to a decision, I think. As soon as my ankle has healed and I have my strength back, I'm going back to the States. This place holds too many memories for me, and without James or his baby I really don't belong here. I'd end up like Lady Margaret someday – an isolated autocrat with no one to love.'

Roger hastily set down his coffee and came to kneel at Allison's feet. 'Oh, my darling girl, don't go,' he implored her. 'Don't leave me all alone in this huge place. I'll end up like one of my butterflies – I'll forget how to speak from having no one to talk to. My life will pass in an instant.'

He took her hand and kissed it. 'I'll do my best to take care of you. You can marry again someday – marry Adam – I won't mind. Fill the house with children. We'll find some way to break the entail – I'll adopt you – you can start the family all over again. With new, wholesome American blood.' He was babbling, and he probably knew it, but the emotion behind his nonsense was real.

Allison took his head in her free hand and kissed his forehead. 'Dear Roger. You've always been so kind to me. I wish I could stay, for your sake. But I think I would go mad. And I could never marry Adam. I can't imagine ever marrying anyone, though I suppose one day that may change. Anyway, my dream of carrying the Fitzhugh legacy into the future died with the tiny life in my womb.'

She sat back with her hand on her abdomen, as if cradling the child she would never hold in her arms. Then her face changed. First her brows drew together in confusion, then her eyes widened in shock. Finally, something dawned that was halfway between astonishment and joy.

'Allison, what is it?' Emily rushed to her side.

'Emily – tell me I'm not dreaming. Tell me you can feel it, too.' She took Emily's hand and placed it on her belly.

At first Emily felt nothing, but in a few seconds she thought she could discern the barest fluttering. 'I–I do feel something. But – well, don't you think it's just . . .' She didn't want to speak her thoughts, both because she didn't want to dash Allison's hopes and because she didn't care to discuss the workings of the digestive system while they were all still digesting.

Allison shook her head. 'No. I mean, logically you're probably right, but this goes beyond logic. I can feel it in my heart.' She looked Emily full in the face. 'Twins do run in the Fitzhugh line. Roger and William, James's father, were twins.' Roger nodded his confirmation.

Emily's heart leaped at the possibility. 'Yes, I know – I read the family history. But do you really think – is it possible for one twin to miscarry and the other survive?' She looked at Luke, for no reason other than that she always looked to him for support. She didn't expect him to have information on this point.

Surprisingly, he did have something to contribute. 'It's possible. I've known it happen. One of my cousins would've been a twin, only my aunt miscarried her sister after a car accident.'

Allison beamed. 'There, you see? I'm almost certain. If you'll drive me to the doctor tomorrow morning, we can find out for sure.'

The next morning, all four of them piled into Allison's more spacious car and Luke drove them into Oxford to the hospital. Allison had been due for a follow-up visit with the orthopedist anyway, so she took care of that first, confirming that her recovery was proceeding satisfactorily. Then they helped her to the obstetrics ward, where she had scheduled an appointment for an ultrasound.

Allison balked at having Roger come in with her, and Luke was perfectly happy to wait outside with him. But she wanted Emily at her side.

The ultrasound technician prepped her, rubbing the jelly over her abdomen. Allison winced at the cold. Then the tech turned on the machine and slowly passed the wand across her skin. A semicircular picture began to form on the screen.

Emily had never witnessed an ultrasound before, let alone undergone one; her one pregnancy had not progressed that far.

She gazed in wonder as the image resolved into a head, a torso, slender half-formed limbs.

Allison gripped her hand. 'I was right, see? There is a baby.'

'There certainly is,' the technician said. 'Look there. You can see the heart beating.' She pointed to a minuscule pulsation within the tiny torso. 'And it's a bit early, but if baby will cooperate, we might be able to tell the sex.' She glanced at Allison. 'Do you want to know?'

'Oh, yes! Absolutely.'

The technician moved the wand around and the picture shifted. Then the baby changed position, and she said, 'There you go.' She pointed at an almost indistinguishable blip. 'You're going to have a little boy.'

Emily's heart flooded with the same joy she saw on Allison's face. A boy. A little Fitzhugh to carry on the line. A piece of James that would be with Allison forever.

And then it struck her: This was the answer to her prayer at St Margaret's well. Profound gratitude swelled to match her joy. Allison had received her miracle.

Allison was speechless as she got cleaned up and dressed. She could only smile beatifically, as Emily had feared she might never smile again. When they rejoined the men, all she could do was nod. Her eyes told the story.

Roger gave her an un-Britishly enthusiastic hug. 'Oh, my dearest girl, I couldn't be more pleased.' He held himself back from saying more for the moment, though Emily could read the rest of his thought in his face – *Surely now you'll stay.*

They were all silent on the way back, respecting the intensity of this moment for Allison. But when they pulled up in front of the manor and Roger helped her out of the car, she stood, took her crutches, and turned herself in a circle to survey the house and grounds.

'This is little James's inheritance. He belongs here, so I belong here.'

She beamed at Roger. 'Yes, Uncle Roger. I'll stay.'

TWENTY-SIX

With the mystery of James's death resolved, and with Allison on the mend both physically and emotionally, Luke and Emily felt their work at Fitzhugh was done. They'd seen most of the places they wanted to visit in the area, and Emily had a hankering to see more of the country. She managed to find a vacancy in a charming eighteenth-century inn in the Lake District, and they planned to make their way there after a detour through Wales.

But first they had some unfinished business to attend to.

'I have to go back to Lower Gloaming,' she said to Luke after breakfast. 'I can't leave here without seeing Rose Cottage one more time.'

Luke heaved a sigh but agreed. 'I know you won't be able to rest easy unless we go back,' he said. 'But I hope you'll take off those rose-colored glasses you had on the last time.'

'I will. Too much has happened since then. I think my vision of England as some idyllic land that time forgot has been shattered forever.'

They set the GPS for Lower Gloaming. This time, even though they took the more rural and picturesque of the two routes offered them, the trip went faster simply because they had a specific destination in mind. When they rounded the last bend and drove into the sunlit village, Emily's original sense of discovering a place akin to Brigadoon was lost. Lower Gloaming was a town on a map like any other.

They pulled up in front of the estate agent's office and went inside. The girl at the front desk glanced up from her phone and yelled, 'Dad! It's those Americans for Rose Cottage again!'

Emily thought business must be awfully slow for the girl to remember them after almost two weeks had passed. Either that or they were the only Americans ever to patronize this office.

Or – a third possibility – they were the only people who had ever asked to see Rose Cottage.

Mr Forsyth bustled out of the back office to greet them, shooting his daughter a furious glare along the way. 'Ah, Mr and Mrs Richards, isn't it? Lovely to see you again.' He shook their hands. 'Come to take another look at Rose Cottage? It does rather linger in the memory, doesn't it?'

'Yes, please,' Emily replied. The cottage lingered in her memory like a beautiful dream, but she knew that for Luke it was more of a nightmare.

They crossed the street, and the weathered stone façade with its welcoming windows greeted Emily like an old acquaintance, inviting her to come in and have a nice cup of tea. She entered to see the same sitting room with the same chintz and lace, the same ancient ceiling beams (which Luke now knew to duck), the same enormous fireplace. But this time she also noticed the slope of the pictures on the wall and the definite downhill grade as she walked from one end of the sitting room to the other.

In the kitchen, she felt the extra tug needed to open each drawer, with its accompanying muffled shriek, and thought about what it would be like to tug those knobs and hear that shriek multiple times a day. Ascending the steep, narrow stair-case with its several bends, she considered how her knees would feel about climbing these steps every time she needed to use the bathroom. And how had she not seen before that the bedrooms had no closets or built-in cupboards at all, and the master bedroom had barely space for a freestanding wardrobe that would hold the merest fraction of her clothes?

She stood at the front bedroom window, a dormer that even she had to stoop to see out of, and regarded the high street through the wavy, settled panes. The day was cool, and a distinct draft blew in around the window frame. This was June – what would those drafts be like in a winter storm? And winter would be the best time for them to vacation, in general, since Stony Beach became a virtual ghost town from January to March, and Luke had little to do.

A vision of the library at Windy Corner rose before her eyes: a blazing fire undisturbed by drafts, her three cats dozing on the hearth as she sat peacefully with Luke, knitting while they chatted about their day. Katie bringing in tea, with scones as mouthwatering as any Mrs McCarthy might provide. A bathroom on every floor, ceilings high enough for Luke to move freely, closets and storage galore. The ultimate in domestic comfort.

And Windy Corner had its own sense of history – the history of Emily's own family. She felt a sudden intense pang of missing everyone at home – Katie, Jamie, and little Lizzie, now an adorable toddler; her brother, Oscar, and his fiancée, Lauren; her dear old Reed friend Marguerite, and her newer Stony Beach friends – Veronica, Devon and Hilary, Doctor Sam, Beanie from the yarn shop and her bookstore boyfriend, Ben. What could she ever have imagined was missing from that life?

We shall not cease from exploration . . .

Luke came up beside her, or as close as he could get given the sloping ceiling. 'Penny for your thoughts,' he said.

She started, lost in her own world. 'I was thinking about some of my favorite lines from T.S. Eliot's *Four Quartets*. He talks about going exploring and coming back to know the place you started from for the first time. I've always loved those lines, but I think I'm just beginning to understand what they mean.'

He turned her to face him. 'Does this by any chance mean you're getting homesick?'

She smiled. 'Just a little. Mostly, it means I've realized I have a home. I don't need another one. Neither here nor at Fitzhugh.' She traced the lines of distortion in the glass with her fingers. 'Though I would like to come back and visit again sometime.'

'We can absolutely do that.' Luke bent down to put his arm around her shoulders and look out of the window. 'I see the teashop's opening. How about one more cream tea before we go?'